The Lizard Returns

BONNIE PEMBERTON

To Dee
Happy Reading!
Best Regards

Pemberton

D1366447

To Kristin, who is the sun

In memory of all creatures whose stories have never been heard.

Also by the author

The Cat Master

ACKNOWLEDGMENTS

Thanks as always to my friends at Trinity Writers Workshop whose unbridled enthusiasm for the written word always keeps me going. Kisses to Sharon Rowe and my husband Kipp Baker...whose editing skills are equal only to their loyalty, love, and talent. To Liz Wilson, Peggy Laskoski, Brenda Ladd and the Arkansas bunch, whose enthusiasm for and belief in this story never wavered, even when mine did. Also a big smooch to Connie Holland and her wonderful Frank, and to Nicholas Kantzios; nephew extraordinaire and number one fan.

And finally, to all the people who loved The Cat Master and urged me to write a sequel... this one's for you..

PROLOGUE

In the dimly lit room, a creature watched from the shadows. It wasn't alone in the cramped enclosure. Rows of cages extended up the wall, their desperate inhabitants clawing in frenzied hysteria, or lying in filth, too traumatized to hope. Terror was an emotion the creature had only experienced through others, and it noted their struggles with detachment.

From a lone window near the ceiling, flashing colored lights intermittently illuminated the darkness, and the hollow whistles of a calliope filtered through the lonely gloom. Occasionally squeals of excitement or murmurs of awe broke through the hum of faceless voices outside, but in the little room, there was nothing but ragged breaths of dread, and the sour stench of dry mouthed fear.

Between two file cabinets, a metal table overflowed with papers, while opened wooden crates almost blocked a single doorway, their sides stamped with documentation of exotic places. Dried excrement, rotting seed, and an occasional small carcass littered the concrete floor; twisted shapes barely discernible in the blackness, and from a corner, an oscillating fan spewed tepid air, round head scanning like a robotic sentry.

The creature observed this in silence. By all appearances, it was no different from the other captives; its cage inadequate, food just as stale, water bowl empty. But there the similarities ended. For where the others were hapless pawns in a world beyond their control, this one prowled the earth with confidence; tainting the world with his presence and wielding the power of death.

PEMBERTON

CHAPTER 1

A mild fall sun beamed against the window and Orie clung to the screen engrossed in his daily calisthenics. Tail extended, throat puffed, the lizard moved up and down in classic reptilian hydraulics, inhaling the tangy aromas of change. Already the oak leaves were turning yellow and the crisp dry scent of autumn filled the air. The peaceful moment was ruined by the ring of a telephone, and the lizard scowled at the ancient machine's interruption.

"Colin? Honey? This is Mom," the recorder boomed. "If you're there, please pick up." There was a pause. "Well, gosh, you're hard to reach today. Anyway, I want to remind you that Alice Wayne and I are leaving at two o'clock for that New England Fall Leaves tour. Her niece is pet-sitting the cats and also that *thing* you're keeping in the bathroom. Oh! There's a roast in the crock pot, and you're looking thin, so come get it. Be back in a week! Love you."

There was some static, and Orie continued his exercise, pleased with his superior powers of concentration, and feeling particularly buff, he did two more sets of ten, mentally recapping the day. This was easy since the schedule never varied: Up at dawn, crawl through mail slot, have sow bug breakfast by driveway, check birdbath for mosquitoes, avoid the ferret, and back inside for exercise and then a nap. The phone rang again, and this time he jumped, startled by another intrusion so soon.

"Dude! This is Graeme. Some guy's been trying to reach you through the biology department...says he sells exotics, that he's calling local herpetologists, and mentioned having a black mamba which is way too intense for me, but I figured you might be interested, so I gave him your cell which you're not answering for some reason. You're getting famous, dude...let's drink beer or shoot hoops or something."

"Yes, lets," the lizard muttered, completely repulsed by such a suggestion. Orie had never understood humans. In his opinion, their behavior was tasteless and crude, with moments of deviance too vile to mention... so, why was he living with one? Scurrying onto the window sill, he huffed beneath dust motes, the bright day suddenly ruined.

It had been years since his old friend, Tenba's, death, and for a while, the lizard tried to settle back into life in the O'Connell's crawlspace...but soon it was apparent he couldn't. Too many memories crowded the dusty darkness. Sometimes they were of Buddy, the yellow tom destined to rule as Cat Master, or Jett, the cat's murderous brother, but more often than not it was the German shepherd, Tenba, whose wise and gentle face stared from the soft shadows of recollection. She was his first and only friend, and the emptiness left by her death provoked a period of wanderings far from Sixth Avenue.

For a time, Orie tried the alleys, which quickly proved too dangerous, and most neighborhoods were filled with children, their sticky little hands grabbing at him wherever he went. By the fourth year, solitary and disgruntled, he stumbled upon an empty guest house behind a dilapidated Victorian home and settled in. Two uneventful summers passed before the snuffling nose of fate found him again. The home was sold, restored, and the cottage rented sight unseen. Furious at the inconvenience, Orie was preparing to move, when footsteps of the new renter echoed down the hall. That sound! How many times had the old crawlspace reverberated with these same thumps from above? His mind zoomed to the past...the scurry of paws as the O'Connell's cats, Zekki and Pris ran through the kitchen, the measured clicks of Mrs. O'Connell's high heels...and the languid scuffling shuffle of... The Boy! Hiding behind a rusted pipe, Orie waited, prepared to see the thin, scabby-kneed child of Sixth Avenue. What he saw was an earnest young man of at least nineteen, tall and fit, with brown hair and rimless glasses.

Colin O'Connell had grown up as Orie had grown old, and the lizard found strange comfort in The Boy's big familiar feet; roaming the house at night, slapping the floors like a 'hand bone' lullaby.

"Hey Orie!"

A raucous voice jolted his thoughts, and the lizard sighed with dread. It was Monday, and Monday's meant The Meeting of the Spoken Word by the river. It also meant Bennett, an African Grey parrot with a big mouth and no boundaries. Orie nodded towards the bird now fluttering on an oak branch. "Hey, Bennett."

"I saw you exercising," the parrot said, "so I thought I'd drop by and remind you about the meeting."

"Yes, I'm looking forward to it." Orie lied. He hated it. The members were stupid and boring and he didn't like talking to other animals anyway. But it was necessary. All creatures were compelled by The Law of Sho-valla to pass on the stories of their lives. For years he'd carefully ignored this obligation, traveling from one place to the other, avoiding as many living things as possible, and assuring himself that no rules ever applied to him. But the situation had changed. Eight years had passed since The Cat Master's ascension to power, and during that time, generations of species had died along with their memories. Orie sighed. There was no denying it; his legendary feat was fast fading from animal lore. Soon, nothing would remain of his story but a silly yarn about cats told by idiots.

With no mention of him.

He puffed his throat at the thought. That *wasn't* going to happen...he would tell his story, careful to include Tenba whom he'd always felt was the true hero anyway.

The parrot watched with pale grey eyes. "You're a little cranky since the exterminators sprayed the house last week. I'm guessing that cut down on your menu. Have you been eating?"

"Yes. I've been eating." Orie clenched his jaws in anticipation of the next question.

"Good. Well, since I'm already here... do you want to head to the meeting together?"

There it was; the ritual he despised. For the last four Mondays, Bennett found him no matter where he was, remarked that the lizard seemed grouchy for a multitude of reasons, reminded him of the meeting and suggested they could go together. And every Monday Orie said no.

"No," he said.

The bird started to answer, but the phone rang, and both creatures cocked their heads at the interruption.

"Hey Colin, where are you?" A girl's voice chirped through the speakers. "I thought we were meeting at the carnival at noon. Kristin and I are standing by the Ferris wheel, and we know you've been here, because, guess what I'm looking at?" Someone giggled in the background. "Your nasty backpack! We knew it was yours 'cause it's held together with that big, stupid looking safety pin!" Music blared from an unidentified instrument. "We're going to hang out for a little longer...so, if you want the backpack you'd better get out here, 'cause we know who you are and we're holding it for ransom!" Squeals of laughter were followed by a beep. "Oops. I've got another call, so anyway, you've got a cell, use it!"

Orie felt strangely unsettled by the messages. The Boy's friends and his mother called frequently, what was different about today?

Something...something.

"But you *are* going, right?" the parrot persisted, oblivious of the beeps and clicks of the ancient machine. "There should be a lot of good stories today. Let's go together."

"I'd rather go alone."

"Good!" Bennett croaked, flapping towards the street. "I'll wait for you downstairs!"

Orie frowned with resignation. The African Grey had appeared in the area six months ago. Word was he'd lived with a film critic and his wife for ten years until the couple divorced. After her departure, Bennett began serenading guests with perfect impersonations of the ex-wife's most annoying moments. "Robbeeee!" he'd screech with perfect pitch and phrasing, "You didn't flush the toilet...*again*!" After a particularly bad weekend of Bennett's relentless renditions, a window was 'accidentally' opened and the parrot found himself homeless. This was strictly rumor, because Bennett often confused his own life with movies he'd seen with the critic, and no one was really sure what his true story was.

Plopping to the floor, Orie scuttled toward the door with every intention of meeting Bennett by the mailbox and explaining *again* why they wouldn't be traveling to the meeting together, when inexplicably, he was drawn to The Boy's bedroom. The lizard rarely came here, preferring to stay beneath the kitchen sink. Standing in the doorway, his lip curled with distaste. Great loops of sheets and blankets twisted beneath soured towels; underwear was draped on shelves stacked with dusty books on herpetology, biology, and zoology. The space was disgusting as always, but Orie had learned to ignore that as he'd aged, more interested in safety than sanitation. What he couldn't ignore was the pulsing red light on the answering machine, and the equally steady throb of a more disturbing fear that buzzed his brain like a wasp; had The Boy simply gone...or disappeared?

CHAPTER 2

Warm Australian winds blew through the wood pile, rocking the spider's web and drenching the air with the sharp scent of red gum. Beside her, an infant lay in the sunshine, chubby pink fist clutching a toy, huge blue eyes gazing at her with wonder, and the spider was so thrilled to see the child, that her eyes filled with tears that plopped to the ground in big, noisy splashes. Wanting a better look, she tried to move but the tears now puddled high around her legs and that of the baby's until both of them floated from the yard, the child in one direction, the spider in the other. "Don't leave!" she tried to scream, but the water gushed in huge, briny waves until the baby's head was barely visible, tumbling in the surge, bobbing out of reach in a burning sea of sorrow.

"Theda," a quiet voice said with urgency, "wake up."

The spider jerked, still groggy from the dream, aware of salty wetness on one delicate leg. Trembling, she squinted through the musty light. Nothing had changed. Cages reeked of waste, creatures fretted, and the formless voice still whispered impossible requests from the shadowy corner of the room. She'd heard it before, on the first day she'd arrived from her homeland, and now it was calling her again. "What do you want?" Theda mumbled, still troubled by the dream.

"Watch and listen." The answer floated from the darkness.

As if on cue, brisk footsteps clicked towards the shed, and a rattle of keys searched the lock.

Panicked, she tried to scale the slippery glass enclosure, legs flailing, fangs drawn, until she fell backwards, quivering with frustration. There was no place to hide, and sick with dread, the spider hunkered in a tiny lump of black, legs drawn close to her abdomen, red striped back hidden from view.

The door squealed open accompanied by a blast of air that doused the room with memories of freedom, and two men entered the room. One was in his thirties, short and powerfully built, with red hair and freckled weathered skin. The other was fiftyish, tall, and morbidly obese. A dark purple birthmark blotched one cheek, swirling beneath his nose like a magenta mustache.

"I don't get the problem here, Stuart." The smaller man picked at a pimple beneath his jaw, and casually assessed the cages. "I brought you a lot of good stuff this time, and all you've done is bitch."

"First of all, Jerry, I don't bitch, I observe." Stuart waddled to a crate and kicked it, his massive belly jiggling with each step. "See this?" He prodded a small, body with his toe. "Every bird in it was dead when it got here. I don't pay for dead birds." He paused, watery blue eyes piercing and sly. "I also don't pay for things I didn't order."

Jerry's biceps twitched. "What are you talkin' about, dude?" His voice rose with indignation. "You ordered everything here, and I've got the list to prove it!"

The large man huffed, lurched to a shadowed cage, and tapped it with a rosy nail. "Really, Jer? Because I didn't order *this*, I don't even know what it is."

They stood by the crate, staring in silence.

Something shuffled in the darkness, and Jerry moved back, beard stubbled face pinched with disgust. "Geez! Whatever it is, it stinks to high heavens!" He took another look. "Is that a hyena?"

"I hope not, Jer, because nobody gives a shit about hyenas. They want rare things, dangerous things, things they can hunt or sell. Get it? And by the way, it's not a hyena, or a dingo, or anything else I'm familiar with. The crate's marked Egypt and the identification tag says," he fumbled in his pocket for glasses, balanced them on a red-veined nose, and squinted at the neatly lettered paper taped to the wire. "A."

"A?" Jerry repeated. "So what does "A" stand for?"

9

"I haven't a clue," Stuart said, "but when you find out, I'll be glad to pay you. Until then, thanks for dropping by, and I'll call when I make some contacts."

Jerry's chin jutted in anger. "Listen, you tub of lard! It wasn't easy getting this stuff in, and I want my money!" He shoved Stuart's chest, and watched him stumble backwards, flailing at crates, and finally righting himself against a tall metal enclosure. Hooking powerful fingers between the wire on either side of the big man's head, Jerry leaned close. "Don't mess with me, Stu..." He stopped, eyes wide with surprise.

From inside the cage, a supple form crashed against the pen, a quick burst of liquid spraying Jerry's shirt.

Both men jumped away, altercation suddenly forgotten.

"Oh my God!" Jerry screamed, frantically checking his arms and hands" Oh Geez! Did it get me?"

Stuart's forehead glistened with sweat, skin white beneath the scarlet blotch. "Keep your voice down!" Hands shaking, he covered the cage with a stained canvas "It's a black mamba, Jerry. If it bit you, you wouldn't be asking, you'd be in the process of dying."

Jerry stared, chest heaving, mouth agape.

"Can we please just cool it, here?" Stuart croaked, wiping his dripping neck, "There's no need for violence okay? I understand your concerns." His voice lowered in a transparent attempt at sincerity. "But I can't pay you until I move some of this stuff, Jer." With paternal care, he guided the trembling man towards the door. "I spoke to a fellow today about the redback spider, and I've had some interest from the website, so come on, you know me, I wouldn't stiff anybody."

"To—today's Friday." Jerry sputtered, shrugging the corpulent arm aside. "I'll be back on Monday for the—the money, and you'd better have it, man, 'cause I know where your trailer's hidden, and I don't have a problem in the world with just bustin' in there and whipping your butt!"

Stuart raised a pudgy palm in submission. "That won't be necessary..."

..."and I don't care what you do with that—that hyena thing," Jerry screeched, spittle flying. "But you're paying me for every frikkin' crate I hauled in here!"

"Fair enough, fair enough, Jer." Stuart smoothed an errant strand of hair from his balding head, and took a deep breath. "I never meant for you to think otherwise. Just pull yourself together before we leave."

"I *am* pulled together! Just let me outta' of here!"

With a quick nod, Stuart undid the lock, and both men hurried into the sunlight, the door slamming behind.

Feathers and debris swirled from the draft, and Theda rose on shaky legs, trying to understand what she'd heard. It wasn't the first time she'd smelled their darkness, or sensed her own fate in their hands.

Melbourne

She raised her head, fangs primed at the memory.

The child crying.

Awash in grief, the spider sank to the floor, drops of venom trailing from her jaws. She had loved the baby, spending hours on its crib, watching. Usually, the infant only stared back, laughing and cooing, but that day, it reached out, grabbing the spider's leg, its soft hand surprisingly quick. "I panicked." Theda reminded herself for the hundredth time. "It was an accident." But the bite had been deep, and having never seen the child again, she feared her little friend was dead. No, she reminded herself miserably; not dead; murdered, and by someone it had trusted. But that would ever happen again, the spider vowed, wiping the wetness away. Not ever.

Something below her jiggled its cage, and her enclosure listed slightly. For a moment she froze, illogically afraid Stuart was back, net poised to scoop, but then she remembered that her tank had been bumped during the men's scuffle. She'd prayed it would fall, shattering to pieces at their feet, but instead, the lid had only rattled and the rocking stopped. Peaking upwards, Theda stared in wonderment.

The mesh cover had slipped, and drifting directly above it, a soft, green feather floated serenely through the tiny opening and into the tank, finally resting with one end propped against the side like a ramp.

"Leave this place, Theda." The voice from the shadowed cage whispered. "What you have witnessed is the beginning, and only the reptile can end it."

The redback scrambled against the glass, trying to see who was speaking. "What do you mean? What reptile? Where?"

"The answer is at the carnival."

Theda's heart pounded. "What answer?"

"I would say that depends on the question."

CHAPTER 3

Orie slithered through brambles, anxious to reach the gazebo before the meeting began. The Boy's absence had darkened his mood, and he'd debated going at all, wondering if he should stay and wait. But, why? What was the big deal? The Boy was a grown man, fully capable of taking care of himself, and besides, at nine years of age, Orie was a very old lizard, with few meetings remaining. Besides, his story was far more important than a couple of phone calls which weren't his business anyway.

Phone calls.

The thought poked at his brain like a rude finger. What about the phone calls? Thrashing through nettles, he replayed them in his mind to no avail. There was nothing unusual about making plans with friends or dodging your mother. He wrinkled his brow in concentration and felt almost on the brink of discovery, when a cheery voice shattered the moment.

"Come on, we're late!" Bennett fluttered above, his stout, grey body darting behind yellowing foliage only to reappear, outlined against the topaz sky.

The Boy's guest house overlooked Trinity Park, and normally it didn't take long to cross the shallow stream leading to the zoo and beyond to the picnic area and the pergola. But today, Orie's mind was elsewhere and the parrot's voice was annoying. "Back off, Bennett!" he shouted. "I'm going as fast as I can."

"But everybody's waiting at the gazebo! They'll all be mad. What should I say?

Orie longed to tell him; loudly, and with lots of expletives, but feared it might upset the bird, and everyone knew it was best to keep Bennett calm. Fear and excitement triggered a barrage of ear splitting, mechanical imitations that was hard to stop. "Don't worry about it," he panted, "just say I'm coming."

"Will do!" Bennett soared ahead, finally vanishing amidst the stand of oaks.

Orie stopped, stretched, and winced. Lately, he'd noticed stiffening in his back legs, a condition of age he imagined, but still annoying, and the trip seemed to take longer each week. He was almost to a bend in the path, when a pointed pink nose pushed through a clump of fading fern to his right. "Hi," the ferret said. "Are you busy?"

"Very," Orie said, feeling trapped. "I'm late for the meeting." Blitz had appeared only weeks before. She was emaciated and sick, and Orie had patiently waited for her to die. Unfortunately, The Boy had nursed her back to health and though the lizard carefully avoided her, it soon became clear that the ferret was stalking him. He wasn't sure why, and he didn't particularly want to find out.

She slunk forward, her long slender form winding liking a snake, small sable ears upright and alert. "I've been trying to talk with you, but it almost seems like you're hiding from me or something." She blinked; her eyes a little too bright. "You're not, are you?"

Orie averted his head, repelled by her musky sweetness Blitz was more than a pest, she was dangerous. Ferrets ate lizards and ending the day as her snack wasn't appealing. "I'm not hiding, just a loner." Orie forced a hollow laugh. "Old lonely lizard, that's me."

Rap music echoed through the park, and a lion roared from the zoo, its exotic ferocity strange amidst the calm Texas day.

"It's nice to finally meet like this," Blitz watched him closely, her body taut with nervous energy, "because I've heard an awful lot about you."

So that was it! Orie relaxed. She was simply one of his many admirers and understandably wowed. "Of course you have," he said, "I'm famous." Suddenly disinterested, he searched for a reason to leave, and remembered the meeting. "Would love to chat, but I'm late. So…goodbye, and have a long, sneaky life or whatever it is that ferrets have."

"But you *are* the lizard that saved The Cat Master," she persisted. "That's right, isn't it?"

So the Legendary Lizard *did* have a following, he thought with satisfaction. How good to know. "Yes," he said, feeling smug and grand. "It is I."

Blitz slunk closer, her expression anxious. "Well, I'm headed to the meeting too, and we need to talk about something, something really important."

Devotees were crucial, so Orie feigned interest, trying to judge her age and wondering how long a ferret's life span actually was.

"Here's the thing," Blitz said. "I've wanted to tell my story for a long time, but it's...well it's not very interesting."

Like this was a surprise. Orie shifted and gave a prolonged sigh.

"I see you're in a hurry, so I'm going to get right to it. I need you to tell everyone that I'm your friend."

Here it was; another star-struck wanna-be who had no sense of protocol. Orie stretched his mouth into what he hoped was a gracious smile, which was hard to know since he'd never felt gracious. "I don't have a clue what you're talking about...but the short answer is no."

"You don't understand." The ferret paced in agitation. "You have to do this. I can't tell my story unless I'm sure that *my* story is part of yours."

"What?" The lizard felt a tingle of fear, as though a hawk's shadow had glided above.

"With all due respect," she said, tone anything *but*, "you're name is still known by some, but hardly anyone actually remembers your boring old story, so let's reinvent it with a little twist. Me."

Had she said boring? Orie's startled mind did a double take.

"Think of it as marketing, a new look for a tired, old theme."

Had she said old? Blitz moved so close that her whiskers grazed his snout, and the lizard pulled back.

"So, here's the deal; it's too late for me to do something memorable on my own, but, if I'm considered a trusted friend of someone sort of famous"—she leaned forward—"which would be you, then by association, I'm sort of famous, *too*. That's how it works. So, all I want is for you to include me in your story."

Orie stood in shock. Blitz wasn't a worshipful fan, she was a nut. Worse than that, she was a nut with a plan. This was a very bad combination, and potentially fatal. "You know," he said, casually backing away, and praying Bennett would come back, "I've never thought of things that way before, but, sure; why not share a little notoriety? Tell you what; why don't I just lead off with some memories of our best times together when I tell my story?" His heart bonged like Big Ben at midnight.

Blitz's ears perked. "What kind of memories?"

"You know," thoughts bumped through his brain like three blind mice, "interesting stuff…like the time…well, the time…"

"…like the time we saved the Cat Master together?" The ferret blocked his path, her eyes narrowed. "I'd like you to say *that*."

A dark silence squatted between them.

Two beetles blundered into the opening then bolted in panic, and a brisk fall breeze sprinkled leaves onto the ground.

"I said," Blitz repeated slowly, "that I want you to say that the two of us saved The Cat Master together." Her voice was flat and quiet.

The lizard was stunned by such audacity. It was one thing for *him* to be considered legendary when the German shepherd, Tenba had done all of the work, but to immortalize a loony weasel through his own efforts was out of the question. "Honestly," Orie said, trying for nonchalance, "It's not that I'd mind embellishing things a little, but the rules are pretty plain about telling." He furrowed his brow with forced concern. "There are plenty of animals who still consider me heroic. If anyone at the meeting thought I've been lying all these years, it could be bad."

"True." The ferret nodded thoughtfully. "But what would *really* be bad," she smiled, canines needle-sharp, "is if you never *made* it to the meeting."

Her meaning was clear and Orie's dread morphed into pissed. He was Orie, the Legendary Lizard! Did this skulking weasel believe she could kill an icon and get away with it?

Blitz watched him, a shaft of fall sunlight reducing her pupils to tiny slits.

Yes, Orie decided, she did. Flicking his tongue, he thought. It appeared that there were only two options for escape. One, he could try to outrun her and hope she died laughing, or, two, lie like heck, and live. "You're absolutely right," Orie said, "I'll start working on the story."

"And you'll do it today, at the meeting?"

He pictured her corpse swinging from the jaws of a Rottweiler, the visual so soothing that he smiled. "Why not?"

The ferret's face relaxed in a quicksilver mood change "Well, this is just wonderful. Here I've been so scared to approach you, and now I think we really *are* going to be friends." With a whoop, she shot down the path, did two forward somersaults and careened back, eyes sparkling with exuberance. "Ferrets call that 'dooking'." Her long tail twitched. "I could show you how."

"I'd love to, but I'm feeling a little under the weather today…so," Orie gave a cheery wave. "I'll just be limping along."

Blitz scowled. "No one's going to believe we're friends unless we hang out a little. I'm beginning to think you'd rather be with that ridiculous parrot." Her ears flattened. "Wait a minute. You wouldn't mention *him* in our story, would you?"

"Are you kidding?" Orie inched further along the path, waving one claw in a gesture of dismissal. "I feel sorry for him. What a nut…just pitiful."

"Totally." Blitz's manner brightened. She fell in beside him; demeanor so brazenly intimate that Orie's skin twitched with revulsion.

She slowed to a stop. "Don't mean to be rude, but I like to be early, so I'm gonna' run. Do you want me to tell them you're coming?" She smiled warmly, her black lips pulled taut over bright pink gums. "After all, if we're both going to tell our stories tonight, we should start acting…*you* know; close."

Orie tightened his jaws to keep from screaming. "That would be… *great*… would you?"

"What are friends for?" With a joyful squeal, she shot up the path, bounced off a tree trunk, leaped twice in the air, and disappeared towards the gazebo.

"Travel safely!" He called, waving patiently until she was clearly out of earshot, "You freaking psychopath!" Shaking with fury, he stood in a patch of shadow, his tongue thick with disgust. He'd suspected Blitz was trouble, but this was worse than he'd imagined. Resolutely, he shook his head. It didn't matter, he'd never do what she'd asked, no matter what the cost.

Outraged by her insolence, he struggled through the underbrush, rich scents of vegetation wafting from beneath his feet. Why couldn't something rip her to shreds, he thought, stopping to eat a tick. Where were wolverines when you really needed them?

* * *

Stuart Krell slumped on a stool in the warehouse, fleshy fingers massaging his temples. Donut crumbs trailed down his shirt, Twinkie wrappers littered the floor, and the remnants of cotton candy clung in spidery pink strands to his multiple chins.

Outside, vendors hawked their wares; the smells of grease and sugar mingling with the sounds of squealing preschoolers…their small, rapid footsteps only yards away.

Panting at Stuart's feet sat a pit bull. Restrained by a long, leather leash looped twice around the stool's slender leg, the dog shifted positions, and fought down panic. This wasn't good. Hard experience had taught him it was dangerous when Mr. Krell was silent, and he'd been ominously quiet since they'd come back from the trailer. A phone trilled, and the dog jumped, spattering the man's shoes with droplets of saliva.

"Axel!" the man shouted twisting the choke collar until the dog coughed. "Move! Get back!"

Accustomed to harsher punishment, Axel eased away, careful to keep his jaws tightly shut.

The ringing continued, and Stuart flipped opened a cell phone. "What do you want, Jerry!" he yelled. "How many times do I have to say this? I don't care who's interested in the redback. It's gone! Just forget about that…we've got bigger problems than selling a spider! Well, go ahead then, I'm listening."

Above them, an aquarium listed to its side with nothing but a feather inhabiting its dusty interior, and Stuart peered at the emptiness with an intensity the dog didn't understand.

Twenty yards away, the calliope bellowed, a barker shouted from the Tilt-O-Whirl, and children screamed with excitement.

Axel cocked his head at the sounds, and whined. Unlike Stuart, he always enjoyed their walk through the carnival grounds to the warehouse which was right behind a snow cone stand and hidden from view by a row of bushes. Food littered the ground and laughing people were everywhere, some with kids. He sighed. Children were a never ending source of fascination. He'd never been allowed around them, mainly because everyone seemed so afraid when he came near, but he'd watched them play with other dogs. They were the happiest, funniest humans he'd ever seen... and small. When they hit you it probably wouldn't even hurt. Axle's thoughts drifted to the trailer and what was now locked inside it, and felt a burst of joy. He hadn't wanted to leave his new friend, but Mr. Krell never gave him many choices. A blip of worry tugged at his mind and he frowned, wishing they were home.

"I don't care about that!" Stuart finally bellowed in to the phone. Swaying to his feet, he clutched the table for support.

Alarmed, the dog squirmed as far away as the leash allowed, and gagged as Stuart yanked him back.

"What am I, Jerry? Stupid?" the big man asked. "You think I'm gonna' stay here after what happened today? I'm shutting the place down, and I need trucks here by tomorrow night to load everything." He lowered his voice to a whisper, and moved to the door making sure it was locked. "And I think you know what I mean by *everything* Jer, 'cause you're in this as deep as I am."

The pit bull relaxed. Good. Mr. Krell was mad at someone else. With a groaning sigh, he lowered his head and considered the happy surprise waiting back at the trailer.

"God Almighty, Jerry!" Stuart roared with frustration. "For the hundredth time, I *know* we've got a buyer for the redback spider, but it's *gone!*" Stuart paced the room, the birthmark a livid gash across his pale face. "Give it a rest! We've gotta' get out of here! There's a guy in Brazil who'll take the whole shebang but we have to move fast." He plucked crumbs from his shirt, and licked them from trembling fingers. "Who cares what he pays us? Half the shipment's dead anyway..." The big man's demeanor suddenly changed, and his voice softened. "Whoa now Jerry, calm down...we're all a little tense right now. Yes, yes...you're definitely going to get your cut, but we've got to do something about the...I know that, but what if someone..." Stuart grimaced and ran a pudgy hand through his hair. "Okay, Jerry, fine...you're absolutely right, money is money. I—I'll look for the spider."

Shoving the cell phone in his pocket, Stuart grabbed a flashlight by the wall and scanned its pallid beam against the cages. "Where are you, you poisonous little shit?" Pushing debris aside with his toe, he carefully checked every recess, his forehead lined in concentration. Suddenly, Stuart stopped, shining the light into a large, dark cage to his right, and squinting at the carefully printed tag. "What are you looking at, and what the heck does 'A' mean? I didn't print that." He banged the cage with frustration, and something inside moved.

A mélange of scents wafted from the enclosure. At first there was an overpowering stench of decay, as though a thousand sewers had disgorged their contents into the sun. And, yet beneath it all there lingered something oddly sweet and appealing. Sunshine, rain drops... the sea.

Axel sat up, a sudden chill bristling his fur and his dry nose probing the air.

The man's voice rose with annoyance. "I've lost the only thing anyone's wanted to buy since I got here, and no body's offered a freakin' dime for you! Know why?" Face flushed with fury, he shoved the cage until it rocked. "Cause you're ugly and you stink, and nobody even knows what you are!"

Primal dread tightened the dog's throat.

That smell.

He knew it from long ago, like in a dream. No, he corrected the thought. Not in a dream, a nightmare. Breath shallow, tail tucked tightly against his belly, he slowly turned, forcing himself to confront the thing behind the wire.

It stared back, and blinked in silent greeting.

With a howl of terror, Axel scrambled backwards, toppling the stool to the floor, and releasing the leash from its tether.

"What the...?" Stuart kicked at the dog's flank in a futile attempt to block him.

Dodging the foot, Axel raced across the floor, slamming against the door with such force it popped on its hinges.

"Axel! Come!" Stuart's voice shouted from behind, but the dog kept running, winding between legs of startled people, scurrying behind flapping tents and whirling machines until he was in the open, racing through autumn tinged grass and dappled sunshine, beyond the carnival, Mr. Krell...and the golden eyed thing that had seen him.

CHAPTER 4

Orie trudged over the last bit of pathway leading to the meeting and stopped to catch his breath. From his place beneath a juniper he could see the group assembled and waiting in the gazebo. As usual, the cockroach, rabbit, armadillo, and parrot were ready and in place, and as usual, he wasn't. He assessed the structure and began his painful trudge up the steps.

A relic from decades past, the gazebo was rotted, unpainted, and set so far into tangles of overgrown greenery that humans seemed unaware of its presence. But all animals wishing to join the Meeting of the Spoken Word congregated within its crumbling protection. Though some were regulars and others were new, the rules remained the same. One; the Meeting of the Spoken Word was considered sacred, a free zone where no animal need fear another, and two; All participants were to be on time, which he wasn't.

Again.

With a sigh of resignation, Orie clambered up the last step and tried to look relaxed.

"Well, what do ya' know," the cockroach jeered, one antenna waving for emphasis. "His Reptilian Majesty has decided to join us. In case you haven't heard, rule number two is for this thing to start on time."

Orie forced himself to ignore the remark, partially from disdain, but mainly because his mind whirred with the growing threat from Blitz. Jangled and tired, he took his place beneath Bennett who perched on a rotting beam above him.

"I tried to tell them you were coming," Bennett jabbered from the brittle roost, "but Blitz butted in and..."

"...that's because you don't know anything about him, he's *my* friend!" The ferret interrupted from her place on the steps.

She smiled at Orie who looked away, desperate to form a plan. He needed to get Bennett's attention. There was no way to judge Blitz's reaction once she realized she'd been betrayed, and though small, the parrot was a formidable protector. Orie motioned to him with his claw, but Bennett gazed happily around the gazebo, completely oblivious.

The rabbit stamped in frustration. "Can we please hurry up and start? I'm not waiting around to get eaten." Her nose twitched with anxiety. "It's going to be dark soon, and I feel like a darn buffet up here."

She had a point. Summer days stretched forever, but fall was different. Already the sky strained towards sunset, and everyone knew the River Cats hunted at night. More than one small member had left after dusk never to be seen again.

The skunk, who'd been the undisputed leader of the group for as long as anyone could remember, cleared his throat. "For any new members, my name is Sarge, and The Meeting of the Spoken Word is now in session. Please repeat after me. "It is my intention to tell my story for the good of my species. I shall honor the free zone and no violence shall be done here. So says the Law of Shovalla. So say we all."

"So say we all!" the animals echoed, then took their usual places; armadillo, rabbit, and skunk sharing an unbuckled space of floor, Blitz stretched on a vine covered railing, and Orie and the cockroach on the first step. The only new member was a gaunt coyote who sat quietly to the side of the structure, his drooling attention on the rabbit, who mouthed, 'help me' to the skunk.

"No predatory behavior allowed," Sarge admonished, "let's get started. I believe our armadillo was telling last time, so he's first."

The cockroach groaned audibly as the creature ambled forward.

"So, I think last week we stopped where I'd been born and I'd just seen a grub worm for the first time."

"Oh God." The roach muttered, rolling his eyes.

Unperturbed, the armadillo droned on, his story so excruciatingly dull Orie considered hanging himself on a trumpet vine. Usually, he drifted off during these times, reliving moments with Tenba, or planning the week's schedule, but today his tail twitched with apprehension. The ferret's demands had temporarily overridden his concerns about The Boy's unexplained absence, but the fear was now back, rooting through his brain for answers. Something about one of the phone messages disturbed him; what was it? The recollection slowly took shape, teetering between discovery and forgetfulness. It was something about …"

"That worm," the cockroach mumbled, breaking the lizard's concentration. "If he mentions 'grub worm' one more time…"

Mouth tight with fury, Orie decided he'd eat the bug, rules or no rules, and then noticed that Bennett was following the armadillo's story with glassy eyed rapture. He knew that look from past experience, and it wasn't good.

"So then," the creature continued, "I walked into the street and this *big* car came over the hill, and…"

Rumblings of a diesel engine filled the gazebo, followed by an assortment of horns honking and tires screeching.

Orie stood in alarm.

Above them, Bennett flapped his wings with excitement, perfect road imitations boinking and clanging from his throat.

"And then what happened?" The parrot squawked, sound effects now including a freight train. "I mean, after the car?"

"What are you doing?" Blitz screamed. "This isn't your story! Nobody asked for that racket!"

"Relax," the cockroach smirked, "it's the best thing I've heard since I got here."

"Order! I want order right now!" Sarge bawled, trying his best to be heard over Bennett's impersonations. "Somebody shut that bird up!"

"Stop looking at me!" squealed the rabbit, dodging the coyote and running through the brush.

"Excuse me, please?" A strong voice called above the chaos.

Something about the tone commanded attention, and the animals turned towards the steps and stared.

A small black spider stood on eight trembling legs, multiple eyes blinking with undisguised distress. " Is this...is this The Meeting of the Spoken Word?" she asked, voice quavering.

The skunk nodded. "Who're you?"

From left to right, she carefully assessed each animal until she reached Orie and then stopped. "My name is Theda," she said, her eyes locked on his, "and I've come to tell a story."

CHAPTER 5

Theda hadn't expected the sudden quiet that gripped the gazebo. She cleared her throat. "But, I mean if it's not the right time or...."

The skunk, who appeared to be the leader, moved toward her. "No, no. Everyone's welcomed here, though I have to say," he paused glaring at the animals behind him, "I'm not too pleased with the rule breaking going on today!" His voice rose with frustration and his right eye began to twitch. "However," he took a deep breath, "we'd love to hear your story, but Rule Number Five says whoever has the floor can finish without interruption, and a member was right in the middle of telling..."

"Before the bird butted in!" the armadillo shouted.

Sarge turned in its direction, and raised his tail in silent warning.

Bennett perched placidly on the beam, seemingly unaware of his outburst. "Yeah, go on with the part about the car coming. I love things with engines."

"Forget it," the armadillo muttered, "nobody's interested, anyway." With a huff, he waddled down the steps. "And it was getting good, too!" he shouted, disappearing into the foliage.

The cockroach nodded at Theda. "So, talk. We haven't heard a spider in a long time. By the way," he fluttered his wings, "I like that red stripe on your back. Classy."

"Good grief," Sarge groaned, "get on with it! This isn't a dating service."

"So, what are you exactly?" The cockroach continued. "Some kind of black widow, or...?"

"I'm a garden spider!" Theda interrupted loudly, her fangs raised in warning.

The roach recoiled "Of course you are." His eyes narrowed with mistrust. "And I'm a butterfly."

A dark anger lazed through the spider's mind. She'd been caught in a lie, and now they all knew. Scanning the animal's faces, she probed for sinister intent. What else did they know? Most stared back with simple curiosity, but plainly the roach was on to her. A gust of paranoia crushed what little resolve remained. She wanted to go home.

"Both of you knock it off!" Sarge's voice cracked with impatience. "Look, we don't care what you are. Everyone is accepted. If you want to tell, we're here to listen, but hurry up, the sun is setting."

There was an awkward silence. A gust of wind twirled leaves into the enclosure, their lifeless forms brightened by shades of yellow and red. "Well?" The skunk said. "Are you telling or aren't you?"

"Yes," Theda blurted, then suddenly stopped, mute with horror. Where were the words? What was she supposed to say? Mandibles clenched with anxiety, she turned towards the lizard, took a deep breath, and prayed for guidance. "A man put me in a cage and wanted to sell me, and..."

"Did she say 'smell'?" Bennett cawed, "Why would some guy want to smell her?"

"Sell! She said 'sell' you idiot!" Orie shouted, the day's anxieties finally taking their toll. "That's it, I'm done!" Turning, he limped towards the stairs, his jaw jutted with fury. "The grub worm story was bad enough, but this...."

Theda watched helplessly. The lizard was leaving, she'd done something wrong.

"And then someone else came in!" Her voice rose with desperation.

Ignoring her, the lizard descended the second step. "Arachnids," he called over his shoulder. "Too many legs, not enough brains."

"But this human was young and kind and saw the man was evil!" The memory was so frightening that tears welled in Theda's eyes, finally spilling onto her legs. "He saw we were dying, what the evil man had done to us, and he was mad…"

"Where do you think you're going, Orie?" Blitz called from the railing. "You can't leave now, we had a deal!"

"You're speaking out of turn, ferret!" Sarge roared.

Theda watched the scene with terror. The animals had forgotten her. They were arguing amongst themselves, the skunk shouting for order, the parrot screaming from his perch while the ferret hopped in fury. But Theda didn't care about them. The voice in the cage had been plain. It was only the lizard who mattered, and he was almost to the last step. If she didn't speak now, she'd lose him forever. "I've come about a young man!" She screamed, voice cracking with effort. "He came to the carnival to see *Stuart Krell!*"

Young man? The lizard jolted to a stop and turned. "What…?" his lips formed.

Scuttering toward Orie, the spider remembered her instructions from the mysterious voice. "Your friend is hurt and in trouble, and I think I know where he…"

A shadow flickered above.

Theda looked up, joy fading to shock.

Rocketing from his perch, the parrot descended, wings outstretched, beak open. "Get the net, get them!" Bennett boomed in a man's deep voice, "get them all!"

His pale eyes fixed on hers, the feathers along his head spiked in a ferocious display of anger, and a rolling wave of panic engulfed the spider. The voice sounded horribly familiar, but amidst the noise of the meeting she couldn't place it.

"Shut up, Bennett, I can't hear a thing!" Orie screamed, struggling back up the steps. Theda!" His eyes locked with hers. "What did you say?"

The spider wanted to respond, to fulfill her mission, but the bird was so close the draft from his wings almost lifted her body. With a gasp, she scurried backwards along the buckled floor. The bird plummeted, talons extended, razor beak opened, and she dropped by a slender silken thread between two boards, just as he landed.

"Theda!" the lizard's voice echoed, but she ignored it, lowering herself to the dirt, and scrambling over rotted pecans, and pebbles, until she was well beyond the gazebo. Blindly she ran, fearful of predators, but too afraid to stop. Gnarls of wisteria vines sent her tumbling, but she pushed on through weeds and ivy, until the sudden scent of wet earth and decay pierced her senses and she stopped. A familiar burble murmured beyond the brush. Pulse thudding, she followed the sound until, finally, through a small clearing, she glimpsed what seemed to be a river, its gentle waters winding to the left, while stands of sycamores rose like monoliths along its banks. For one vague moment, she considered walking into the glistening wetness, spinning through the murky darkness, legs limp and floating, and finally sinking to the bottom, much like the baby in her dream. But self-preservation won.

Racing to the closest tree, she scaled its trunk and hunkered beneath the sheltering bark. Engulfed by the loneliness of such anonymity, she curled in a tiny ball, legs tight against her abdomen, and gave way to angry sobs. She'd tried her best, and look what had happened. The voice in the cage had betrayed her. And no matter how loud it shouted, she'd never listen again.

* * *

"This is insane!" The cockroach screamed at Sarge. "You're the leader, why didn't you do something?"

Sarge snarled, the coyote howled, and all that remained of Bennett were three small gray feathers floating along the wooden plank.

Orie stood on the top step of the gazebo, transfixed by what Theda had said and amazed at how suddenly snippets of the telephone conversation had slammed to the surface of his memory. "I thought we were meeting at the carnival at noon." The girl's message had said. "…you have a cell, use it."

Meeting at the carnival at noon.

The Boy's friends and his mother had all tried to reach him…and no one had. Why? The lizard's heart pounded. There was more to the message, but he couldn't remember what. It didn't matter; the important thing was that The Boy was never without his cell phone. He was obviously in trouble, and the spider had come to the meeting specifically to tell Orie… but how had she known where to find him? And what had happened to Bennett? Orie had never seen the bird so agitated, or heard him mimic that particular voice before. What did "Get the net" mean, and where was Bennett now? After Theda's escape, he'd flown from the gazebo, unresponsive to the lizard's shouts of concern. Orie shook his head, desperate for clarity amidst the pandemonium now rocking the gazebo for the second time that day.

"Everybody quiet down!" the skunk screeched.

Startled, the animals stood solemnly in the grey haze of twilight.

"Okay." Sarge took a deep breath and looked around. "What in the heck just happened here?"

"Whadda ya' *think* happened?" The coyote slunk up the steps, thin sides heaving. "The spider looked good. The bird decided to eat it. Badda-bing. End of story!"

"You're wrong." The cockroach minced to the center of the gazebo, his antennae waving for attention. "Bennett's a parrot, right? And parrots have a curved beak." He shot the group a look of disdain. "Well, no curved-beaked bird eats insects. They only eat seeds and berries. So, sorry my misinformed friends," he sneered at the animals who listened in stony silence, "he wasn't trying to eat the spider."

Orie watched the insect, wondering how fast he could run it down and stomp it.

"And just how do you know that?" Sarge asked

"Because I live in the Fairmount Library, that's why," the roach said with prissy smugness. "And if I'd ever had a chance to tell *my* story, instead of listening to the insipid tales of every grub worm that's been eaten, you'd *know* this!"

"Oh bull!" the coyote barked. "When I look at a rabbit you guys are all over me. When the bird tries to eat the spider, it's excuse city. I should've known canines wouldn't get a fair shake from a group like you!"

"This thing is over!" The skunk shouted. "I've got a horrible headache, every rule in the book has been broken, and I'm sick of all of you."

"Over?" Blitz shouted, fur bushed. "But you'll love my story, it's very, very important!"

The gathering erupted into chaos, the animals pushing and shouting to be heard.

"I agree with the ferret! the coyote howled. "There's only one more meeting left before the hibernation break. Can't we just go on?"

"No!" the skunk screeched. "There's no telling allowed after dark. Rules are rules, and I can't help it if you're all undisciplined losers." He trotted down the steps, his black and white tail dangerously curved toward his back.

Only one more meeting? Stunned, Orie realized what had just happened. In the confusion, he'd completely forgotten about his decision to tell. Another opportunity had passed and there was only one Monday left. He watched Blitz, now screaming at Sarge and felt a tug of dread. She wouldn't forget their talk, and her threat had been clear. The answer was plain, Blitz could wait as well as the story...The Boy's safety couldn't.

Ignoring the arguments now escalating to curses and slurs, Orie ran to where the spider had disappeared, and slithered between the slats. He had to find Theda...she held the key.

CHAPTER 6

The pit bull crouched beneath a sprawling privet bush and stared at the vine covered structure. His intention had been to run as far from the carnival as possible, but then he'd smelled the animals and stopped...mesmerized. Clearly, he'd stumbled upon a Meeting of the Spoken Word, something he'd heard of, but never seen. For one sweet moment he thought of joining them, walking right up the steps to the gazebo and basking in an imagined cocoon of acceptance that he'd always longed for. But to tell his story would betray Mr. Krell, and canine law forbad disloyalty to any master. And besides, his life was too humiliating to share. With a sigh of resignation, he settled into the bushes by the gazebo, head resting on his tangled leash, his ears straining to hear the stories.

That was before the redback spider's arrival. Now, Axle's heart pounded and he strained to see through the approaching twilight. Before the parrot had interfered, she'd been trying to tell them about The Boy. Now the gazebo rang with hateful accusations, and the dog huddled beneath an indigo sky trying to understand what had happened.

Why had Theda told the meeting about what Mr. Krell had done, and why would these animals care?

Did The Boy belong to them in some way? No! The Boy was with him and Mr. Krell now. Axel lurched to all fours. He shouldn't be lying around listening to stories; he should be protecting the trailer; make sure nothing happened.

Stuart Krell's image loomed in his mind, and the pit bull cringed back onto the ground, whimpering with anxiety. Axel had almost forgotten about the scary thing in the cage, and the fact that he'd broken his leash and run away. None of this was good. Mr. Krell was probably really mad about it, and when he was mad, bad things happened.

The pit bull trembled. What should he do? Forget his new friend in the trailer? Go back to where he came from? Shadowed memories clouded his mind; his siblings' torn ears and ravaged faces…the sandy floored fighting pits splattered with blood, and the drunk and screaming men shouting for more. Axel licked his chops; tongue dry with apprehension. He couldn't go back there. Mr. Krell wasn't perfect, but at least he didn't fight dogs. A sharp recollection of Theda's story sent prickles of worry up his neck, and he shivered. Something was wrong, and he needed to get back. Forcing himself to stand, Axel headed through the bushes. The crisp air brought tears to his eyes, and his leash snapped and snaked behind him in the thorny weeds. Suddenly, he realized that he was running…toward what, he wasn't sure.

* * *

"Get the net!" Stuart Krell's booming voice reverberated in her ears, and Theda jerked to alertness. Was she dreaming? "Calm down," she whispered to herself. "You're hidden in a tree. Mr. Krell could never find you here." But it was definitely his voice, there was no denying it, and he obviously had a net! He was going to catch her and take her back! Horrified, she burrowed deeper into the wood, praying he would pass her by.

Something rustled close to her head. She held her breath, waiting to be recaptured… and then there was silence. Heart pounding, she straightened her legs and peaked from beneath the bark cover.

A pale, grey eye stared back.

It wasn't Mr. Krell; it was the crazy parrot from the meeting! With a shriek, Theda pulled herself into a tight ball, desperately looking for an escape route. There wasn't one.

The bird pecked at the tree, methodically stripping the bark until moonlight filtered through the last shred of wood, and he could see her plainly. Theda raised her fangs, hoping the parrot would back off. Instead, he hopped closer, his stare glassy and unfocused.

"Get the net," he repeated.

The spider felt confused. Maybe she'd only imagined that she'd heard Stuart's voice. It was obviously the parrot who was now speaking, and he was saying the same things she'd heard at the gazebo, only this time the voice sounded different; small, flat, and achingly sad.

"What do you want?" She asked, squirming as far from his beak as possible.

The bird clung to the tree and fluttered his wings. "I—I want to talk to you." He shook his head and as though just awakening. "My name is Bennett."

"Are you going to kill me?"

"What?" The parrot seemed shocked. "Gosh, no. I was listening to your story at the meeting." Bennett stopped and swallowed hard. "And—and you mentioned a name. Was it—was it Stuart Krell? Is that what you said?"

Theda stared. Why was he asking about Mr. Krell? The mysterious voice in the warehouse had been very specific that any information she had should be given to Orie only, and she assumed this included things concerning Krell. But she couldn't ignore the question. The bird seemed calm now, and she didn't want to anger him. Theda gave a vague shrug, hoping to discourage further conversation.

Bennett cocked his head, the feathers above his eyes ruffled with concentration. "Could that name be a character from a movie or maybe a soap opera?"

"I've never seen any," Theda said, happy for a question she could answer, "but I doubt it."

"How about a sit-com?" The parrot's eyes brightened with hope. "Or a documentary? There're always lots of names in those."

The spider shook her head.

Bennett blinked and sighed. "I didn't think so."

"Why do you ask?"

He shrugged. "Because the name sounded familiar and my old owner watched a lot of TV."

Beneath them, the river gently gurgled and tangled leaves swirled by its banks.

"So," Theda said with nervous cheer, "have you told your story yet?"

Bennett glanced away. "No. I probably never will."

"But, why?"

"Because I can't remember it," he said. "I don't know why...but I can't."

* * *

Orie's chest hurt and his breath was coming in a hoarse, ragged wheeze. He didn't know how long he'd been pushing through the park. It seemed like hours, but he knew it couldn't be, because the moon was still high overhead, and the lights had just gone out in the zoo. Desperately he flicked his tongue, trying to taste the spider's scent, but it was no use. He stopped, and grimaced. At some point he'd stepped on a bramble and a thorn had lodged in his toe. Now, every step hurt, his joints ached, and his night vision was awful.

Bats soared overhead, hawks watched from tree tops, and snakes slid beneath rocks and twigs. This was no place for a lizard, especially one with bad eyes and a puncture wound.

"Theda!" Orie called, his voice a tiny squeak amidst the busy silence of the night. Giant oaks rustled above him, their leafless branches suddenly sinister. In the distance, lights twinkled at the carnival, but here the park was dark, its perimeters hidden by bamboo and fences. What had ever made him think he could find a spider amidst this vastness? Never had he felt so small, and he hated small. "Come on!" he shouted with fury. "I've almost killed myself getting out here! Let's talk!"

"So talk," a voice said from behind.

Startled, Orie whirled in alarm.

Sitting in the grass, expression bright with intelligence, was a small, female lizard. Her back was a mottled brown, her skin looked spiny and rough, and her chin had a serious under-bite.

She was lovely.

With a provocative stretch, she pursed her lips in a mock kiss. "What's up, handsome one?"

Orie's head felt hot and there was a tingling in his snout that felt strangely exhilarating. No. He shook the feeling away. He was many years her senior and her behavior was disrespectful. This

34

upstart needed a lesson, and Orie was just the one to teach her. He decided to be kind but firm. Tell her who he was, allow her a moment of awestruck mortification, and then end with a scathing lecture on social morays that would leave her reeling. "I have a sticker in my toe," he said

"Awww." She gave a little frown of sympathy and got up. "Maybe I can pull it out."

The female was approaching! In a matter of moments they would be touching!

"No, no," Orie protested in a shrill and silly voice he didn't recognize "I'm fine." He tried to move, but his legs felt glued to the ground.

"Sit down," she said.

He sat.

She wrinkled her nose. "This is gonna make you feel a whole lot better." With quiet authority, she bent over his foot, delicately grabbed the splinter in her mouth, and pulled it out with one quick tug. She spit it onto the leaves. "There," she said, "good as new."

Orie felt a burst of what? Relief? His foot did feel better, but no, that wasn't it. Happiness? Certainly not, he was a lizard of importance with much on his mind. Hope? That rang a bell... but hope about what? "Nice job," he finally said, "very professional. I usually avoid stickers, but, this one was big and..." he knew he was rambling and wondered why he couldn't make eye contact, "are you a healer of some kind?"

"Me?" She howled with laughter. "A healer? That's great!"

The sound was loud and gravely, and leaning toward crude. In fact, her mouth was opened so wide that Orie could see straight down her throat.

It was adorable.

With a snorting giggle, she wiped her eyes. "Holy cannoli! All I did was pull out a sticker. Any dope can do that."

She had called him a dope. He was fascinated.

The female moved closer. "My name's La De Da. I heard you shouting out here and just wondered what was going on." She playfully bumped his shoulder. "So, what is going on?"

Orie hated to be touched, but suddenly, couldn't remember why. He bumped her back, and fought a rush of giddiness. "I'm Orie," he felt slightly hysterical. "I'm looking for a spider."

La De Da nodded, "me too...very tasty."

"No. I mean, I'm looking for a spider who wants to talk to me. I'm also looking for a parrot."

She stared. "That's very weird."

It *was* weird. Orie wished he had told her something else. "So—so anyway," he stammered, "thanks again. I'll see you around."

"When?"

Orie felt a twinge of terror. "When?"

"Yeah, you're cute. I want to see you again. So…when?"

She wanted to see him? Orie's mind whirled like a cyclone. What did that mean? The thought was repelling and interesting, and basically frightening as heck. "I'm very, very busy right now,"—he stalled—"and I'd—I'd have to check my schedule…"

"Ohhh," she interrupted with a knowing nod. "I get it. Hey, you don't have to be embarrassed. I mean, if you think you're too *old* and not up to a little companionship…." Her voice trailed off and she casually sniffed some grass.

Old? Orie scowled. What was she implying? Wait a minute. He experienced a sudden flash of insight, and his jaw jutted with resolve. He knew *exactly* what she was implying! Puffing his throat, he straightened his stance. "Does this look old to you?" Aching joints forgotten, he did an intricate little mating dance and flicked his tail like a whip. "You want to hang with me, fine…but I've got lives to save, sister, and it's going to be dangerous work. So if you think you're up to it"—he looked her dead in the eyes. —"Let's go."

Her smile was wide and hot as lava. "I'm right behind you." she said.

CHAPTER 7

Stuart Krell paced the trailer, his massive weight causing the dilapidated structure to shift and creak. He hadn't found the redback spider, which would piss Jerry off, and now the idiot dog was gone, which pissed *him* off. But that was nothing compared to the trouble that was tied up in the bathroom. He slouched to the curtain separating the toilet from the living area and pushed back the soiled cloth.

A young man lay on his side by the sink, his mouth covered with duct tape, his hands and feet tied. At first Stuart thought he might be dead because Jerry had hit him pretty hard. But the kid's eyes had finally opened, and a quick check of his injuries showed only a purple lump on his forehead. Stuart had quickly placed a bag of frozen peas against the wound, though he couldn't tell if it had helped. "Can you see this?" Stuart asked, holding a plump index finger in front of the kid's face. The boy nodded. "How many am I holding up? Blink once for one, and two for more." The boy squinted, and then blinked once. No double vision. That was good. The only problem was that the kid seemed to sleep a lot. Maybe he was just bored, or maybe he had a concussion, which would make things much harder for both of them.

The big man stamped his foot. "Hey Mr. College Boy!" he shouted, grabbing the curtain and shaking it hard. "Wake up! My friend wanted to kill you and I probably should've let him!" But Stuart would never allow that to happen, not until the kid gave him the information he so desperately needed.

College Boy had a ploughshare tortoise, one of the rarest reptiles in the world. Just the thought of what a find like that meant to Stuart's future made him light headed. If he could get his hands on that baby, he'd be set for life. No more crappy little carnival and stinking warehouse filled with animals. The big man's eyes narrowed, and better than that, no more Jerry. The kid hadn't moved, and Stuart shuffled down the hallway to the kitchen.

The young man's name was Colin O'Connell, and Stuart had read about the tortoise on Colin's college website. Apparently, someone found the injured animal smuggled in an unclaimed bag at the Dallas/Fort Worth airport. The local zoo had agreed to let the university biology department nurse it back to health because Mr. College Boy had quite a reputation as an up and coming herpetologist. Stuart had already checked with the university. Apparently the turtle was still in Colin's care. It hadn't taken much to lure the kid to the carnival and things could have gone so smoothly if he hadn't turned out to be one of those tree hugging, bleeding hearts! Stuart had barely mentioned the tortoise when the kid looked around the warehouse, saw the animals and threatened to call the cops. That's when Jerry walked in, freaked out, and things became violent.

A two liter bottle of Coke sat on the counter, which Stuart opened and chugged dry. He belched loudly. Where was the tortoise, and how was he going to get it without his idiot partner, Jerry knowing? Because he wasn't sharing this stroke of luck, not with anyone. The big man's temples throbbed. Things could get tricky. People would start asking questions when the kid didn't show up for class on Monday. He had to work fast.

Ambling to a sagging couch, Stuart lowered himself onto a cushion. Somehow he had to get the boy to talk by tomorrow, because he needed to empty the warehouse and get out of town fast.

Stuart loosened his belt, scratched his belly, and thought. As much as he hated involving himself in dangerous activities, there was only one way out of this: First, no matter what it took, he'd locate the tortoise. After that, he'd tell Jerry he'd changed his mind about killing the kid. They'd crate College Boy along with whatever animals they could sell to the dealer in Bolivia, and just send the kid on. The brokers always used a private plane, and those guys would know what to do with the body, they disposed of people all the time. Everything would be clean and simple, with nothing connecting him to the murder at all—Stuart reached for a bag of Fritos—except, of course, for Jerry.

There was a sudden banging at the door, and Stuart jumped, sending a fistful of corn chips into the air. A digital clock on the side table read eleven o'clock and his thoughts turned again to his missing pit bull, Axel. Where was the stupid dog when he needed him? Stuart turned and peered through the blinds. The trailer, which stood beneath a towering mesquite, was concealed from public view by rambling vines and bushes, and the soft glow of his camping lantern was the only thing visible in the darkness. Stuart used the trailer because of its isolation, but, now, with possible danger lurking in the shadows, he regretted that decision. Tightness gripped his chest, and slid like a serpent towards his throat. Could it be the police? No, they would make themselves known right away. Could it be kids…or some drunken locals trying to rob him… or worse?

The hammering sound grew more persistent, and Stuart's heart accelerated to an alarming speed. He massaged his chest and wondered if was having a heart attack. Grabbing a baseball bat that he kept by the couch, he tip toed to the door.

"It's Jerry!" a hoarse voice shouted. "Open up!"

A thick saliva filled Stuart's mouth, and he fought the urge to gag. Jerry never came to the trailer, especially not at this time of night. Sweat trickled down his forehead and into one eye. He blinked at the sting and willed himself to calm down. The situation with The Boy was getting to him. Stuart pressed his forehead against the coolness of the door. All he needed was aspirin and a little sleep to come up with a plan. Maybe if he just stood quietly, Jerry would go away. They could talk in the morning, in the more rational light of day, and things would feel normal again.

Footsteps crackled in the leaves, and a sudden pounding by the window rattled the glass, Stuart jumped.

"I know you're in there!" Jerry shouted.

There was no way out. Stuart squared his shoulders, took a deep breath, and unlocked the bolt. "It's late," he said, surprised at the steadiness of his voice. "What are you doing here?"

Jerry ran to the steps, his pock marked skin glowing like a moonscape in the hazy light. "I've just come from the carnival," he mumbled, pushing his way inside. "Something's happened, and it's bad."

* * *

"Bennett?" The spider asked. "Are you okay?"

The parrot started at the sound of her voice. He didn't know how long he'd been clinging to the tree, staring into the gloom of the park. The trance-like state was a familiar one that he often used to block unpleasantness. He'd been doing it since he was small, though usually in private. Embarrassed, he turned toward Theda who still crouched by the shredded bark, her many eyes kind but worried. "I'm fine," he said. But he wasn't. Ever since the meeting, an unsettled feeling had crawled through his mind, bumping the walls of his past like something blind and lost. Though Bennett was use to missing blocks of time, this particular incident troubled him. Did the nervous feeling pertain to the spider? It didn't seem likely, since they'd just met. Shaking his head, Bennett sighed. Already the night's events seemed foggy and far away. He recalled something about a man's name, one that had triggered fear and sadness, but now he couldn't remember what it was or why he had cared.

"I'm sorry I ran from you." Theda's voice interrupted his thoughts. "I'm not from here, and I've never been around parrots."

The bird looked up. "You ran from me?"

"At the gazebo." Theda fidgeted. "You don't remember?"

"Oh yeah," Bennett lied, "that's right." Despair tightened his throat. The spider had run from him, but he couldn't imagine why. The truth was; he could hardly remember the meeting at all. Frustrated, he pulled a clump of feathers from his chest, and both animals watched as it drifted in a fuzzy grey tuft to the ground. "Let's just drop it," he finally said. "Everything's fine now."

"Perfectly fine," she agreed, but her jolly tone suddenly dissolved into hitching sobs. "Sorry." Her voice cracked with misery. "I guess I'm just homesick."

"Where are you from?" Bennett asked. Homesickness was something he understood.

Theda hunched into a ball, tears rolling down her legs. "A long way from here."

The parrot bobbed his head in sympathy. "I know how you feel. The guy I used to live with kicked me out of the house a couple of months ago. I'd be dead right now if The Boy hadn't found me."

"The Boy?" Theda blinked with confusion. "You mean the young man I saw at the carnival?"

"Sure, The Boy. A lot of animals know him. Orie and I live with him. So does the ferret." Bennett felt confused by her question. "Do you know him, too?"

"Not exactly." The spider tapped three legs against the tree with anxiety. "I'd like to explain, but I'm not supposed to talk about this to anyone but the lizard." She looked hopeful. "Do you think Orie is still at the meeting?"

"No," the bird said, glancing at the star spattered sky. "It's late. Meetings always end by dusk. But if you want, maybe I could help you find him." Bennett hopped to a branch and steadied himself on a twig. "I saw a movie once where a dragon flew around with a kid on his back. My former owner was a movie critic, and he gave it three stars for originality. I personally thought the animation wasn't quite up to par, but it was entertaining."

Theda blinked. "I don't understand."

"Well, you're pretty small and the park is really big." The spider was nice, he thought. Maybe they could be friends. The dark feelings faded into excitement, and Bennett felt good again, like when he heard engines. "Why don't you crawl on my back and we'll fly around like they did in the movie, and look for Orie?"

Theda unfolded her legs, scuttled forward a few steps, and then stopped. "Are you sure you actually want me *on* you?" Her multiple eyes shown with wonder. "I mean...I could be...well, you don't know anything about me."

"What's there to know?" The parrot cocked his head. "You're a garden spider, right?"

"Right," she said, with a happy smile. "That's exactly what I am."

CHAPTER 8

Darting through the underbrush, the ferret scanned every shadow for danger. In addition to dogs and children, the River Cats were a well-known threat for any small animal that blundered into their territory. Though Blitz didn't fear most felines, large colonies of hungry ferals were another matter.

The ferret sat and yawned. She'd been trailing Orie ever since he'd left the meeting, and she was tired. At first, his odor was strong and easy to follow, but then a decaying rat's carcass had thrown Blitz off, and she lost valuable time back-tracking. Raising her slender head, she perked her ears. Dark branches swayed in the autumn breeze, and squirrels chattered from above, their nests temporarily camouflaged by fading leaves and shadows.

The zoo, with its surrounding park and soccer field, was vast and finding something as small as the spider would be difficult. However, Blitz thought, scratching an itch beneath her chin, it was only a matter of time before she tagged Orie's scent again. The ferret sniffed the ground, her pointed nose rooting beneath pecans and twigs. The meeting had dissolved into chaos, and though she hadn't heard much above the commotion, whatever the spider said had shocked Orie. Something big was happening...big enough to stop the meeting and derail Orie from telling 'their' story.

She stopped, jumped and zigzagged in a war dance of anger. The darned spider was spoiling everything! Blitz's mouth tightened with determination. Things were finally looking up, and she wasn't about to share her imminent celebrity with a bug.

A fat yellow moon glimmered against the velvety sky, and Blitz detected a twang of winter beneath the brisk air. Soon the nights would be cold, and she felt a surge of gratitude for The Boy and his kindness. Human companionship was an oddity to her, since most of the ferret's life had been spent in a cage pushed to the back of a pet store. It wasn't that no one wanted to adopt Blitz; the problem was that no one kept her, and the reason for this was clear; She stole things...interesting things...things that people cherished and searched for with astonishing tenacity. And she enjoyed it. Unfortunately, no matter how ingenious her hiding place, humans always discovered the stash and back Blitz would go to the pet shop, to be exchanged for some bland little creature, less exotic, but more appropriate for theft-free living.

After three embarrassing returns, luck intervened, and a woman finally took Blitz home. Things progressed nicely, and just when her future seemed secure, the lady's malevolent dachshund butted in. Blitz bristled at the memory of his aggressive arrogance. His final betrayal had been despicably complete, and if the ferret hadn't escaped at the last minute, the pet store might have been her final resting place.

But it wasn't. After weeks of wandering, The Boy discovered Blitz shivering behind a woodpile and things fell into place. In fact, they turned out so well that today, with only the teensiest bit of intimidation and some good old fashioned blackmail, Blitz had finally clinched a deal with Orie that had 'Ferret Fame' all over it. Now all that remained was for Orie to tell their story before he died, forgot, or both.

With a determined sigh, Blitz pushed her nose along the ground, sorting through a hodgepodge of odors. Something sharp poked her lip, and she shook her head. A small thorn tumbled to the ground. The sticker reeked of Orie's familiar scent, and she poofed her cheeks with surprise. He'd definitely been here, and not long ago. Raising her muzzle, she breathed deeply. There was another smell, too, with the same tartness of Orie's, and a hint of minty pheromone. Blitz sniffed again. It was plainly reptile, the ferret scowled, and female. Orie had a new friend! Now, in addition to the spider and the bird, there was another interloper. Clenching her jaws, Blitz fought a flush of panic. Females of all species were tricky opponents. What if the new lizard prevented Orie from telling their new and improved story, or worse yet, talked him into sharing it with *her* instead of Blitz? "No!" the ferret shouted, startled by the sound of her own voice in the chilly silence. That wasn't going to happen. After locating Orie, she'd explain her concerns to whomever he was with, and then invite the stranger to get lost or die.

The solution was perfect, and Blitz relaxed. Fate had handed her a brand new life with a celebrated friend whose heroic story would soon be hers. In addition: the kleptomania was under control, and she was a whisker away from the kind of adulation she'd always dreamed of. A burr of concern pricked her consciousness, and she scowled. There *had* been that one little incident at The Boy's house. Blitz's tail swished with anxiety. But it was such a small thing…just a naughty little relapse brought on by nerves and boredom, certainly nothing that would be discovered before the meeting. And besides, she thought, trotting briskly through the leaves. The Boy hadn't even noticed, and as all ferrets knew; if they didn't notice, it didn't count.

* * *

La De Da and Orie lay on top of a picnic table, their bodies barely touching. The search for Bennett had proved discouraging. Tired and hungry, Orie suggested a rest. The decision was a lucky one, because a Popsicle had melted among the table's littered surface, its sweet, red puddle alive with ants. Within minutes, the two lizards consumed every last insect, leaving nothing but a gloss of stickiness in their wake. Now, stomachs bulging with contentment, they relaxed in silence.

Orie sighed and assessed his surroundings. Paint chipped Jungle Gyms and grimy barbeque grills dotted the park landscape. Beside each picnic table, garbage spewed from the tops of black wire receptacles and tumbled onto the dusty ground. They were lovely in a modernistic sort of way, and the lizard wondered why he'd never noticed the splendor of trash before. In fact, suddenly everything shone with a golden glow he couldn't identify. A car alarm screamed in the distance and he smiled at its musicality. A raccoon scurried past the table, two babies in tow, and Orie almost wept at the wonder of motherhood.

Motherhood?

The lizard jumped to his feet. What was wrong with him? He turned toward La De Da, a coil of suspicion strangling his fast fading euphoria. This embarrassing drivel had all started with *her*. Orie narrowed his eyes and watched the female intently.

She dozed on an empty hamburger bag, her body twitching with wheezing snores, and a stream of drool pooling beneath her chin.

Orie wrinkled his snout with distaste. Without a doubt, she was the messiest, loudest, most unrefined animal he'd ever met. Not only did she chew with her mouth open, spewing food with a gusto usually reserved for middle school lunchrooms, but she belched for fun, snorted when she laughed, and had stepped on his sore toe so many times it now throbbed like a boom box. Orie set his jaw with resolve. He had completely lost track of his mission, which was to find Bennett and the spider. The female was a distraction, and she had to go.

As if on cue, La De Da-Da opened a round yellow eye, twisted onto her side, and grinned. "Hi, handsome one," she murmured. Her languid gaze turned skyward, and the moon's reflection bathed her face in a silvery shaft of light.

Flecks of ant remains still stuck to her forehead, and the urge to wipe them off was so overpowering, that Orie forgot what he'd been thinking. He wondered if he was going insane and destined to wander the streets, babbling, and incontinent. He didn't care. Tenderly he brushed the crumbs away from her mottled skin.

Stretching, she flashed a lazy smile of gratitude. "Was I all dirty again?"

"Sort of." Orie took a deep breath. "La De Da, there's something I want to tell you."

"Okay," she said, "but there's something I should tell you, first"

Orie felt the jolt of anxiety that came whenever she spoke to him. "What?"

"Well," she raised one slender foreleg and pointed high above them. "I think I've found the parrot."

CHAPTER 9

"What are you talking about, Jerry?" Stuart shut the door and allowed his body to relax a little. He had over reacted. His partner's visit wasn't about the boy, it was about the warehouse. Putting down the bat, he leaned against the wall. "It's late, I'm tired. If this isn't about cops, it can wait 'til tomorrow."

"You're not listening!" Jerry shouted. "Something weird is going on in the warehouse! I'm not crazy, so don't even look at me like I'm crazy, man, because I know what I saw!"

A sickly stench of sweat and alcohol wafted through the room, and Stuart wondered if Jerry was drunk. If so, though he seemed more agitated than dangerous, it was better to placate him. "Okay." The fat man lowered himself on to the couch, kicked off his shoes, and crossed his ankles in an attempt to appear casual. "What did you see?"

Jerry ran a thick, freckled hand through his hair. "Well, I—I decided if you couldn't find the spider, maybe I could." He stopped and gave Stuart a confrontational stare which the big man ignored. "So, I grabbed a flashlight, went on over to the carnival, let myself in the warehouse, and started looking around." Jerry licked his lips, sat in a chair, then stood up again. "But, pretty soon I got this creepy feeling, like…I don't know. Like something was watching me, or…." his voice trailed off and he wiped his palms on his jean.

"Of course you were being watched," Stuart said, wishing the man would either pass out or go home, "you were in a room full of animals."

Jerry took a ragged breath. "Yeah, it was an animal all right." In spite of the drop in temperature, a bead of sweat rolled from his sideburns and coursed down his jaw. "It was that stinking hyena thing..."

"You came all the way over here for that? Stuart huffed with disgust. "If it bothers that much...put a cover over the cage."

"It wasn't in the cage," Jerry said, slowly, "it was sitting behind the door."

Stuart sat forward with such force that the couch's back legs tipped off the floor. "What?"

"Yep," Jerry muttered, his eyes fixed and glassy. "Old 'A' was just sittin' there, staring at me with those crazy gold eyes. And not like some wild animal, Stuart...but more like the family cat...watching me real calm, like it had lived in that hell-hole all of its life. Like it was happy there."—Jerry paused—"like it was waiting for me."

Stuart struggled to his feet, and the couch righted itself with a thump. Obviously Jerry was more than drunk...he was delusional.

"And here's the best part, Stu, the really best part." Jerry moved closer, his voice lowered to a conspiratorial whisper, his breath a tepid mix of beer and onions. "The door to its cage was closed. Understand what I'm saying? The door was closed and *locked*, but old 'A' was...*out*."

"That's not possible," Stuart said, turning away, and shaking his head so hard that his jowls flapped and jiggled. "Everything was secured when I left, and I have the only key." He patted his shirt pocket. "See? It's right here."

"I don't care about your key!" Jerry shrieked. "He was out!"

Stuart took a protective step back and felt the crunch of a corn chip flatten beneath his heel. Jerry had always been paranoid, but this was extreme even for him. Obviously, kidnapping the boy had pushed him over the edge. "Keep your voice down. I believe you," he said, careful to make his tone friendly and calm. "Maybe in all the confusion, I just *thought* I locked the door." The big man steadied himself on a side table, eyed the discarded baseball bat, and casually brushed the crumbs from his foot. "Tell you what;

you're tired. I'll go to the warehouse, put...put Mr. 'A' in his cage. Okay?"

"You don't have to do that," Jerry said, his voice flat and low.

Stuart frowned. "I can't leave a dangerous animal like that running around. It could kill the birds, or..."

"It's not running around."

"But you just said..."

"...I know what I said," Jerry interrupted. His face was flushed, and small black moles dotted his throat like ticks. "I haven't told you everything. See, I got real freaked tonight, sort of lost it, if you know what I mean." He gave Stuart a belligerent glare that wavered between rage and desperation. "Hey, I'm not proud. I got scared, so what?"

Stuart said nothing. The sooner Jerry told his crazy story, the quicker he could get him out of the trailer and figure out what to do.

"When I saw that locked cage," Jerry continued, "I ran out of the place as fast as I could, and slammed the door behind me. But half way to my car, I realized I'd left my keys in the warehouse. So, I crept around to the side of the building, climbed on top of a couple of crates, and looked in the window to see where our old pal, 'A', was. I mean, I didn't want to waltz back in there and get eaten or something." He paused, his mouth suddenly stretched into a sly grin. "But I didn't have to worry about that, Stuart. You know why?"

The big man shook his head.

"Because 'A' was back in its cage!" Jerry howled, his eyes bulging from their sockets. "How did it do that, Stuart?" Froth bubbled at the corners of his mouth. "Could you tell me how something just moves in and out of a locked cage?"

Stuart suddenly felt clammy, as though he might pass out. Had someone been in the warehouse? His mind flickered to the boy tied up in his bathroom. Was it possible that an unseen witness had called the police or that the kid's friends were already looking for him? "I don't know the answer to that," Stuart said, desperately trying to think, "but I promise we'll figure it out in the morning." He placed his hand on Jerry's arm and gently pulled him toward the door.

"And—and there was something else, dude," Jerry babbled, clutching Stuart's shirt-sleeve, "something I noticed when I first walked in."

"What's that?" Stuart asked, turning the door knob, and firmly guiding Jerry through the opening.

Jerry turned on the steps, his face stark in the moonlight. "It's name's not 'A'...anymore."

CHAPTER 10

Orie looked up in shock, his eyes following La De Da's pointing claw to a swag of branches swaying above them. Nestled in the crook of one moon-outlined limb was a gray blob of feathers, hunched in formless silence. Orie knew that lump; it was Bennett.

"Bennett!" he shouted. "Bennett, wake up!"

The parrot squirmed, pushing his head further beneath his wing, and slept on.

"Wow," La De Da said, "is he deaf?"

"No," Orie scowled, "just annoying". Silently, he paced along the picnic table, ignoring the gummy drag of syrup sticking to his claws and tail. A muscle ached by his left knee, his toe felt inflamed, and he wanted nothing more than to go home, crawl beneath the sink, and forget the whole thing. But The Boy was in trouble, and time was wasting. He looked up. The oak tree loomed skyward, its angular limbs bare, black, and spread like a witches hand. In younger days the lizard would have scrambled up the rough surface in seconds, but now... "Bennett!" he screamed again, despising his infirmities and everyone who witnessed them. "It's Orie! Come down! I need to talk to you!"

The bird remained motionless.

La De Da nudged his side. "You should probably just go up there and wake him." She peered into his face then patted him protectively on the shoulder. "Forget it, hon, I'll do it."

Orie drew his mouth into a tight little line. So it had finally come to this; a female was telling him what to do.

And she'd called him, 'hon'.

Well, the lizard thought, with an inward sneer, he didn't need help from anyone, especially some pushy little upstart from the wrong side of the park. Orie widened his stance. No matter how much it hurt, he and he alone would climb up the tree and awaken Bennett. "Stay where you are," he commanded. Marching forward, his eyes followed the trunk up to the first branch, then to the second, third and fourth...and finally to the one so impossibly far away that held the sleeping parrot. This was more than a tree, it was a twenty story building covered with bark.

Orie shifted his eyes to La De Da who now stood to the side, watching. On second thought, he reasoned, this was war. Generals didn't risk their lives in battle. He brightened...that's what privates were for! "I've changed my mind," Orie said, his voice brisk with assertiveness, "get up there, and make it snappy."

La De Da nodded, and in one motion leapt from her spot on the table and began a quick ascent to the first branch. She turned and waved one claw.

Orie waved back, and then blinked, his front leg suspended in midair, his mouth dry as a Texas July.

A large dark form fluttered onto an adjacent limb, and steadied itself against a protruding knot hole. Its head swiveled to watch La De Da as she scurried upward; it's large, round eyes glowing in the moonlight.

"La De Da!" Orie bellowed in a voice he hardly recognized as his own. "There's an owl above you! RUUUUUUN!"

Panicked, La De Da spun on the bark trying to locate the predator.

Orie took a running start and flung himself onto the tree. Something in his hip popped and spasmed, but he ignored it and with a blast of renewed energy scrambled higher. "Hey!" he shouted, his breath coming in hitching wheezes. "It's me, Orie, The Legendary Lizard! Check it out!"

Rotating it's neck to the right, the owl blinked once, and then turned its attention back to La De Da, who now found herself trapped between the huge bird and the oncoming rush of Orie bearing down from behind.

Beak open, the owl lunged towards La De Da, when suddenly, a blur of grey rocketed through the branches and body slammed the bird from behind.

"Go, Orie!" Bennett shouted, disappearing behind some branches, and then streaking downward to deliver another blow to the predator's head.

The owl whirled in fury, its wings flapping wildly, as the two lizards swirled down the tree and under the picnic table.

"We're okay! We're safe!" Orie screamed from the shadows.

One last blow from the agile parrot sent the owl soaring towards the zoo, its angry screeches harsh against the sleepy stillness of the park.

Bennett fluttered to the ground, his feathery brow furrowed in concern. "What in the heck are you doing all the way out here?" He peered beneath the table. "You could have been killed!"

Orie's heartbeat thudded in his ears, and every time he moved, his hip grated and cracked in a symphony of pain. Behind him, La De Da pressed against his flank, her body trembling, and Orie realized just how close they'd come to disaster. And why? His eyes narrowed in anger. Because of the stupid parrot! If it hadn't been for Bennett, the spider would never have run away and none of this would be happening. "What are you talking about!" Orie screamed, charging the bird. "Do you think I like stumbling around in the dark? I've been looking for you all night!" A horrible thought gripped his mind and he stopped in mid stride. "You didn't... kill the spider did you?"

"No!" Bennett hopped backwards, his face blank with bewilderment. "Why does everyone keep talking like that?"

Orie turned on the parrot with renewed fury. "Because you acted like a lunatic at the meeting, that's why!" He scuttled closer, until his snout almost touched Bennett's chest. "Do you know what it's been like for me out here?" He raised his foot and wiggled the sore toe for inspection. "See this? The bird hung his head in misery, and Orie's voice cracked with self-pity. "I'm tired, Bennett, tired and cold. I've been limping around in this God forsaken place all alone... "

"What do you mean, alone?" La De Da's voice interrupted. She marched out of the shadows; mouth set with disapproval.

"Well, not—not totally alone," Orie sputtered. He scuffed one claw at a discarded Popsicle stick and avoided her gaze. "I've had too much sugar, I don't' know what I'm saying."

The female pushed past him and smiled at the bird. "I'm La De Da. Thanks for saving our lives."

"No problem." Bennett said. He flew to the picnic table, and waited for the lizards to join him. "I'll admit I don't quite remember the meeting, but I would never hurt the spider. Theda's my friend." His pale eyes widened in sudden surprise. "And how about this for a coincidence; she's been looking for you, too!" The bird twisted his head around until it almost faced his back. Frowning, he rummaged his beak beneath each of his wings, then flipped forward, his head upside down, his eyes peering between his legs.

"What are you doing?" Orie's voice was breathless from the climb.

"I'm looking for Theda." The parrot said, preening through the feathers on his belly. "She was on my back." Carefully, he raised each clawed talon, checking between his toes, then straightened up, his expression confused. "That's funny. I don't know where she is."

A tsunami of fury engulfed the lizard. The entire day had been a nightmare. He wished he'd never gone to the meeting, he wished he was back at the house…but mainly, he wished for teeth so he could kill the parrot. "You idiot!" He shouted, launching himself at the startled bird. "You lost the spider!"

"I'm not lost." A muffled voice called from the darkness. "Look behind you."

CHAPTER 11

The pit bull crouched beneath the trailer, watching as Jerry stumbled away through the trees. He'd been listening to the two men's voices for some time now, and his legs felt weak with anxiety. The thing in the warehouse was out and Jerry had seen it! Axel gave a keening whine of fear.

The door slammed open, and Stuart's massive frame filled the opening. "Who's there?" He squinted into the darkness. "Jerry? Is that you?"

Squirming into the open, the dog cowered in the dimness of the gas light, suddenly aware of the frayed leash twisted around one hind leg.

Stuart stood silhouetted in the yellow light of the door, a wooden bat clenched in one hand. His small blue eyes flitted first to Axel, then darted nervously from side to side finally settling on the shadowed stand of Mesquite trees that formed a natural protection between the trailer and the park. "I've got a big pit bull here!" Stuart shouted into the night. "So if someone's out there, you'd better keep going!" Squirrels rustled in their nests, and a roof rat scampered across the top of the trailer and onto a branch. Stuart jumped at the sound, then stepped back, and slapped his thigh. "Axel! Get in here!"

Low to the ground, Axel crept up the steps. He'd been hit with the bat before, and steeled himself for the first blow. Instead, Stuart unhooked the torn leash and delivered a half-hearted swat to the dog's flank as he bolted into the trailer. Amazed by the reprieve, Axel scurried to the kitchen, and quickly curled into a tight ball on the rug below the sink, his eyes fixed on Stuart.

The man paced the length of the trailer…his bare feet white against the linoleum, his pudgy hands clutching the bat to his chest. Finally, he stopped at the bathroom and yanked the curtain open.

Axel tensed. He heard the sound of something hard crack against metal and then a muffled cry from The Boy. Jumping to all fours, he cautiously approached the hallway.

"Listen, kid, don't make me hurt you!" Stuart's voice shrilled and Axel detected the familiar stench of his sweat. "All I want is for you to agree to tell me where the turtle is. Okay? Just tell me where the freakin' turtle is and then I'll let you out of here."

The pit bull inched closer, until he stood beside the curtain. Slowly, he nudged a grimy corner of fabric aside with his nose and looked inside the small room. The Boy was sitting up with his back against the tub. A piece of tape covered his mouth and his hands were bound by electrical cord that coiled from behind his waste like a snake.

"You're name's Colin, right?" The fat man leaned forward, the purple birthmark livid against his lip. "Nod your head for 'yes'."

The Boy nodded.

"Okay, Colin. I'm going to remove the tape." Stuart raised the bat at a threatening angle. "And if you shout for help or anything, I swear I'm going to hit you with this."

Axel felt a surge of panic that made his guts roil. "Please." He prayed silently, "Please do what Mr. Krell says."

The Boy nodded again, and Stuart pulled the tape off of his mouth with one motion.

Colin worked his jaws and blinked in the dim light. "Where are my glasses?" he asked in a croaky voice. "I can't see without them."

Stuart slowly lowered himself onto the rim of the bathtub, and stretched his legs. "Tell me where the turtle is and I'll give you your glasses."

Shifting his position, The Boy grimaced. "What turtle?"

Stuart banged the bat against the sink and the metallic crack made Axel whine involuntarily. Krell didn't notice, and the dog panted with relief.

"Don't play games with me, college man." Stuart said quietly. "I'm talking about the ploughshare turtle you've been rehabbing. Where is it?"

The Boy seemed surprised. "How—why—why do you want to know that?" he stammered.

"Because I'm the question guy, Colin." Stuart nudged the boy's jaw with the bat. "And I'd like an answer before I break your face."

* * *

"Theda?" Orie spun around on the picnic table, his eyes straining into the chilly gloom. "Where are you?"

"From the smell, I'd say I'm in a garbage can." Came the spider's faint reply.

Bennett hopped to the rim of an overflowing trash container, and peered into its murky depths, feathers ruffled. "How did you get in there?"

"I fell off when you went for the owl."

"Who cares how she got there!" Orie bawled. "Just get her out!" He joined the bird beside the wire container and looked in. Fast food sacks and soda bottles tumbled from a mountain of newspapers, paper plates and cigarette butts. "It's okay, spider." Orie said in a voice he hoped was comforting, but which actually came out as pinched and annoyed. "The owl is gone."

"What about the lizard?" Theda's muffled voice asked.

Orie stamped his foot in frustration. "I *am* the lizard for cryin' out loud!"

"The *other* lizard." She said quietly.

Bennett and Orie looked at one another, and then turned to see La De Da who was poised on the rim of the trash can, her tongue flicking, eyes hard and predatory.

"I can taste her scent!" La De Da whispered. "She's right behind that plastic stuff. I'm going in and get her."

"Are you nuts?" Orie pounded the table with both claws. "I need to talk to her which won't be possible if she's dead. So, could you just back off..." he flicked his head, indicating the edge of the picnic table furthest from the trash can—"And stay over there?"

La De Da shrugged, then jumped back to the table. "Sorry. Ants never fill me up." Sashaying to a far corner, she winked at Orie before sitting down. "I'll be good, handsome one."

"Don't call me that. "Orie said, trying to look stern. But he felt a lopsided smile forming on his mouth and he quickly looked away and cleared his throat. "Okay, spider, let's have some answers. We can't stay here forever."

A faint rustling sound emanated from beneath a plastic cup, and Theda slowly emerged one trembling black leg at a time. She stopped, teetering on the lipstick stained rim. Her mandibles clicked with fear. "I think I'll just stay here."

Impatient and tired, Orie leaped forward, then saw the red stripe on her back and instinctively recoiled. "I've had it!" he shouted, tail whipping with fury. "Where is The Boy?"

CHAPTER 12

The ferret slunk quietly through the underbrush, her long body low to the ground. She'd found Orie and his 'friends' and allowed herself a moment of smug satisfaction before moving on. Carefully, she maneuvered past brambles and vines as she approached the picnic table and the little group assembled there. Blitz stopped, her nose quivering. The parrot's scent was easy and strong to detect, as was Orie's. But the female lizard's presence wasn't apparent until Blitz saw her move in the shadows...and the spider was only detectable through voice. Tired and hungry, she decided to make her presence known and escort Orie home, when the spider suddenly broke the silence. Intrigued, Blitz sank behind a cement water fountain and listened.

"I was only supposed to tell Orie about this." Theda said. "But I guess it doesn't matter since all of you are here anyway."

A horn honked in the distance, and the animals jumped at the intrusion.

"There's a warehouse behind the carnival. It's just up the road, that way." The spider gestured with one delicate leg.

Orie sighed with impatience. "We know where it is. It's been around for years."

"Well, right now it's filled with animals," Theda paused, and cleared her throat, "some of them dead. A man stole us from our homes all over the world, and brought us here to sell. Somehow your boy, *The* Boy," she corrected, "ended up there this morning. I saw him." Her voice quavered. "The fat man wanted something from him, but The Boy was so upset when he saw the condition the animals were in that he threatened to call the police. He said we were endangered species and it was illegal to trap us, and that's when it happened."

Orie drew a quick breath. "What? What happened?"

Theda jumped off the cup and swung onto the picnic table by a silken cord. Her voice rose with anger. "That's when the other man came in and hit The Boy! He fell down and the two of them dragged him out the door! They're bad people! You have to help!"

Bennett fluttered to a branch, his beak gaping with fear. "Orie!" He squawked, grey feathers ruffled. "Do something!"

Blitz backed away from the water fountain, her ferret mind racing. So that was it. The Boy was hurt and kidnapped. Stealthily, she inched along the shadows, stopping behind the tree where Bennett perched, careful to keep downwind.

"Where did they take him?" Orie asked.

"To the fat man's trailer."

"Trailer?" Bennett cocked his head.

"Yes. I think it's where he lives." Theda shuffled her legs with anxiety. "But the thing in the cage didn't mention a trailer. He said that the answer is at the carnival."

Orie's head shot up. "What thing in the cage, and what answer?"

"I don't know what it is, and that's all it said." The spider fidgeted with distress. "Its voice told me what to do when I escaped this morning and where to find the meeting. I was so scared and it was so dark in there, I never looked back. She shrugged. "But somehow it knew exactly where you'd be. It—it seems to know things…" Her voice trailed off.

A soft wind blew through the park, and the stars faded into a drowsy twilight.

"We're going to the carnival, right?" Bennett asked.

"Maybe." Orie said. "But first we find the trailer."

* * *

Stuart Krell leaned closer to The Boy's trembling body. "I'm going to ask you once more: Where is the turtle?"

"I don't have it anymore." Colin answered in a calm tone. "We sent it to a zoo up north."

The birthmark above Stuart's lip seemed to pulse, its color deepening into a bright, hot fuchsia against the pasty skin. You're lying." Stuart said, his voice a little too patient. "I've done my research, kid. It hasn't gone anywhere."

"Can't help you." The Boy's eyes fixed unblinkingly on the big man's face. "It's gone."

The air was thick with silence, and horror flooded Axle's mind. The Boy wasn't going to tell! The dog could feel the truth of this in every nerve of his body. He paced in the hallway, trying to think of some way to divert Stuart's attention. Short of attacking his master there was nothing he could come up with, and frustrated and frightened, he stood in the bathroom doorway whining with anxiety. Stuart looked up at the sound, and flashed an unexpected smile. "Come on in, Axel." He said.

Mr. Krell's voice held a breezy good will that the dog had never heard before. He licked his chops and took a tentative step forward.

"Good boy." Stuart patted his massive thigh with encouragement. "Come here and meet someone."

Axel felt a burst of joy. His prayers had been answered! His master was happy. Maybe The Boy was telling the truth and wouldn't be harmed. Wagging his stump of a tail he slunk to the big man's side.

"You really are an animal lover, aren't' you kid?" Stuart asked, positioning the dog's body between the two of them and slowly stroking the pit bull's massive head.

The Boy nodded, but his eyes were tense and watchful.

Stuart encouraged the dog to lick Colin's arm, and chuckled. "You're such an honorable guy, I'll bet you'd let me break your head rather than tell me where the turtle is." Stuart pulled Axel closer and rubbed his ears. "Do you like dogs, Colin?" The Boy didn't answer, and Stuart scratched Axle's rump until the dog's leg thumped with pleasure. "Because this one has sort of a sad story." He leaned forward, and a bead of sweat dropped from his nose and onto The Boy's cheek. "A guy I knew owed me money, and asked if I'd take a one of his pit bulls in trade. I said sure because I really do admire the breed." Gently, he bent down, pushed Axel onto the tile floor, and massaged one thick paw.

Axel mouthed the man's hand in gratitude. No one had ever touched him with affection before, and he wondered if he was dreaming.

"But instead of giving me one of his fighting dogs," Stuart continued. "He brings me this…" Stuart gestured at the fawning dog at his feet. "You know why?"

The Boy swallowed and shook his head.

"Because the guy was using Axel as bait to teach the other dogs to fight, and didn't care about him anyway." Stuart moved his hand to the dog's neck and stroked it. "Can you imagine doing something like that to an animal?" He looked up, his brow furrowed with sincerity. "You strike me as a guy that wouldn't approve of that sort of thing." Stuart reached down and grabbed the dog's muzzle, playfully shaking it. "Doesn't he, Axel? Doesn't Colin look like that kind of a guy?"

Axel squirmed on the ground, his mind adrift in a happy fog of acceptance and love. He would have preferred that Mr. Krell not mention his past to anyone, especially The Boy, Mr. Krell was the alpha and it looked like they were a pack at last.

"Now, I realize you're a white knight and all that." Stuart continued. "But I feel everyone responds to incentives, and here's one for you. Nothing bad is going to happen to that turtle because he's too valuable to harm, but if you don't tell me where it is," he grabbed Axel by the scruff of his neck and yanked him on to all fours, "I *am* going to kill this dog."

The pit bull yelped with pain and surprise, and then stood quivering with confusion beneath Stuart's pinching grasp. What had just happened? What had he done wrong?

"So this is what I'm going to do." Stuart wiped his now dripping face on the back of his sleeve and shoved Axle's hindquarters into a sitting position. With a grunt, he pushed up from the edge of the tub and ambled through the doorway toward the living room. In a moment he came back, Axle's leash in his hand. Breathing hard from the effort, Stuart bent down on one knee, attached the leash to the dog's collar and then tied the other end around The Boy's ankle with two hard knots. "I'm going to let you two bond tonight…sort of get to know one another if you get my meaning." Stuart heaved himself to his feet. "Then, in the morning you can tell me what it's going to be; you can either hand over the turtle and the whole thing will be over…or you can watch me shoot this nice dog." He brushed off his pants and winked. "It's strictly up to you."

CHAPTER 13

Pris and Zekki relaxed on Mrs. O'Connell's favorite chair, their soft bodies entwined in a circle of legs, tails and paws. Moonlit shadows danced across their faces and the house smelled of rosemary and garlic from a roast simmering in the crock pot.

There had been a time when Zekki would have preferred sitting in the window sill, his eyes squinting past the front porch, his heart aching to leave the safety of 6th Avenue and explore the wonders of the Outs. But that was before Jett had lured Zekki and Pris into an adventure that almost resulted in Pris's death. The white cat's breath quickened at the thought. How could he have been so foolish? Never mind, he thought, licking his shoulder. That was years ago, and after Buddy's ascension to Cat Master and the death of his malevolent brother Jett, Zekki accepted his life as in Indoor with genuine contentment. Of course, The Boy had grown up, and he and Pris missed Buddy, but Frank, the neighboring dachshund, and Soot, Buddy's feral son kept them apprised of things beyond the house. As far as Zekki was concerned, stories about the Outs were definitely preferable to living there.

He gazed at the sleeping Pris with affection. No longer the timid young cat of their youth, the plush calico now strode through the house with confidence, firmly reminding Zekki that The Boy and Mrs. O'Connell had been the best thing that could happen to any animal. The white cat agreed. Though they rarely saw The Boy, his mother was a great source of comfort and both felines loved her dearly. The fact that she was gone for the week made Zekki slightly uncomfortable, but the pet sitter seemed efficient and friendly. Thankfully, she'd left after breakfast, and the cats were glad to be alone.

Well, not entirely alone, Zekki reminded himself. There *was* the 'thing' in the bathroom.

With a wide yawn, he stretched, shook his long white fur, and jumped from the cushion.

Unconcerned by his departure, the calico readjusted her position, then pushed her head further beneath one plump paw, and slept on.

Zekki trotted down the hall to the open doorway and stopped. This was the uncomfortable part. His and Pris's litter box was kept in Mrs. O'Connel's bathroom, and for the last week something else had been sharing the space with them…a turtle.

It wasn't that Zekki disliked turtles; but all Indoors considered their litter box as sacred territory. The bathroom had always served as a nice, quiet place for Zekki and Pris to take care of business, ponder life's mysteries, and stretch out on the cool white tiles for a nap if they wanted to. Now their privacy was compromised by scuffling, scratching sounds coming from inside the tub which invariably ended with a leathery face rising over the porcelain siding and peering in unabashed interest at whatever the cats were doing. Zekki hated this, but Pris hated it more. On more than one occasion, Zekki had stopped the calico from using a potted plant in the living room instead of her box. But the longer the interloper remained, the harder it had become to dissuade her.

Slowly, Zekki crept to the litter, stepped over the box's rim and stood quietly in the dusty gravel, hoping that the turtle was asleep.

It wasn't.

"Hey," a muffled voice said from inside the tub. "Who's there?"

With a sigh, Zekki jumped from the box and leapt onto the the tub. "It's me. If you're sleeping or something, don't let me bother you, I'll be gone in a minute."

The turtle blinked, and moved with excruciating care past a large pan of water and made his way in slow motion closer to the cat. "You're not bothering me." There was a pause, followed by more scraping and shuffling.

Zekki's mind drifted to thoughts of Buddy. The yellow tom would have been patient and kind to this creature, which was the exact opposite of Zekki's current feelings. But in the eight years since Buddy had left 6th Avenue, Zekki and Pris had carefully followed the teachings of their spiritual leader and former housemate, and patience was definitely one of his edicts.

Making sure that his voice was kind and even no matter how violated he actually felt, Zekki smiled. "I'll just be in and out of here. So, go back to"— he stopped, his attention turned to the pie-tin sized gold and black patterned shell that covered the turtle in a dome like peak—"Or go back inside that thing, or whatever it is you do."

The turtle's clawed feet scrabbled against the tub as he made his way forward. Finally, he stopped, staring up at Zekki, his wizened face small and dry.

There was a long, uncomfortable silence.

"How's the weather?" The turtle finally blurted.

"I really don't know." The white cat's skin twitched with barely suppressed irritation. "I never go outside."

"You should." The turtle said solemnly. "You look a little pale."

Zekki rolled his eyes and jumped to the floor. Cat Master or no Cat Master, the situation was becoming impossible. His bladder was at the bursting point and Pris's potted plant idea was sounding more appealing by the minute.

"Are you still there?" the turtle asked.

"Yes, and I'd appreciate a little privacy."

"Okay, but don't leave! You won't leave will you?" There was a pause. "Oh nooooo!" It screamed. "You're gone! You've left! I'm A L O N E!"

The creature's voice rose with hysteria and Zekki stood on his hind legs and looked into the tub. "Calm down, what's the matter with you?"

"Where's The Boy? The turtle asked, his worried face creased with a thousand wrinkles. "I thought he was coming back for me yesterday."

Where *was* The Boy? Zekki thought hard and a vaguely remembered conversation between the sitter and Mrs. O'Connell drifted back to him. Apparently, exterminators had sprayed The Boy's house and the turtle was staying in the bathtub for a couple of days. That was it! A happy flash of hope warmed the cat's ears. The situation was only temporary. "Something's going on at The Boy's place." Zekki said reassuringly. "When it's safe for you, he'll be back."

"How can you be sure of that?" The turtle's voice increased in volume. "I realize that you and the other cat enjoy this room, but with all due respect, I don't want to spend the rest of my life in a bath tub, because…because…" The turtle began to hyperventilate in small wheezing breaths. "…because I'm claustrophobic! It's so bad I can't even go into my shell!" Its claws scrabbled wildly on the sides of the tub. "I can't breathe! Everything is going black! Let me out of here!"

"Relax!" Zekki called, hunkering in the box and trying to concentrate amidst the chaos. "I've known The Boy for a long time, and if he says he's coming back for you, he will."

There was sudden silence from the bathtub. Slowly a leathery neck stretched over the rim, and the turtle tapped his beaked lip on the porcelain. "You don't know that."

"Yes I do." Zekki said, furiously digging in his litter until clay particles flew in puffs around his head. "He'd rather die than let something happen to us." An unexpected chill coursed up the white cat's spine and he stopped and drew a sharp breath.

He'd rather die than let something happen to us.

Suddenly anxious for the warmth of Pris's sleeping body, Zekki leapt from the box and ran from the room.

"Where are you going?" wailed the turtle. His cry reverberated in the silence, bouncing off the tiles and finally fading in the dusty air.

CHAPTER 14

The ferret waited until Orie and his entourage disappeared into the darkness, and then slinked into the open, her mind alive with questions. The lizard was heading for the trailer to find The Boy, but the spider said that the carnival was where the answer lay. Answer to what? Twitching with frustration, Blitz plopped in a patch of grass and scratched behind one ear. It stood to reason that once The Boy was located, Orie would head to the carnival, because whatever waited there seemed somehow tied to the rescue plan.

Blitz sighed remembering how happy she'd felt during the Meeting of the Spoken Word, and her whiskers drooped with disappointment. Why hadn't Orie included her in this new adventure? She sniffed with self-pity. The lizard was an awful friend, nothing like he'd seemed that morning. She mentally replayed their earlier conversation and felt a twinge of optimism. Maybe she was wrong. After all, Orie had agreed to include her in his story, and they still had one more Monday meeting left. The thought made the ferret feel better and she wiped a dangling tear from her snout. Perhaps they simply needed more time to bond, which was hard to do with the tacky La De Da hanging around, not to mention the rest of his dopy entourage. But now there was another issue. The Cat Master legend was fast becoming old news compared to this new turn of events. If Blitz didn't think of something quick, the Meeting of the Spoken Word would find her newly acquired story quaintly passé.

The ferret rubbed her flank against a nandina, its berries draping her back like bright, red pearls, and thought hard. Maybe now was the time to join him. She could catch up with Orie's gimpy pace in no time. Happily, she started forward, and then stopped, shrinking back against the bush's brittle stalks. What if Orie told her to go home? The ferret's past bulged with rejections, and she had no intention of enduring more. Surely there was something she could do to insure the lizard's acceptance. An idea slowly took shape and Blitz jumped in the air, dooking with stiff-legged delight. The 'answer' was at the carnival! Ferrets were masters at puzzle solving. She would find the place; interpret whatever riddles were hiding there, and then present them completely solved to Orie. The Boy would be saved, and Blitz hailed as a hero. Now *that* was a tale worth telling! Blitz pranced in place then frowned, her forehead creased with worry. But where was the carnival? She was relatively new to the area, and the park's boundaries stretched deep into the murky darkness; huge and unknowable.

The wind shifted and the ferret backed into the grasses, her nostrils flared. A rich smell of mud and vegetation signaled the river, but suddenly there was another scent, stronger, pungent, and close. Panicked, she turned, almost colliding with the dark figure standing in the shadows.

"What are you doing here?" A whispery voice asked.

Blitz jumped back, her eyes straining for a place to hide.

The creature took a step toward her and the moonlight illuminated its face.

The ferret breathed with relief. "You're a cat."

"And you're in River Cat territory. Why?"

Blitz took a closer look at the visitor. She was slender, with a round head and thin body. Her black and white fur was speckled with mud, and though her eyes appeared sleepy and indifferent, Blitz suspected that they weren't. "I just left The Spoken Word gathering, and I guess I got lost," she said.

The cat threw back her head and laughed.

The sound echoed in the still night air, high pitched and eerie, and Blitz felt a shiver of apprehension. What if the feline was signaling her friends? Blitz could handle one cat...but not a colony.

"Boring little animals telling boring little stories," the cat chuckled, rubbing her ear against a shrub. "What a stupid way to spend an evening."

"Stupid?" Blitz arched her back with indignation. "To honor the Laws of Sho-Valla?"

Something dangerous flickered in the cat's amber eyes. "Sho-Valla is for the weak and frightened. The River Cats live by their own rules."

The ferret swallowed. This wasn't going well. The cat was rude and aggressive and her attitude wasn't good for Blitz's new image. "Weak and frightened?" Blitz asked. "I'll have you know that The Legendary Lizard, Orie, attends those meetings." She tossed her head with disdain. "Maybe you've heard of him?"

"Orie?" The cat's eyes were no longer sleepy. "The great friend of The Cat Master?"

"Yes." Blitz said, pleased that the conversation had taken a more positive turn. She hadn't planned to tell her story before Monday's meeting, but now that she had the cat's attention, why wait? "Orie is my oldest and dearest friend." The lie felt good in her mouth, and she longed for the chance to repeat it.

"That's not possible." The cat spat. "There's no way he's still alive."

Blitz blinked with uncertainty. Fame should illicit awe, not antagonism. "Well—well of course he's alive." She stammered. "I just spoke with him." The cat's reaction was confusing. Maybe she hadn't heard enough of Blitz's story to be impressed. "Not many animals know this." Blitz continued. "But I helped Orie save The Cat Master. I was right by his side the whole time"

"Really?" The cat's voice dragged with sarcasm. "And who exactly *are* you?"

Her fur smelled dank and sour like the river, and the ferret took an involuntary step back. "Blitz." She said. "My name is Blitz."

The cat was quiet for a moment, her sloe-eyed stare regarding the ferret with a silent intensity. Finally, she moved a step forward, her muscles tensed despite her pleasant expression. "And my name is Aluna. Sorry I was so rude, but my colony has claimed this territory, and we don't allow just anyone to pass through." She flashed a dazzling smile, her fangs gleaming. "But any friend of the legendary Orie, is always welcomed here."

Blitz tingled with importance. This was more like it. "Well, thanks. That's very kind."

"So," the cat said, "when will you see the lizard again?" Nonchalantly, she licked a spotted paw pad, but her eyes glittered with interest. "I'm sure the colony would love to meet him," Aluna's mouth pulled into a tight smile, "and, of course, you, his *best* friend."

"Well, he'll be at the Meeting of the Spoken Word next week." Considering how much greater her own story would be by then, Blitz could barely contain her pleasure. "You should join us, because Orie and I will be telling. Of course, you'll have to hear some other member's stories, too. The cockroach, the coyote..."

"Coyote?" Aluna interrupted, drawing back in alarm. "There's a coyote at the meeting?"

"Yes, but his story shouldn't take too long."

The cat licked her chops with uncertainty. "On second thought, I wouldn't want to disrupt the group." Her expression brightened. "I know!" Why don't you bring Orie to *me?*"

Blitz felt a bubble of concern. Orie didn't strike her as a lizard who could be 'brought' places and somehow the request sounded odd. "I'm not sure that's such a great idea," she said, "he's sort of retired, and doesn't travel much."

"Well, maybe you could tell me where he is now, and I'll go to *him*," The cat watched Blitz carefully, "unless you've been lying about your friendship, and don't know him at all..."

"Of course I know him!" Blitz interrupted, hopping with rage. "I just saw him talking to that stupid parrot by the picnic tables. They're headed somewhere very important right this minute." She tossed her head in triumph. "*Now*, who's lying?"

Aluna ignored the challenge and cocked her head. "Somewhere important?"

"Very," Blitz said with haughty disdain, "but I can't tell you where." She leaned forward, careful to make her voice low and mysterious. "It's a secret."

The cat gave a derisive snort. "Which means you don't know."

"I do, too!" Blitz shouted. "They're looking for a trailer!"

Aluna dipped her chin. "I apologize. You're obviously what you say you are; the lizard's trusted friend."

The lizard's trusted friend.

That's exactly what she was. Blitz's thoughts drifted in wispy puffs of sentimentality. Orie hadn't forgotten her, he was simply old and stressed. After saving The Boy, they would have many more adventures together, each one more amazing than the last, and none of them involving his current gang of toadies. Eventually, of course, the lizard would die and Blitz would be famous in her own right; a clever, daring creature whom all animals admired. She glanced in the cat's direction and smiled inwardly. Another thought pushed to the surface. The River Cats' territory was vast. Maybe Aluna would know where the carnival was! "Actually," Blitz said, "I'm supposed to meet Orie later on at the carnival. But, I've never been in the park at night, and I'm sort of"—the ferret shrugged apologetically—"lost. I was thinking that maybe you could take me there."

"The lizard's looking for a trailer?" The cat said, ignoring Blitz's request. "Why?"

The ferret blinked with confusion. The question surprised her, but she couldn't see any harm in answering honestly. "We both live with a human who's in some kind of trouble. I guess that's where he is."

"So you live with a human." Aluna's nose wrinkled with distaste. "That explains the smell," she grimaced, "or at least part of it."

The cat was being deliberately rude. Blitz wanted to tell her so, but there were more important issues at hand, and they needed to stay on track. She sighed with annoyance. "The Boy feeds me, end of story. The point is, I need to get to the carnival. Can you take me?"

"Unfortunately, no. The River Cats' province doesn't extend as far as the carnival. It's too close to the highway and we avoid human infestation as much as possible."

Blitz squeaked with irritation. Somehow she hadn't expected the cat to deny someone with such impressive connections. "That's disappointing," she said, choosing her words carefully, "because I could introduce you to Orie as a reward for helping me get there." Blitz looked at the ground, trying hard to seem humble. "No offense, but he's very wary of cats and would never let you get near him without my say so." She rolled her eyes and shrugged. "What can I say? He depends on me for so much."

"I can imagine," Aluna said blandly, "but not even seeing the Legendary Lizard is worth risking the carnival." A brisk wind blew from the north ruffling the fur around the cat's neck, and a broad smile transformed her face. "I have an idea! You said that Orie is headed to the trailer, *first*, right?"

Blitz nodded, unsure where this line of questioning was leading.

"Well, the trailer is between here and the carnival." She stopped and stared hard into the ferret's eyes. "Why don't I take you there instead? That way, you won't get lost, and I can meet the lizard."

Blitz felt a warning buzz. There was an icy current beneath the cat's goodwill that disturbed her, but the offer had possibilities. There was still much to learn about The Boy's situation. Maybe going to the trailer first was actually a better idea. "Smart thinking," Blitz said, "and thanks for the offer."

"Of course, you *will* introduce me to Orie, right? Since you were there when it all happened, you know that Buddy's brother, Jett, died trying to claim his place as the old Cat Master's heir." Her eyes narrowed. "What you don't know is that both Jett and Buddy were my uncles."

The ferret frowned. Why was Aluna saying all this? They needed to get started. "I don't believe I did know that. You must be proud."

"Very. Both my uncles were extraordinary felines, but as a feral, Jett was my colony's choice for leadership. No one blames the Legendary Lizard for taking sides, and he has the River Cat's unquestioned respect as our spiritual leader's sacred comrade." She blinked. "That's why meeting him would be so meaningful to me."

There it was again, Blitz thought with annoyance, the whisper of contempt beneath the flattery. Or maybe it was just her imagination. After all, passion often bred zealots which could explain Aluna's intensity and persistence. "Orie told me many times how fond he was of both your uncles," the ferret lied, "it was a hard choice for us all, but what can one do?" She shrugged helplessly, "may the best cat win, and all that."

"I couldn't agree more." Aluna murmured.

The night sky stretched above, its ebony depths tinged with purple, and the ferret felt a thread of cold beneath the balmy breeze. October was almost over and a hint of winter charged the air.   "Shouldn't we get moving?   It's going to be morning soon, and I can only imagine Orie's joy at meeting a direct descendent of The Cat Master."

Without comment, the cat sprang into the bushes and Blitz followed her disappearing form.   There were many ways of dealing with aggressive fans like Aluna, Blitz decided, as they turned from the river and headed west.   She hated to fib about the promised introduction, but Blitz had no intentions of spending any more time with this creature than was necessary.   At the first scent of Orie, she'd lose Aluna in the darkness.   The Boy's abduction was a legendary story in the making, Blitz reminded herself.

She might have to deal with birds and spiders to be included, but she wasn't about to share it with a cat.

CHAPTER 15

Orie and La De Da scrambled through the grass, their eyes fixed on Bennett's fluttering form which darted among the trees like a shadowed beacon. The night was fading and Orie felt a sense of urgency that bordered on hysteria.

The answer is at the carnival.

But according to Theda, The Boy wasn't at the carnival, he was in the trailer, so what did that mean? Why had the spider been instructed to seek Orie out and by whom? His head ached with dangerous scenarios and complex questions. But amidst it all, one thing was clear: tree lizards weren't exactly warriors in the animal world, especially elderly lizards with sore toes and aching joints. No matter how daring the Legendary Lizard stories had made him seem, the truth was that Orie had never physically saved anything in his entire life. But Tenba had. The lizard thought of his old friend, and the chow she'd so valiantly fought to protect the Cat Master. How he longed for the shepherd's wisdom and strength; a message from beyond that might help.

Messages

Snippets of memory tickled Orie's mind. The answering machine! What had all the messages had in common? His eyes widened with discovery. The Boy's phone! No one had been able to reach him. Where was it?

"I see the trailer!" Bennett shouted from above. He swooped to the ground, and Theda scurried from his back and onto a rock.

"It's a big, white bus looking thing!" The spider's front legs waved with excitement, and the waning moon cast a pale light on the red stripe marking her back. "And it's parked by a stand of trees. No one is around, either, so all we have to do..." She stopped and stared from the lizards to the bird. "...What *do* we do?" Her many eyes turned in worried unison toward Orie.

La De Da and Bennett followed her gaze; their faces tense and waiting.

Orie's thoughts lurched to a stop, half formed ideas flashing like lights on a pin ball machine. "The first thing is to get inside the trailer and find The Boy. If he's still there, we must locate his cell phone and get it to him." The lizard bit his lip. "It's the only shot he has at calling for help."

"How big is it?"

The animals turned to see La De Da, stance wide, brow furrowed.

"What do you mean?" Orie asked, knowing exactly what she meant and wishing he'd left her in the park.

"I mean," she said, her eyes moving from one small creature to another, "is it heavy? We're all pretty small. Even if we find the cell phone, whose going to carry it?"

Everyone stared at Orie and he puffed his throat, praying he looked confident. "We'll figure that out when we find it."

"Are you kidding?" La De Da slapped her tail for emphasis. "We've got to have a real plan, something to..."

"...wait." Theda stepped forward. "If the voice in the warehouse trusts the Legendary Lizard, shouldn't we?" She blinked at Orie. "You've got something in mind, right?"

The others waited, and for a moment Orie fought a swell of panic. He'd never asked for anyone's trust; which was an annoying word embraced by the needy, and leading to cult-like adoration. Which, in retrospect was worth a lie. "Of course I do," he said in his most confident voice. " Push on."

Amazingly, no one protested, and the animals moved toward the trailer, its hulking form dimly illuminated by a camping light that hung on a drooping nail by the door. The wind shifted and primal scents from the zoo mingled with the stench of bird droppings and rust from the filthy vehicle.

Bennett lifted his wings. "I'm going to fly up there for a minute and check things out." He waited for Orie's terse nod of approval and then flapped onto the roof. His talons scrapped against the metal, and a dog barked once from somewhere inside the trailer.

"Do you think you could be a little louder?" Orie sputtered from below. "Why don't we just form a marching band and play some Souza?"

Theda dropped by a silken thread from Bennett's beak. "No one can hear *me*. I'll take a look around." With a four legged wave to the lizards, she darted across the roof and disappeared down the other side.

Bennett waited on the trailer, a silent sentry, carved in stone, while the lizards paced by the tires, anxiously waiting for Theda's report.

"What if something eats her?" La De Da whispered. "We'd never know. We could sit here for a week and never know."

"How about a little optimism here?" Orie sniped, secretly wishing he'd thought of the question first. "Of course she hasn't been eaten, that's a ridiculous idea. Bennett!" he hissed in a hoarse whisper. "What if Theda's dead?"

"I'm fine." The spider's tiny form appeared from behind a tire and scrambled to the ground. "Everything's okay. She looked at Orie. "Can you climb up this thing?"

The lizard puffed his throat and scowled. "Of course I can."

"Good." Theda said. "Because there's something you need to see."

* * *

Axel fretted and panted by The Boy's leg. As soon as Mr. Krell had left, The Boy pushed away from the tub and flopped onto his side against the bathroom tile. Axel was worried. He didn't know a lot about humans, but this one didn't look good. An angry bruise on the young man's temple was puffy and red, and it was obvious from his dried lips and scratchy voice that he needed water. The dog crept close to The Boy's face and tentatively licked his cheek.

The young man's eyes fluttered open. "Hi, big guy," he croaked, before drifting off again.

Axel whined softly. The night was turning cold, and he'd tried to provide warmth for The Boy by curling beside him.

Unfortunately, the room was too small and he'd ended up squashed between his new friend's feet and the wall. A soft grey light shown through the little bathroom window, and Axle's heart raced. Mr. Krell was in his bedroom asleep, but soon it would be morning, and then what? Even if The Boy told, he'd never be released. Axel knew this as sure as he'd always known that Mr. Krell would eventually kill him, too. The dog just hadn't expected it quite so soon.

A scratching from the roof caught his attention, and instinctively, he barked. The Boy didn't stir, and Axel crept as close to the window as the leash would allow. Slowly he rose on quivering hind legs, one paw touching the tub for balance.

A form moved against the window screen, and the pit bull growled low in his throat.

"Stop that, we're here to help!" Something called from somewhere by the window.

Axel barked again, and then cocked his head in confusion. This wasn't a human voice, and it sounded oddly familiar. "Who's there?" He demanded.

There was more shuffling against the screen, and slowly, a small form clamored into view. It was a lizard.

"My name's Orie and I live with The Boy. Is he in there?"

Orie? Could it be the lizard he'd seen at The Meeting of the Spoken Word? Axel gently tugged at the young man's t-shirt, pulling his limp body along the tiles, and closer to the window. "Yes." He said, straining against the leash until he was within inches of the shadowed shape. "And he's hurt." There was more movement from outside the trailer and the dog heard muffled whispers.

"Can you push the screen open so I can get in?" The lizard finally asked.

Even on his hind legs, the window was too high and the dog whined with frustration. "No, I can't reach it. But there's a little hole up at the top. Can you squeeze through that?"

"It's too small. I'm sending a friend in. Her name is Theda and she's a—a garden spider. Don't step on her."

Axel watched with interest as a tiny form scurried up the screen, slid through the tear and dropped by a thread to the floor.

"Hi." She said. "Can you tell me what's happened?"

Axel strained forward for a better look, saw the red stripe on her back, and instinctively placed himself between her and his friend. "The Boy's been kidnapped." The pit bull indicated the sleeping figure on the floor. "He has a turtle that Mr. Krell wants, but he won't say where it is. Mr. Krell doesn't like it when he doesn't get what he wants." His voice quavered. "He's given The Boy overnight to think about things, but if the answer is still no, Mr. Krell is going to…" He swallowed hard. "… kill us in the morning."

"What?" The spider scuttled back in shock. "Kill? Both of you?"

Axel nodded.

"Hurry up!" The lizard shouted from outside the window screen.

With a flurry of movement, Theda scurried over the dog's white tipped paws and onto The Boy's body. Quickly she darted to the wound, peered at the young man's unresponsive face, and then made her way along his shirt and in and out of his jean pockets. "His phone!" she shouted, scrabbling up the tub and perching on the dirty rim. Her black eyes stared into Axle's. "Orie says The Boy has a cell phone. Where is it? He could use it to call for help!" Axel thought hard. "Well," he said. "The Boy came to the carnival to meet Mr. Krell at the warehouse. But suddenly, they began arguing about the animals, and that's when Jerry came in and The Boy was hurt." The dog growled at the memory. He didn't recall a phone other than the ones Mr. Krell and Jerry used. "I'm positive." he said sadly. "I saw them go through his pockets. There wasn't one."

"That can't be right!" the lizard screamed from the window ledge. "Theda! Get back up here, and let's get to the warehouse!"

Axel felt a pinch of hope that was quickly destroyed by a sudden slice of fear. "Hang on a minute!" he shouted at the spider's retreating form.

She stopped and dangled upside down from a wobbly nail. "What's the matter?"

"You can't go inside the warehouse." The dog's voice was hoarse and strained. "There's something bad there."

"I know." Theda nodded with understanding. "It's an awful place, full of suffering and…"

"...I'm not talking about that." the pit bull interrupted. "I'm talking about the, I mean..." his voice trailed off into a bleak silence. "I can't explain it." Listlessly, he plopped back down beside The Boy. "Just don't go in there."

"I promise we'll be careful." The spider sprang onto the wall and made her way to the window ledge. "By the way; what's your name?" she asked, staring down at the dog's upturned face.

"Axel."

"Well, don't worry, Axel." Theda said, her eyes bright with encouragement. "We'll come up with something."

The pit bull watched helplessly as she disappeared through the hole in the screen. "Wait!" he called. "What do I do when Mr. Krell comes back?"

There was silence, and then the lizard's silhouette appeared against the mauve tinged backdrop of approaching dawn.

"I'm only a lizard." Orie's voice answered from the window. "But I know what I'd do if I were a dog."

"What's that?" Axel whispered, knowing the answer before he asked.

"I'd stop him," came the stony reply, "no matter what it took."

CHAPTER 16

Blitz followed the black and white cat's thin form through the bushes. They'd been running for some time now, and beneath the smoky smells of autumn, she had detected Orie's unmistakable scent on the wind. "Wait up!" she shouted.

The cat glided to a halt and turned around. "Why?" She asked. "We're almost there."

"Really?" Blitz craned her head for a better look. "How close is it?"

Aluna indicated a stand of trees in the distance. "The trailer is just beyond those, you can barely see the light through the branches. Come on."

"I'm a little winded." The ferret stalled, her eyes quickly sizing up the quickest escape route. "Guess I'm out of shape." The time to ditch Aluna was now, and Blitz hoped she hadn't waited too late. "So, I'm going to mosey behind those fern and make a little pit stop. Guess I drank too much water."

"Me too." Aluna said, not moving. "I'll go with you. We can watch each other's back."

The ferret felt a throb of worry. This wasn't working out! She only wanted a guide not a pal, if Orie saw her with a River Cat; he'd never trust her again. Blitz's eyes darted to a shadowed stand of crepe myrtle bushes. If she could sprint to those before Aluna realized what was happening, perhaps her solo plan was still doable.

The cat's eyes narrowed. "What's wrong?"

"Nothing." Blitz tensed her hindquarters, preparing to bolt.

A dog's bark cut through the silence, and both animals froze as it reverberated through the park.

"That came from the trailer!" The cat hissed, whirling toward Blitz. "You didn't say anything about a dog. What are you trying to pull?"

"P—Pull ?" Blitz stammered, her mind struggling to understand. "Nothing! I—I…"

The dog barked again, this time more aggressively, and Aluna scrambled half way up the trunk of a sycamore where she slid and clambered on the smooth bark in awkward panic. "You were never lost!" she screamed from her perch. "This was a trick to get me killed!"

Blitz flattened her long body in the grass unsure of the best course of action. She wanted to run, but not into the jaws of an angry dog. Where was it? And what was the cat talking about?

"You lured me here on the pretense of introducing me to Orie." Aluna shouted from above.

The barking stopped, and both animals listened intently, their ears perked and scanning. Wind rattled dry leaves, and a distant horn honked from beyond the zoo, but otherwise, danger seemed to have passed.

With a grunt, Aluna dropped to the ground, landing inches from the ferret. "I should have known better than to trust a friend of the lizard!"

Blitz sprang to her feet and hissed a warning. Startled, Aluna pulled back, but the ferret felt that whatever intimidation she'd managed to achieve was short lived. The cat was fast, and running away was no longer a workable solution. "We both need to relax, okay?" Blitz tried to sound calm despite the swelling wave of terror threatening to drown her. "I don't know what you're talking about.

"Of course you do!" Aluna's scraggly tail bushed in anger. "This was going to be an ambush. Who cares about one less River Cat, right? They're disposable." She leaned in closer. "But no one gets rid of us that easily, and, believe me, smarter beings then you have tried."

Blitz blinked, this sounded personal. What was going on? Her heart thudded and she wished that she'd paid more attention to The Cat Master legend. "Look, this is crazy, I don't have anything against you and I don't know a thing about cats, river or otherwise. I *am* a close friend of Orie's, but I've—I've been away for a while and maybe I've missed something?"

Aluna gave a snort of disgust. "Then let me bring you up to date, *ferret.*"

She moved so close that Blitz could smell her breath. It was foul from decaying teeth and rotten food.

"I told you the Legendary Lizard was important to my colony"—Aluna's expression darkened into a sneer—"but not because we revere him. The River Cats don't need to worship some stupid reptile; we have a legendary figure of our own."

"Perfectly understandable." Blitz said, hoping to distract the cat until an escape plan came to mind. "And who is that?"

"Jett." Aluna's eyes were strangely bright in the moonlight. "Martyred hero of the River Cats, and true heir to The Cat Master."

"Jett." Blitz repeated. The name sounded familiar.

She leaned forward, her face devoid of emotion. "He was my uncle, and the lizard killed him."

The animals stood in edgy silence. Leaves dropped onto their backs, and a cloud skimmed across the moon, obscuring the cat's face in darkness.

"This doesn't make sense." Blitz said, finally breaking the stillness. She tried to smile but her mouth was so dry her lip stuck to a fang and hung there. "Orie's just a lizard. I mean, he's 'special' and all that, but he couldn't actually kill a cat."

"Not physically." Aluna backed beneath a fern, its shadowed fronds draping her body like tattered lace. "But murder comes in many forms." She dipped her head in exaggerated politeness. "You'll forgive me if I don't take you the rest of the way, but I'm sure we'll meet again." Without a sound, the cat sprang toward the river, her paws spinning dust in her wake.

* * *

Stuart Krell awoke with a start, his pulse thrumming with fear. Despite the trailer's chill, the sheets stuck to his bare back and chest in soggy patches of sweat. What was wrong? Struggling into a sitting position, he groped for the lamp, turned it on, and stared around the room. Everything was in order. Clothes had been hung in the tiny closet, a high backed rocker sat adjacent from the bed, and a cheap chest of drawers and mirror stood against the wall beneath a high, narrow window with faded striped curtains.

The wall clock read four a.m., and Stuart shivered. He'd obviously been dreaming. Dragging a threadbare afghan from the foot of his bed, he pulled it over his rotund belly and bunched it tightly beneath his sagging chins. Taking a deep breath, Stuart tried to relax. It was no use, strange and disjointed images darted through his mind, and he stiffened at the memory. He'd imagined waking to a murky from crouched at the foot of the bed, its saffron eyes glowing like cinders, its thick nails clutching the sheets. But there was something else, something even more chilling about the dream that he couldn't recall. The big man gnawed his bottom lip and thought hard. Vaguely, he remembered Axel barking, but the dog often did that during the night, and Stuart usually went right back to sleep. Could that have triggered such terrible hallucinations?

Something scurried across the roof of the trailer and Stuart tensed, waiting for Axel to respond from the bathroom...but the dog was quiet. Should he get up and check things? The thought of putting his bare feet on the floor was oddly unsettling. "No." Stuart answered out loud. "Go back to sleep. You're just tired and stressed." That was it, the big man decided, turning off the lamp. He'd had an old fashioned nightmare complete with creepy noises and a first class Halloween boogieman. None of this was hard to understand considering the strain he'd been under. Still clutching the throw, Stuart snuggled down into the mattress. "Jerry is an idiot." He mumbled, straightening his rumpled sheets, and punching the pillow into a plump mound. "Everything is going to work out." He struggled on to his side. "Tomorrow I'll get the turtle, dump the kid and get the blue blazes out of here. No more worries."

Purple sky peaked through a tear in the curtains, and Stuart watched it until his eyes slowly closed with fatigue. Soon it would be morning, he thought in dreamy surrender. Everything would look better in the morning. Yawning with contentment, he relaxed, enjoying the floating descent toward sleep.

Suddenly his eyes opened wide.

The chilling thing he couldn't remember barreled through the dreamy mist and roared into blazing clarity. The smell! There had been a smell with the nightmare form at the foot of his bed; a gagging stench that even in sleep had jarred his memory ever so lightly. It was strange, though, because now that he thought about it, beneath the sickly mixture of sewage and decay…was a whiff of rain and the barest scent of the sea.

CHAPTER 17

Orie stood beneath the trailer trying to sort things out. The Boy had been injured, and if the dog was telling the truth, both would be killed by the man who'd held Theda and the other animals in the warehouse.

"What now?" The spider's mandibles snapped and clicked with worry.

Bennett fluttered from a pecan tree and hopped closer. "And how about the dog? I've watched quite a few 'Lassie' movies, plus the series, and you know how dogs are with humans. Should we trust him?"

Theda waved her front legs in frustration. "Why would Axel lie? They're both going to be killed if we don't do something!" She looked at Orie, her many eyes swimming with helplessness.

"Tell me more about the phone." An authoritative voice said from the shadows. La De Da made her way from behind a tire and looked at Orie.

She had been so quiet during the trip to the trailer that Orie had almost forgotten about her. Now he was strangely comforted by the confident tone of her request. "The Boy always carries a cell phone with him." He explained. "I thought if he still had it on him, maybe we could open the window, crawl in and push the phone close to his mouth and ...." Orie stopped, his eyes shifting from Theda, to La De Da, to Bennett. Regardless of their good intentions, none of the animals had the size or strength to do what he'd proposed. What they really needed were opposable thumbs, not claws and hairy little legs. Orie felt tired and annoyed and made a mental note to cultivate more evolutionarily advanced friends in the future. "Not a good idea." His shoulders hunched with defeat. "Forget it."

"But it is a good idea." La De Da said firmly. "The Boy probably lost the phone during his abduction, or maybe the man has it. But wherever it is, we'll find it."

A sudden memory exploded to the surface of Orie's mind, and he stiffened.

The answer is at the carnival.

"Wait a minute!" he shouted, twitching his tail for emphasis. "Right before The Meeting of the Spoken Word, there were lots of messages on The Boy's answering machine, but there was one in particular." Orie wrinkled his brow, desperately trying to remember the exact verbiage. "Something from girls waiting at the carnival and knowing that he'd been there because…because." He stopped. Because why? The answer bounced through his brain like a flea on a trampoline.

'Kristin and I are standing by the Ferris wheel, and we know you've been here, because, guess what I'm looking at?' A girl spoke from behind them.

The animals turned in unison, their mouths agape.

Bennett was poised on a log, his beak slightly opened and a perfect imitation of an exuberant young woman's voice emanating from his throat. *"Your nasty backpack! We knew it was yours 'cause it's held together with that stupid looking safety pin."*

"That's it!" Orie screeched, stamping his feet with joy. "That's the message!" He turned to the parrot with begrudging respect. "Bennett, how did you do that? I thought you only did engines."

The parrot shook his head and blinked. "I don't know. I hear things and then they just come out of my throat at the weirdest times." He fluttered his wings and looked from one animal to the other. "So, was that what you wanted? There might have been more, but that's all I can remember."

"It's exactly what I wanted." Orie squeezed his eyes shut and tried to sort through this new information. The girl said she was looking at his back pack which meant it wasn't with The Boy. But that didn't make sense. The Boy carried it everywhere he went, and he never threw anything away. Where had the girls seen it?

"Do you think the phone is in the back pack?" La De Da asked.

Orie frowned and scratched his snout. "We won't know 'til we find it, but The Boy would never throw it away. That was done by someone else." He thought of the messy bedroom waiting at home and felt an unexpected pang of sadness. "The Boy treasures his old things."

La De Da bumped his shoulder and winked. "So do I."

"I don't know what you're talking about." Orie sniffed, but he bumped her back.

A gentle breeze swirled bright red leaves beneath the trailer, and Orie realized with a sense of shock that it was no longer dark. "We need to get to the carnival as fast as we can. Maybe the phone's in the backpack.," he said, "and if we can find it before the man wakes up…" Orie stopped. And then what? Ask the cell to follow them to the trailer? He'd think of a way to move it, he thought fiercely, but finding it came first.

"I have an idea!" Bennett said with excitement. "I saw a cartoon once where the…"

"Shhh!" La De Da interrupted, holding up one claw for silence. She turned to Orie. "I heard a noise," she whispered, indicating a stand of oak trees behind the trailer. "Over there."

The animals held their breaths, all eyes strained towards the area in question. Both lizards flicked their tongues, trying to discern a scent, but after a few moments they stopped.

"I didn't get anything." Orie said. "Did you?"

The female shook her head, but her mouth was tight with suspicion. "Something doesn't feel right. We need to get out of here."

Morning unfolded around them, and the moon so vibrant in the ebony sky, had faded into pallid obscurity against the soft white of dawn.

"But shouldn't we tell Axel something before we leave?" Theda turned to the La De Da, for support. "Shouldn't we?" The spider's voice shook with intensity and for an instant she exposed her fangs before quickly withdrawing them. "I—I mean, I told him we were going to help."

"The dog already knows what to do." Orie said with finality. "If he fails…" The lizard looked away. "Then, no matter what we find…The Boy is lost."

* * *

Blitz waited until Orie and his friends disappeared from sight before shinnying down the oak tree where she'd been hiding. For one tense moment, it seemed that Orie and his tacky lizard girlfriend had detected her scent. But no, reptiles were lousy trackers, and Blitz had crouched low amidst the protection of a gnarled limb until they'd given up and left. This was good, because in the last few moments much had happened to alter her plans, and the ferret needed time to think.

Thanks to the unexpected delay with Aluna, Blitz had been late reaching the trailer and arrived just as Orie and Theda were descending from its window. From her hiding place, the ferret watched the animals, and though their conversation was fragmented and quiet, she heard it all. The situation sounded grim; The Boy was seriously hurt, and the dog that Blitz and Aluna heard barking, was apparently inside the trailer along with a man.

Once again, Blitz begrudgingly noted Orie's commanding leadership, so calm and cool with all the answers. Well, maybe not *all* the answers, Blitz thought with a smirk. The ferret still had some secrets of her own.

Twigs snapped in the bushes behind her and Blitz sprinted to a more protected area beneath the trailer's makeshift steps. A dove fluttered from the thicket, her white tipped wings whistling as she flew and the ferret relaxed, but not too much. The River Cats populated the entire park area, and wherever they were, Aluna would be close. Though she hadn't had time to process all that the cat had said, one thing was certain; Aluna hated Orie. Perhaps, later, Blitz could leverage this information to her advantage, but for now, more urgent issues prevailed.

Clearly, the key to The Boy's survival rested on finding his cell phone, which had led to an amazing epiphany; whomever's voice the spider heard in the warehouse had lied, because the 'answer' was definitely not at the carnival. Blitz headed for home, a chilly autumn wind at her back. Let Orie and the Three Stooges search every inch of the fair grounds. They wouldn't find the cell phone there, because it wasn't at the carnival. It was in The Boy's room, under his bed…just exactly where she'd hidden it yesterday.

CHAPTER 18

Pris stood up from the ottoman, shook herself awake and stared at Zekki.

The white cat sat on the window sill, his blue eyes dilated to black in the shimmering glare of daylight now spiking through a crack in the blinds.

"What's wrong?" The calico asked. "You have a weird look on your face."

Zekki turned to her, his brow wrinkled, whiskers forward with anxiety. "Where is The Boy?"

"What are you talking about?" Pris yawned, jumped to the floor and stretched her plump body its full length. "He hasn't lived here for years."

"I know that." Zekki persisted. "But didn't he tell Mrs. O'Connell that he'd be back for the turtle last night?"

Licking one plush paw, the calico shrugged. "Did he? I only remember the pet sitter saying she'd take care of everything during Mrs. O'Connell's trip. I figured that meant the turtle, too." "Speaking of turtles." Pris grimaced. "He's still in the bathroom, isn't he?"

"Yeah." Zekki said. "And he's not too happy about it."

"Well, neither am I." Pris's green eyes turned to the potted plant by the couch. "This is ridiculous." She stalked toward the towering Ficus, her round face set with determination.

"No!" Zekki shouted. "Don't use that! Really, I was just in the bathroom. The turtle's not a voyeur. He just wants out."

"And I want privacy." The calico turned from the plant, but her expression was annoyed. "When is he leaving, anyway?"

"That's just the point." Zekki said. "According to the turtle, The Boy should have picked him up yesterday, which he didn't. And another thing," the white cat's eyes widened with concern, "Mrs. O'Connell tried to call The Boy three or four times before she left and never could reach him. I heard her. You know that's not like him. The Boy carries his phone everywhere. He wouldn't ignore his mother, and he'd *never* forget an animal. *Never.*"

As though emphasizing the cat's words, a sudden wind rattled the front windows, and the porch swing creaked and swayed in squeaky protest.

Crouched in the chilly silence, Pris shivered. "You're right. The Boy should have been here yesterday. What should we do?" She looked up in alarm. "You're not planning on escaping the house again, are you?"

Both cats remembered their time in the Outs, and had vowed never to leave the safety of the Indoors again.

"No, I won't do that." Zekki murmured. "But we need to think of something."

"Should we try and reach Buddy?" Pris asked.

"Maybe we're over reacting. Before we panic, let's see what we can find out on our own." The white cat swished his tail in agitation. "If there's trouble, surely someone in the Outs has heard about it."

The cats looked at one another, their eyes suddenly locked together in unspoken understanding.

"Soot!" Pris whispered. "Contact Soot through mind-talk."

* * *

The thin, black cat limped through the alleyway, his crooked tail up and high above his back. During the night, a Texas cold front had swept through, and he was shivering. Winter would soon come, and with it, starvation, disease and desperate times for all creatures of the Outs. He sat for a moment, giving his back leg a rest. The injury had happened years before when he'd been hit by a car, and he still thought of the kind old woman whose unquestioning love had nursed him back to health. The two shared five happy years together before her death. But that was over.

With a groan, he rose to his feet and continued on. His duties concerning the feral colonies along 6th Avenue and Ryan Addition were many, and there was much to do before the first freeze. A leather clad couple roared by on a motorcycle, and the cat darted through an opening in a fence, almost toppling two adolescent kittens playing among the leaves.

Their mother, who lay hidden in shadow, jumped to her feet, and hissed a warning, but then her eyes widened with recognition,. "Oh!" She said, clearing her throat. "Attention, please," she called to her offspring. "We have a very important visitor!"

The two young animals froze where they were, their small tails still bushed with fear. Slowly, they crept to their mother's side.

"This is such an honor." The female murmured, corralling the youngsters, and hurriedly grooming them as she spoke. "I had no idea you'd be in this area today." When every tuft of their fur stood in damp, clean, spikes, she stepped back and smiled at the black cat. "I'd like you to meet my newest litter."

The two little males pushed against their mother's chest, peaking in wonderment at the stranger who stood quietly in the grass.

"And what have you been taught to say?" The gray queen nudged the larger of her offspring towards the black cat and nodded, her eyes glowing with pride.

"Are you The Cat Master?" The kitten asked.

"No!" The mother cat screeched, giving her son a hard swat with her paw. "I've told you a million times who this is!" She looked apologetically at the stranger. "I don't know why he said that."

"It's okay." The black cat smiled reassuringly, and turned to the cowering kittens. "Your mother is right. I'm not the Cat Master. I'm his son, Soot. I'm known as the Crippled Prince because of my leg. The cat wiggled it at the kittens who crept forward for a better look. "Other than that..." He shrugged. "I'm just a feral, born in the alley, like you were."

The mother cat shook her head in protest and turned to her offspring. "The Crippled Prince is much more than a feral. He's also the heir to The Cat Master. He makes our spiritual needs known to The Master who will lead us to Sho-Valla, heavenly resting place of all animals." She turned to Soot, her face troubled. "I appreciate your modesty, but kittens of the alley are becoming rebellious and undisciplined, and they need to learn respect." She leaned forward, her voice lowered for emphasis. "Some of them are mixing with the River Cats, and you know what *that* means."

Soot understood all too well. Aluna, his cousin and leader of the River Cats, had never accepted Buddy's ascension to Cat Master, and her colony was known for their hatred of all who supported him instead of Soot's and Aluna's uncle, the malicious Jett.

Shunned by most felines, the settlement mainly consisted of former Indoors who had been dumped in the park by their owners, and though Soot felt compassion for their plight, the gang's reputation as paranoid misfits had been earned.

Soot sighed. Perhaps a visit to Aluna was in order. Her group's increasing infiltration of the alleys was unacceptable. "You're point is well taken." He said to the female who shifted with discomfort before him. "But with vigilant mothers like you, I'm confident that the Laws of the feral will be well taught and our traditions held sacred."

The gray queen relaxed, purring with pleasure at the compliment.

With a nod to her, and a wink to the kittens, Soot launched back over the fence, his demeanor confident but his heart heavy with what the female had said. Aluna had, indeed, become a problem.

CHAPTER 19

Threatening black clouds rolled across the sky, blotting out an earlier promise of sunshine, and Orie was cold. Not only that. His hip ground and caught with every step, and his stomach felt bloated from the combination of too much ants and sugar. Beside him, La De Da strode effortlessly through the grasses, her face upturned and her eyes focused on the horizon. Orie snorted with irritation. The female should be following *him*, not leading the pack while the Legendary Lizard gimped behind, gaseous and drained. He stopped, flexed his sore toe and sighed.

There was no use denying it, La De Da had taken over. This wasn't a surprise. Orie had spent a life time avoiding the opposite sex for this very reason. From his limited experience, they were a pushy sisterhood, sneaky, vain, and incapable of complex thinking. The fact that these attributes more accurately described him than they did La De Da annoyed him even more. The truth, Orie thought sadly, was that in just twenty four short hours, his life had changed. No longer the mysterious lizard of legend, he now meekly limped behind a ragged crew of misfits who actually believed their opinions were equal to his. And the worst part, he hated to admit, was that he allowed it. In short, he'd become the most loathsome of creatures: a team player.

Bennett fluttered to a tree branch, and La De Da stopped and looked up. "Do you see the carnival yet?" She asked.

The parrot plopped to the ground, his pale grey eyes almost opaque in the soft morning light. "Yep, I've already been there.

It's around that corner," he gestured with one wing, "and to the right."

Theda scrambled from beneath his head feathers and blinked. "We flew really low, and didn't see any people yet. But, I remember how the carnival looked when I escaped...humans everywhere. Lizards and insects won't get much notice, but Bennett is different. Parrots are worth a lot of money and when animals are income for humans, it's never good for the animal."

"Lecture over?" Orie asked, impatient to get moving.

"I'm just saying he needs to be careful, that's all." Theda shivered. "The warehouse is an awful place."

"Okay then Bennett, keep out of sight as much as possible. However," he gave the spider an uncompromising stare. "I don't care what you think of the warehouse. Without that phone, The Boy doesn't have a chance."

* * *

Blitz scampered across a ditch and swerved to the west. The Trinity River was close because she could smell the thick, sour dampness of rotting leaves and decay. The ferret paused for a moment, her ears perked to the gentle burble of water in the distance. Her mouth was parched and suddenly it registered how long she'd gone without eating or drinking. Though food could wait, dehydration was worrisome, and it wouldn't do to lose her strength at this juncture. Turning toward the river she moved cautiously through the underbrush. Loamy sand gave way beneath her paws and dark ropes of ivy tickled her belly like soft, cool fingers. The ferret's eyelids dipped and fluttered and she shook her head to stay awake. Blitz knew the area was considered dangerous for small creatures, but it was daylight and most predators hunted at night and slept during the day. This included Blitz, who was suddenly desperate to rest.

Carefully, she picked her way over vines and pecans until she was close enough to the river to drink. Crouching low, Blitz lapped from the murky water, its earthy sweetness refreshing despite the reek of rot beneath. Occasionally, she lifted her head, testing the breeze for any signs of the River Cats, but the air smelled clean and benign. Satisfied, she noticed a stand of bushes on a sloping bluff beside her. Nandina and holly pushed together in a circle of overgrown lushness and Blitz struggled up the gentle berm for a better look. The area was secluded and quiet, and Blitz scurried into its welcoming protection.

Retrieving the cell phone would be easy, she thought, but carrying out the rest of her plan would take strength and endurance. Her tail drooped with fatigue and she realized rest was no longer an option. With a weary squeak, Blitz sank into the welcoming softness of leaves and dirt, tucked her head beneath her paws and slept.

* * *

The river wound in serpentine sparkles through the park, its rippling surface hypnotic in the morning mist, and Aluna crouched on its bank, her round eyes fixed on the small cluster of bushes on the slope above her. The morning's humiliation still burned in her mind and she'd spent hours roaming the park trying to calm down. That was before she'd spotted the ferret, again. At first she wasn't convinced that the creature was actually Blitz, because the ferret and her friends should have arrived at the carnival long ago. But after following her to the river bank, Aluna recognized the brown markings and distinctive scent. It was definitely Blitz, but why was she here? Maybe the plans had changed and the ferret was waiting for the lizard to join *her.* This thought was almost too wonderful to bear. But time passed; no Orie appeared, and now, careful to keep downwind, Aluna watched with confusion as Blitz settled in to the grass and slept.

The cat, too, suffered from exhaustion, but naps could wait. Despite the morning's setback, her pulse quickened with renewed excitement. Orie was alive! There was still time to avenge Jett's murder and earn long overdue respect for The River Cats. Her ears flattened in frustration. She had been so very close to the reptile and then the barking dog had ruined everything.

Aluna's mood darkened at the memory. There was a time when she would simply have scaled a tree and waited for danger to pass beneath her. But that choice no longer existed. Self-consciously, the cat tucked her front paws further beneath her body and tried to block painful thoughts. Like many members of her colony, Aluna had been declawed by her initial owner. She could still climb short distances, but her altered grip was precarious and prone to slippage. It was a shameful condition and one that Aluna hid as best she could. She glared into the river, her fierce green eyes reflected like emeralds in the lapping water. That was in the past, she had learned to cope and there were more important issues than man's many betrayals.

Her mind slid to the ferret's bushy hiding place. Was it possible that Blitz hadn't arrived at the trailer in time, and that Orie and his cronies had left for the carnival without her? She licked one dingy white paw and thought. This scenario didn't sound reasonable, especially if Blitz had been truthful about her friendship with Orie. Felines would never ignore a planned meeting, but who knew about lizard loyalty? Whichever the case, she didn't intend to lose Blitz again. With silent stealth, Aluna crept through the brown grasses, her black and white body almost skimming the ground.

Oblivious to her approach, the ferret sighed deeply, eyes closed, breathing rhythmic and calm.

The cat slid closer, nostrils quivering with distaste at Blitz's musky odor. A snarl of scrub trees offered the perfect place for covert observation, and settling behind a tangle of briars, she watched as the ferret slept on.

CHAPTER 20

A wind gusted through the trees, sending a shower of debris onto Soot's back. The black cat stopped, shook the leaves and acorns from his body, and painfully picked his way around the rubble. The female and her kittens had distracted him from the day's task. Late summer litters crowded the alleyways including a litter of his own. Most had no idea where to seek protection when winter came. Stopping to stretch his good hind leg, he mentally reviewed the day's agenda. First, find and mark appropriate shelters in Ryan Addition and surrounding neighborhoods up to the highway. Second, locate reliable cold weather food and water sources, then...

"Soooot!"

The cat's thoughts were interrupted by a sound deep within his consciousness. Someone was attempting to reach him through mind-talk, the unspoken communication of all animals. He cocked his head. Whoever called, was definitely limited in the silent language. In fact, the caller's dialect was so primitive; the cat wasn't sure what species he was hearing.

"Soot!" The voice called again. *"Where are you?"*

The mind talker's voice seemed vaguely feline, and much stronger this time. "I hear you." Soot telepathed back. A blast of static noise burst in the black cat's brain and he winced.

"...The...oy...troub...elp."

Soot frowned, trying to decipher the garbled message. Could this be a prank? Perhaps some bored young cats playing games?

"If this is a joke, stop it!" He admonish mentally. "Mind talk is serious." His consciousness registered silence. The caller was quiet.

A squirrel chattered from its nest and the steady thwack of newspapers being thrown from a car were the only discernible sounds in the crisp morning air.

The mother cat had been right, Soot thought, continuing down the alley. Today's kittens had no respect.

* * *

Bennett flew in lazy circles above the carnival, his shadow flitting across rickety rides and scattered concession stands. From the parrot's perspective, the grounds below looked dirty, deserted and small, a desolate place of manufactured fun and thrills, and nothing like he'd imagined. Movies were so much better. He felt a nagging tickle above one eye and realized that Theda was trying to get his attention. "What is it?" he asked, raising his voice above the wind.

"The warehouse is behind the snow cone stand!" she shouted in his ear. "Veer to your left!"

Bennett tilted downward, skimming the small row of locked kiosks holding stuffed animals and cotton candy machines until a dark, flat roof peeked from behind a fluttering canvas sign that read: 'Good Time Carnival – Old Fashioned Family Fun!'

"That's it!" Theda screeched. "Let's go back and get Orie and La-De-Da!"

Normally, Bennett followed others orders without question, but the warehouse roof top had triggered a surge of feelings he couldn't describe. On one hand he knew Theda's instincts were right, they shouldn't stay here alone, but there was something about the shack, something compelling and irresistible. He fluttered to the signage for a better look.

"Wait a minute! Why are you stopping?" Theda asked. She scurried onto his beak and stared into his eyes. "This is dangerous. We need to find the lizards, search the grounds, and get out of here."

Gently, the bird shook her onto the canvas, where she scrambled for footing on the glossy surface.

"Let's go back!" She wailed.

"Stay here." The parrot said quietly. "I'll be with you in a minute." Before Theda could protest, Bennett sailed to the warehouse roof and then fluttered to the window sill. Though the glass was dirty and cracked, the morning light was strong enough to illuminate most of the building's murky interior. Bennett leaned in close, his beak scraping the filthy panes.

The room was small and cramped, with cages stacked high against the walls. Most contained barely discernible forms the parrot assumed to be animals. In a far corner, a larger enclosure was covered with a tarp and in the opposite corner, another cage stood with its door ajar.

Pressing his forehead against the window, the bird's eyes teared with strain. Something sat quietly inside the opened cage. It was medium in size, and even amidst the gloom, Bennett could see bright amber eyes blinking up at him. The bird pulled back in terror. It had seen him! Bennett furrowed his brow and tried to quiet his furiously pounding heart. Why was he so afraid? After all, it was just a poor trapped animal...ripped from its home and family, hungry and frightened. Bennett shut his eyes against a whirling vision of tropical sunlight and birds screaming in terror.

So many nets.

The parrot caught his breath, talons clinging to his perch as the world rotated in a crazy spin around him. Slowly his dizziness rocked to a nauseating stop, but a buzzing question formed in his brain. *"How do you know this place?"* It whispered. *"How do you know anything about it?"*

"Bennett?"

Startled, the parrot jumped at the sound of the soft voice at his feet. He looked down to see Theda scrambling over his talons and up his chest. Breathlessly, she pulled herself to his head and then onto his beak. "Bennett." She repeated, her front legs waving wildly. "What's wrong? What are you doing?"

"Nothing is—is wrong," the bird stammered. The noise in his head had stopped, and the dreamy feeling he often experienced after such incidents slowly draped his consciousness in a thick veil of nothingness. Disconcerted, he ripped a feather from his breast, and winced. "You were right. Let's go find the lizards and look for the phone."

Surprisingly, the spider sprang onto the window sill, her compound of eyes rolling and refocusing to see through the panes.

"The cage," she said. "The one that's open? I think that's where the voice came from that told me to escape and find Orie." She frowned. "But it's so dark in there it's hard to see." Frenetically, Theda crisscrossed the window, stopping at intervals to stare through the glass, her busy legs carving squiggly trails in the dust. "I mean, I'm not completely sure because I ran out so fast, but I did look back once, and…there it is!" She shouted with excitement. "That's the cage that was beneath mine, the one with the…" Her voice trailed off with uncertainty, and she peered with a sudden intensity into the room, and then pulled back. "Something has changed."

The parrot leaned down, his pale grey eyes wide and confused. "What?"

Theda clenched and unclenched her mandibles. "When I was there before, even though things were awful, I felt a presence that was," she paused. "I don't know…helpful…friendly. But now…"

"Now, *what?*" The bird interrupted, his initial feelings of discomfort roaring back.

"I can't explain." Theda's voice quavered. "But whatever it is, it wants something." She looked up at the bird. "Something we won't want to give."

CHAPTER 21

"It's no good," Zekki said, pacing the room in frustration. "I couldn't make a connection. I heard Soot's voice, but I wasn't able to reach him." The white cat's tail slapped the floor with anger. "Darn!"

"Ze—Zekki." Pris stammered. The stress of not knowing The Boy's whereabouts had brought back a stutter from her kittenhood that she hadn't experienced in years. "Don't be discouraged. You can try again."

"Why bother? It's pretty plain that I don't know what I'm doing." Zekki jumped on to the couch, his ears back, and his whiskers limp with dejection. "I've only experienced mind talk once, and that was when Buddy spoke to me after the Gathering. That was a long time ago, and I've never had a reason to do it again." He gave the calico a tight smile. "I mean, you're the only feline I'm interested in talking with, and you're right here."

The two cats sat in tense silence.

"Hey!" The turtle's voice boomed from the bathroom. "It's lonely in here! What's going on?"

Pris groaned. "What does *he* want? I'm banned from my litter box and now we can't even have a serious conversation without him butting in. I've had it." She turned and trotted briskly out of the living room and down the hall.

Zekki hurried after her. "Wait a minute, Pris!" He called. "Don't hurt his feelings."

The turtle's head was barely visible over the tub rim. His claws scrabbled and slipped against the porcelain and the geometrical design on his brown and black shell shown in bold contrast against the pink walls and soft green accessories of the bathroom.

Pris stretched against the tub, her nose inches from the turtle's wrinkled face. "I—I'm tired of you listening to our conversations, and watching us, and—and yelling all the time."

The turtle blinked. "I wasn't yelling."

"Yes you were." The calico insisted, carefully avoiding a damp washcloth drying on the rim. "What do—do you want?"

A sparrow rustled by the window, and a burst of rain thrummed against the roof, but the turtle said nothing.

"Don't just stand there." Pris said firmly. "What do you want?"

Zekki sat in the doorway, his thoughts a tangle of fear. All attempts to reach Soot through mind talk had failed, and The Boy needed help. He could feel it in every fiber of his being. Zekki let out a long, slow breath of despair. If only he could remember how he and Buddy had wordlessly spoken so many years ago. Maybe then he could...

"Who were you looking for?" A dimly familiar voice interrupted from inside of his head.

The white cat started and looked around. Pris and the turtle were still nose to nose by the tub, and water plunked in tuneless droplets from the sink's leaky faucet. Other than that, the house was quiet.

"I said," the voice continued deep within his mind. *"Who is it you've been trying to reach?"*

"What the...?" Zekki whispered.

"Could you excuse me a moment?" The turtle asked Pris. Slowly, he turned from the calico's angry stare and redirected his gaze toward Zekki. "I was asking..." He enunciated in a loud voice. "Who have you been trying to reach?"

The white cat sat in disbelief. "A minute ago...that voice...that was you speaking to me in mind talk?"

The turtle nodded.

Pris frowned with confusion. "Who—who did? When?"

Zekki leapt into the bathroom, almost knocking her down. "I understood you perfectly!" he shouted, his face inches from the turtle's. "And you heard me trying to reach Soot, earlier, didn't you?"

The turtle steadied himself on the side of the tub and nodded again, a large smile creasing his wizened face.

The white cat sprang joyfully onto the toilet lid and then back to the floor. "Pris!" He screamed, embracing the calico in a giant bear hug which sent them both tumbling onto the tiles. "The turtle knows mind talk and he's good!"

"Actually," The turtle's eyes sparkled with pride. "My dialect's not perfect, but I *was* considered one of the best interpreters in Madagascar. My specialty is multi species language…fascinating stuff." He gave a humble little shrug. "I guess you could say it's a gift."

Zekki disengaged himself from the startled calico and jumped into the tub.

The turtle skittered back in alarm, almost tipping over. "I don't want to seem inhospitable, but I have an issue with claustrophobia, and it's a little tight in here." He shifted with discomfort. "Maybe if you stay… there." He indicated the far end of the tub with one claw and watched solemnly as Zekki moved backwards. "Yes." He took a deep breath and then let it out slowly. "That's better. My name is Cuff."

The calico glared from the bathroom scales. "Can someone tell me what's happening?"

"Don't you get it?" Zekki chortled, his ears and nose bright red with exhilaration. "Cuff is a mind talking genius. Multi species! Head of the class!"

"But—but." Pris stammered. "Can he reach Soot?"

"Are you kidding? This guy is a living, breathing telephone!" The white cat gave a silent prayer of thanks for the aged creature before him. "And if I understand him correctly, he can contact just about anyone he wants." Zekki looked hard at the turtle. "Am I right, Cuff?" he asked. "Can you?"

"Bingo." Cuff said. "I can."

CHAPTER 22

Orie and La De Da crouched beneath a shuttered snow cone stand, their tails twitching in nervous silence. Theda and the parrot should have been back by now, and a few workers were arriving to open for business. Cars rolled into the parking area, their tires crunching through gravel and disintegrating asphalt, and voices called to one another in sleepy greetings.

Once a well-kept park facility with grounds available for community art fairs and outdoor performances, the carnival was the sole survivor of a once prosperous south side. Expanding population had forced a much needed downtown renovation, and the thriving community had shifted west, leaving the zoo, picnic tables and soccer field as lonely relics of a simpler time. But the carnival had held on, returning every September with its quaint promise of family fun in the guise of stale popcorn, outdated rides and carefully rigged games. Through it all, an ancient calliope boomed from the entrance, its monotonous tunes wafting through the park.

Though neither of the lizards had actually seen it before, they were both aware of the fair's presence, and also the danger that such events harbored for animals. Bordering a busy highway, the area was deemed hazardous by domesticated and wild creatures alike, and as all animals knew, one could never be too careful when faced with crowds of adolescent humanity.

"Where in the world are they?" La De Da fretted, her brow furrowed with frustration. "If they don't show up soon, I'm gonna' find the warehouse and start looking for the phone myself."

Before Orie could object, a familiar flapping of wings announced Bennett's return and both lizards scrambled from their hiding place.

"Did you find it?" Orie demanded. The parrot seemed strangely subdued, and the lizard felt a stab of uneasiness. "Well? Did you or didn't you?"

"We did." Theda answered, dropping from Bennett's tail feather. "It's right behind that big sign and some bushes." She pointed to the fluttering canvas above the calliope. "But we can't actually go in there. If the phone isn't on the grounds outside, then we have to go back." She looked away, and scuffled four legs with uncertainty.

"What are you talking about?" Orie asked, his joints throbbing and his patience with all things female finally at an end. "I didn't limp all the way over here to ride the darn merry-go-round! I'm here to save The Boy!" He pushed past the spider, his face a mask of anger. "I'm going to find the phone and if I have to go inside the warehouse, then that's what I'll do."

Theda watched helplessly as La De Da trotted after Orie and finally Bennett joined them, bringing up the rear. "Wait!" she called. "Just hear me out!"

The animals stopped.

"This better be good," Orie said, "Because you're looking less like help and more like lunch by the minute."

The spider swallowed hard. "There's something I didn't tell you. I guess I didn't believe it until now." She sank in to a miserable black ball. "Or maybe I didn't want to believe it."

Orie swished his tail impatiently. "Yes, yes, and what could that be?"

"Right before I left The Boy in the trailer, Axel told me to stay away from the warehouse. He was already so terrified of Stuart Krell, I just thought he was over reacting." Theda's eyes suddenly welled with tears. "But he wasn't. I don't like it in there, either."

"Of course you don't like it!" Orie screeched. "It's filled with dead things!"

The parrot rocked with anxiety. "But, I felt it, too." With rhythmic precision, he yanked clumps of feathers from his

105

increasingly bare breast and watched them drift onto the dirt. "Maybe we should listen to what the dog said."

"Wait a minute." La De Da stepped forward. "Aren't we getting ahead of ourselves? Who says we need to go inside the warehouse? We haven't even looked around here, yet."

"She's right." Orie said glad for a distraction. "Let's check out the grounds before we decide anything about the warehouse."

The animals fanned out, Bennett scanning from above, and Theda, La De Da and Orie moving in ever widening circles toward the warehouse. Empty popcorn boxes, candy wrappers and tattered blue entrance tickets littered the area, and only grease-soaked gravel lay beneath the silent rides. But there was no sign of a cell phone.

"I found something!" Bennett cawed from behind the banner.

The group hurried to where he sat perched on the swaying red seat of a rusted Ferris wheel.

"It's not the phone, but look over there!" Bennett waved his wing, indicating a dark blue lump of fabric dangling from an over flowing trash can. Hanging down the side was a ripped strap with a large safety pin holding the two ends together.

"It's The Boy's backpack!" Orie shouted, racing to the container. "Don't just sit there, Bennett! Pull it down!"

* * *

Axel lay on the bathroom floor, his closed eyes jerking and tracking beneath soft, gray lids. He was running through wavy grasses, a hot white sun warming his back, and a black chain slapping the ground behind him. But that was okay, because The Boy was skipping to meet him, his kind blue eyes magnified by purple rimmed glasses. Bending low, he unhooked the links from around Axle's neck and tossed the shackle high in to the air. For a moment, it slithered and arced against the clouds, a glistening serpent unfettered and free. But the sun burned brighter and brighter, until the links smoldered red and suddenly melted in long, ropey tendrils down the sky. The Boy pointed to the dripping heavens. "Wake up." He said.

Axel frowned. Groaning, he pushed his muzzle beneath his paw and tried to ignore the unwanted feeling of consciousness now paddling to the surface of his mind.

"Axel, Axel! Wake up!"

The dog's eyes opened wide, and he yipped with surprise at the grimacing face inches from his own. The Boy was lying on his side, lips drawn tight in pain. Axel struggled to his feet, stumbled against something soft, and realized that he'd been sleeping on his friend's hand. He scurried backward, and The Boy moaned and rolled onto his back.

"Good dog." He whispered, slowly flexing his fingers.

Axle's brown tail wiggled with joy, and he squirmed closer. Gratefully, he licked The Boy's neck. It tasted of salt, soap, and blood.

Blood!

He jumped back. Sure enough, a sluggish rivulet of blood oozed from behind the young man's ear in slow, sticky droplets. The dog leaned in and whined. The Boy's injuries were worse than Mr. Krell had thought. A purple lump still bulged taut and shiny against the pale forehead, but there was also a deep gash buried beneath a matted swirl of hair.

Suddenly panicked, the pit bull rose onto his hind legs and tried to touch the window sill with his paw. The spider had promised they'd be back with help, but when? A feeling of doom squeezed his chest, heavy and wet as yesterday's laundry. What if his warnings about the warehouse had been ignored? Axel remembered the amber eyed thing staring from the cage and he whimpered. Maybe the lizard and his friends were there right now, trapped and...

A loud cough came from the bedroom, and Axle's thoughts shifted from concern to horror.

Morning had come. Mr. Krell was up.

CHAPTER 23

A cold wind ruffled the ferret's fur and she opened her eyes and stretched. Judging from the sun's position, she hadn't slept long, but the nap had definitely helped. Relaxed and rested, Blitz turned on her back as a cluster of dead leaves drifted above her head. Chortling with delight she batted and kicked at the foliage until nothing was left but brittle crumbles on her belly. It felt good to play, and she sat up, looking for a new diversion. Though open to all forms of fun, what she really wanted was to wrestle. But that was only a dream. The closest she'd come to bodily contact with any animal was the evil little dog at her former home. He hadn't appreciated her brand of camaraderie, and Blitz still remembered the prick of his pointed teeth in her back. Luckily, resilience was every ferret's motto.

The wind shifted and Blitz paused, sides heaving, front paw tucked high against her body. There was definitely a scent, slightly dank and definitely mammal, but it was too fleeting to identify. Satisfied, she took a deep breath. Everything was fine. It shouldn't take long to reach The Boy's house if she didn't stop for food or play.

With a final burst of exuberance, she rolled down the slope, boinked stiff-legged over a rock and headed toward home.

Behind her, a dark figure watched from the bushes. Slowly, it rose from the shadows and silently followed behind.

* * *

"Good job, parrot!" Orie shouted. "You're almost there!"

Bennett stood panting in the dirt, his beak open, and opaque eyes focused on the trash can towering above him. At first, he'd tried to stand on top of the container, and push the back pack onto the ground from there. Though seemingly empty, it wouldn't budge; and after much arguing, the animals finally agreed that a better plan was for Bennett to pull the pack from below, using the safety-pinned strap as leverage. After multiple tries and agonized moments of tugging and grunting, it now teetered over the rim, inches away from either falling onto the ground or rolling back into the trash can.

"Should he take a little break?" Theda asked, scurrying to the parrot's side. "Do you want to rest?"

Bennett shook his head. "We need to get this done before someone sees us. But, don't stand too close, I don't want you squashed."

Wild eyed, the spider skittered to where Orie and La De Da stood. "You can do it!" She shouted.

Bracing himself against the metal container, Bennett clamped his beak around the strap and fluttered backwards with all of his strength. Feathers flew from his beating wings and twirled in the chilly air. Slowly, the back pack inched forward, dangled for a moment, and then plopped with a whomp to the ground.

"Hurry!" Theda shouted. "I hear voices!"

La De Da and Orie rushed forward, their snouts pushing through pockets and gaping zippers. A tube of Lip Chap, and a music CD tumbled from the pack. Encouraged, the animals rooted in the remaining side pouch. One compartment produced two pencils and four colored markers, and the last held an unopened packet of gum… but no cell phone.

Orie stared blankly at the ground, his eyes skimming The Boy's familiar things strewn before them. "It isn't here." He said, as though no one else had noticed. "The phone isn't here."

"Go!" Bennett cawed from above. "People are coming, we can't stay here!"

Orie's mind sank in to a bog of despair, his legs leaden as pipes. They had failed. He thought of The Boy's cheerful voice, sloppy ways, and the multitude of unbearable irritations the lizard had come to hate and to love. His heart squeezed in anguish.

Heavy sounds of footsteps vibrated along the ground and La De Da screamed for him to run. He didn't care.

The cell phone had vanished. The Boy would die.

* * *

Stuart Krell sat on the edge of his bed, massaging the back of his head, and staring with groggy indifference at the disheveled image squinting back from the dresser mirror.

The night had been a restless one, full of anxious thoughts and worry, and today would be ten times more difficult with real dangers wrapped in real consequences. A vein throbbed in his temple, and Stuart rolled his shoulders trying to relax, but it was no use. The nightmare drifted back in hazy patches, the images blurred and rippling, as though seen from the bottom of a swimming pool. Jerry's midnight visit demanded attention and scratching his thigh, Stuart scowled.

Its name's not A anymore.

Despite all efforts to ignore them, the words gnawed at the big man's mind. Could someone really have been in the warehouse? Stuart's thoughts darted to yesterday's abduction and his gut felt hollow with fear. Had they been seen? And what about the kid's back pack? He'd been more than clear with Jerry about getting rid of it. Stuart scrunched his face with concentration. No, all the bases were covered. They'd been very careful and he was certain that he'd locked the warehouse door. He *always* locked the door. Jerry's slack freckled face drifted through his mind. So, why *was* the cage open? Stuart flopped back against the headboard, a slow anger constricting his throat. His partner had been trouble since the day they'd met. He was a volatile drunk. Worse than that, he was a volatile *stupid* drunk. Stuart belched and tasted acid. So, now, in addition to dealing with College Boy, the warehouse needed to be checked, and all because of Jerry and his alcohol induced hallucinations.

Its name's not A anymore.

Stuart felt a sudden and inexplicable dread. Perhaps he should just deal with the kid, get the turtle and blow off the warehouse situation all together. Reaching for the clock, he put on his glasses and noted the time: seven forty-five. His mood lightened. It was still early. He could go by the warehouse now, and then spend the rest of the day finding the turtle.

Pleased with the new strategy, Stuart pushed up from the mattress and threw open the bedroom door with a thud. Success was simply a matter of planning your work and working your plan, he thought philosophically, making his way down the hall. He wasn't sure where he'd heard that, but it was what he intended to do.

CHAPTER 24

A biting wind rattled an awning, and Soot trotted through the neighborhood, his injured leg dragging only slightly. The morning's earlier promise of warmth had faded with an increasing blanket of storm clouds, and the black cat's thin, short coat offered little protection. Soot shivered, wishing he was back beneath the pawn shop, a place he'd called home since the old woman's death. Increasingly, he fantasized about the people who worked there, but he couldn't return yet. One last thing remained on the day's schedule, and that was to find Aluna.

Soot had heard other complaints against The River Cats since leaving the feral mother and her kittens. The River colony's toms had been vying for alley females, and if not handled quickly, the problem could erupt into violence. Apparently, city officials had vowed to eradicate the cat's settlement once and for all, and because of this, some were slowly migrating from the park to the alleys. Soot sympathized with their plight. As heir to the Cat Master, all feline matters were his concern, but Aluna's clan was aggressive and wild. Their history had never been one of peaceful intermingling, and Soot couldn't allow them to disrupt the autonomy of his territory.

Thunder rumbled to the east and Soot turned toward the park. If the weather held, he could still speak to Aluna, and be back at the pawn shop by dark.

* * *

"Move!" La De Da screamed. With a grunt, she dashed forward grabbed Orie's tail and dragged him beneath the Ferris wheel, just as two dirty boots scuffed past.

The lizards huddled in the darkness. Wind whistled through the park, and the canvas sign flapped and cracked above them.

"That man almost saw us!" La De Da said. "You could have been killed!" Her eyes were wide and worried, and her body trembled.

Orie stared ahead and said nothing.

In a moment, Theda and Bennett scrambled beneath the ride, and all four animals sat in silence.

"I don't know how to say this," the spider said gently, "but, maybe Bennett should fly back to the trailer and check on The Boy while we decide what to do next." She looked at the ground. "I mean, we couldn't find the phone, and if the man is already awake…" she swallowed, "…well, you know what Axel said…" Her unfinished thought hung in the air, heavy with innuendo.

Someone turned on the calliope and the animals jumped as 'Down The Lazy River' belched from its pipes.

Bennett huddled beneath the machinery, tears rolling along his bill and splashing in the dust. "This can't be happening," he sobbed, "I love The Boy, he's the best human I've ever known." Theda and La De Da rushed to his side, their sad murmurings strange amidst the cheerful music.

"It has to be in the warehouse." Orie said suddenly.

The spider looked up. "What does?"

"The phone!" He said, his voice rising with excitement. "If it's not in the backpack, it has to be there because the dog claims not to have seen it since the abduction. If it was in the trailer, he would've remembered." Orie stared at the gaping trio as if seeing them for the first time, and glared at the weeping parrot. "What in the heck are you doing, Bennett?"

"I'm crying because I…"

"Well, knock it off!" Orie interrupted "If there's anything I hate, it's a blubbering bird." The lizard stalked into the open, his tail whipping the air.

"Wait!" La De Da shouted, running after him. "Where are you going?"

"I'm going in to the warehouse and look for the phone. If it isn't there…" he shrugged, "then we'll find it somewhere else, but nobody gives up on The Boy." Orie stared pointedly at each of the animals. "Understood?"

La De Da grinned and gave him a wink. "That's my guy!"

"But the warehouse is locked." Bennett sniffed and wiped his beak on a wing. "How will you get in?"

"I don't know yet," Orie's tone was stanch, "but I will."

It was still early, and aside from scattered employees talking and smoking by the stands, the carnival was quiet.

Scurrying to the warehouse, the animals clustered by its door. Though obviously old and weathered, it fit the frame tightly, the base almost sitting atop the cement flooring. Orie pushed his snout along the tiny slit at the bottom, but it was no use, he couldn't fit. Huffing with frustration, he moved along the building's perimeters. Timber had rotted in places, but the holes had recently been patched with plywood. Further investigation proved just as futile. The structure, though poorly built, had been meticulously safeguarded against unwanted entry, even from creatures as small as a lizard. "I need Theda!" Orie bellowed. "She's the only one who can fit under the door." He marched back to where she crouched in a ball at Bennett's feet. "You've got to go in and check for the cell phone."

The spider blinked. "No," she whispered. "I can't. I won't."

"Uh oh," a smug voice spoke from behind, "do I smell mutiny?"

The animals whirled toward the sound, their eyes wide with surprise. Standing behind Orie, his antennae waving with impudence, was the cockroach from yesterday's Meeting of the Spoken Word.

"What are *you* doing here?" Theda remembered the insect and how he'd looked at her.

"I could ask the same thing." The roach gave her a slow once over. "I see you're still hanging out with the riff raff." He pointed to the red stripe on her back. "But shouldn't you be sunning on a daffodil? Because that *is* what you are, right, a *garden* spider?" The roach gave a nasty chuckle and turned to face Orie. "I've been watching you imbeciles since you wandered in here this morning. I don't know why you want in the warehouse, but believe me," he poked a hairy leg in the lizard's direction, "it's an exceedingly bad idea."

Orie stood in silence, his stomach growling. The cockroach needed to die. Not because he'd insulted La De Da and Theda, though that was annoying, and not because he'd called them all imbeciles, which in itself was reason enough to tear him in two, but because Orie was famished and it was way past his breakfast time. But the bug was smart, and there was much at stake. He'd pick his brain first, and eat him later. "So, it's a bad idea, huh," Orie asked, careful to keep his tone even. "Why?"

The roach sniffed and fluttered his wings. "If I remember the spider's story correctly," he leaned forward and lowered his voice, "and by the way, I have an excellent memory and retain details with awe inspiring accuracy...she's already escaped this place once, and it didn't sound like a very pleasant experience. Besides," the insect paused and for the first time, Orie detected a note of uncertainty beneath the arrogance. "I've been in the warehouse today, and I'm not going back until I do a little research."

"Did he say 'research'?" La De Da sniggered with disgust. "Oh, *please.*"

"I can see scientific terms disturb you," the roach's voice was patronizing, "so, let's just say that there's a very interesting animal in the warehouse, one I've never seen before and would like to know more about."

"We've never seen anything like it, either." Bennett said. "Theda and I looked through the glass and..."

"Here's an idea." Orie interrupted, his voice rising with sarcasm. "There're lots of animals in the world we've never seen. Why don't we spend the rest of our lives going through the alphabet until we've named them all?"

"He has a point." Theda said quietly. "It's unknown to us, but so what? Why should that be so scary?"

The cockroach preened one antennae. "That's what I intend to find out."

"And exactly how are you going to do this, smart guy?" La De Da swaggered forward until her nose was almost against the roach's face. "You just said you didn't know what it was."

With a nervous hiss of warning, the roach stepped back. "Because its name is written on a tag by the cage."

"You can read?" Bennett asked, bobbing his head with excitement. "Usually I learn everything from television. What does it say?"

"Of course I can read." The insect sneered. "Can't everyone?" The animals regarded him with tight lipped fury, and snickering, he turned away. "As I mentioned at the gathering, I live in the Fairmount Library." He paused, his tone condescending. "I assume that everyone knows what a library is?"

"Where roaches go to die?" La De Da asked hopefully.

He sniffed. "It's where knowledge is stored, you vapid reptile. A place where every question has an answer if one is clever enough to find it and that includes the origin of the mysterious name in the warehouse."

"Exactly what *is* the name?" Theda asked, stamping four of her legs in frustration.

The roach winked. "That, my little charlatan, shall remain confidential for the moment."

Theda started to speak, then turned with a huff and bustled away.

"Am I the only one on to this germ bag?" La De Da asked. Turning to Orie, she rolled her eyes. "Let's get out of here, he doesn't know any more than we do."

"Are you sure?" The cockroach wiggled one antenna. "Call me overly protective, but I feel all aspects of a situation should be considered before putting my own life", he stared blandly at Orie, "and the lives of others at risk. As the 'captain' of this regrettable crew, wouldn't you agree?"

Orie pictured the bug lying on its back, all six legs twitching in an agonized death throe and felt a buzz of pleasure. But that would come later. "Words to live by," he said, nodding with genuine enthusiasm.

"So, I'm headed for the Fairmount Library." The roach lifted his wings. "If any of you would like to expand your limited little horizons, feel free to join me. It isn't far."

Bursts of lightning illuminated a distant cloud, and the chilly air felt thick and moist.

Theda shivered, and flashed the roach a look of true loathing. "As much as I hate to say this, I think we should go with him. I'm the only one small enough to get inside the warehouse, and I—I just can't do it until I know what we're dealing with."

Bennett nodded solemnly, and even La De Da shrugged in sullen agreement.

The insect turned to Orie, his stare challenging. "Your minions have spoken. What about you?"

Orie's mind churned with possible scenarios. The Boy's life was on the line and checking the warehouse was imperative. Whatever had frightened Theda and Bennett so badly needed to be dealt with quickly. If going with the bug was what it took to find the cell phone, then so be it. Orie smiled. "Majority rules!" He said, trotting towards the roach. "Lead on."

CHAPTER 25

The cats sat on opposite corners of the bathtub, their tails twitching with anticipation.

Okay, Cuff." Zekki said. "Here we go. The friend we need you to call is Soot." He flashed the turtle an encouraging smile. "So, do your thing, let's make contact!"

The turtle slowly blinked and said nothing.

Moments passed in an uncomfortable silence.

"Maybe you didn't understand." Pris finally said. "The name is *Soot.*"

"I heard you." Cuff said pleasantly.

Zekki frowned and shifted his position. "So, what's the hold up? You're a mind talking genius, right? So, talk!"

Cuff scrabbled forward, until his vaulted shell was directly beneath the white cat's gaze. "I was thinking that maybe you'd do me a little favor first."

"Uh oh." Pris said.

"What favor?" Zekki squinted with suspicion. "You never mentioned a favor."

"I'll be happy to contact anyone you want." The turtle stretched his leathery neck toward the cat and cocked his head. "But, first I want to get out of here."

"W—what are you talking about?" The calico stammered. "How on earth can we help with that?"

Cuff picked up a piece of apple and chewed it thoughtfully. "I don't really know. But I'll bet if you put your minds to it, you could figure something out. Take your time," he said, swallowing the fruit and licking his lips. "I can wait."

"Are you out of your mind?" Pris stood up so fast that she almost slipped into the tub.

"Not yet." The turtle panted, beginning to hyperventilate. "But if I stay here much longer, I will be. It's too tight in this tub." His voice suddenly rose in pitch, the cadence edged with hysteria. "I—I can't handle this anymore! I need air! The walls are closing in!"

"Whoa!" The white cat held up one paw. "Take a deep breath. Don't go crazy on me."

The turtle complied, his gasps finally subsiding into shallow hiccups. I'm not crazy." Cuff's lower lip trembled. "I'm tired. The bathroom light is always on and I haven't slept in days."

Exasperated, Pris leapt to the floor. "For Heaven's sake! Isn't that what your shell is for? Pull your head in and rest for gosh sakes."

"I can't." the turtle said sadly.

"Why not?"

"Because, it's too tight in there!" Cuff wailed.

Zekki licked his chops and gave the calico a worried glance. "Look, Cuff. Pris and I are going to have a little pow-wow in the other room, okay? Everything is going to be fine. Just have a raisin, or something, and relax."

Placated, the turtle nodded, and moved to his food bowl with slow, deliberate steps.

The cats trotted to the kitchen and crouched together on the floor.

"We have to think of something," Zekki said, "before he loses it completely and we never reach Soot." His eyes brightened. "How about this? I'll lie down in the tub and let him climb on my back, then you push him up and over."

"I don't really want to touch him," the calico groused," but, okay, let's give it a try."

They filed in and Cuff stood by his food pan, staring at a lettuce leaf. "How's the plan coming?"

"This may or may not work, but you're going to get on my back and Pris and I will push you over onto the floor." Zekki stopped, suddenly worried. "You can do this without dying, right?"

"See my shell?" The turtle gave a crinkly eyed smile. "Think of it as Homeland Security. I'll be fine."

"I'm taking your word for it. "Zekki prayed for luck. "Keep the faith."

Both cats jumped into the tub.

Pris nudged the food and water pans as close to the faucet as possible and Zekki settled on to his stomach as though resting. "Okay," the white cat said, gritting his teeth. "Get on."

With a determined grunt, Cuff clambered forward, his nails scrapping porcelain and catching in Zekki's long fur. "Ow!" the cat screeched, "watch where you're going!"

Startled, the turtle tumbled off, landing on his side, all four legs thrashing. "Give me a push, will you?" He asked, his eyes rolling toward Pris.

The calico grimaced with distaste, and with one tentative paw, nudged him onto all fours.

"Thanks." Cuff pulled himself over the cat's spine, smiled with satisfaction, and promptly fell off again. Finally, after an hour of clutching, prodding, falling, and readjusting, he teetered on Zekki's neck and shoulders. "Now what?" he panted, his beaked mouth resting against a green wash cloth drying on the tub.

"Now we hoist you up and over." Pris said. "Can you raise yourself so that your front claws are on the rim of the tub?"

The turtle nodded and carefully inched upward.

"I'm going to get up as smoothly as I can." Zekki's said. "So hang on." In one fluid movement, the white cat rose onto his feet and at the same time, Pris placed her head beneath the turtle's tail and lifted.

Cuff's body shoved up and forward. For one second he thrashed on the porcelain rim, almost threatening to fall backwards. But, suddenly, he shut his eyes, rolled to the left, and pulling the wash cloth with him, toppled to the tile floor with a hard crack.

Zekki and Pris leapt onto the sink and peered down.

"Are you okay?" The calico asked.

The turtle lay belly up, his glossy ochre underside looking thin and vulnerable beneath the thick shell. "I think so," came the muffled reply. Cuff's head and extremities protruded from the dome, and he carefully rotated his legs. Craning his neck, he stared upside down at the cats. "Yep. Everything feels fine." Slowly, he began a subtle rocking until his body tilted and tipped from side to side, and in one quick movement, he flipped on to his feet. Glancing up at the bath tub, he stretched his mouth into a toothless grin. "There's nothing like wide opened spaces." With a satisfied sigh he turned to the cats. "Okay, kids, let's do some mind talk."

CHAPTER 26

The Boy's guest cottage sat back from the Victorian home, its wooden sides painted a dusty pink with sage trim. Though the main house was occupied, the owners were rarely there, and Blitz had stopped watching for them long ago. With brazen assuredness she scampered along the asphalt driveway, her back arching and stretching like a Slinky toy. The nap had helped but she was hungry, and since The Boy wasn't there to feed her, she nosed through the flower beds looking for insects. Despite the rain, the clay earth was hard, so she turned to a dark green ligustrum bush, its purple berries close to the railing. Flipping wildly amidst the lower branches, she stripped off the fruit, eating and playing until she could barely move. "Can't nap yet," she cautioned, "not until I get what I came for." Luckily, a pet door allowed access to the kitchen and she slithered through it with no trouble.

The house was cold and strangely quiet. Blitz climbed up a chair and onto the window sill. A sprinkle of rain dotted the sidewalk, and she caught herself listening for Bennett's caw from the mulberry tree. Life had been happy here, and she felt a sudden sense of loss. What if The Boy never came back? Where would she go, and with whom? Setting her jaw, she leapt to the floor and darted through the hall. There was no reason to worry. The Boy would be saved and everything would continue just as it had always been.

Except she'd be famous.

Blitz beamed with pride. There was no denying it, kleptomania had an upside, and she made a mental note to include that in her memoirs. With a happy squeak, she slunk down the hall way, heading for her secret place. The old house was a plethora of hidey-holes and after much snooping, she'd settled on The Boy's bedroom.

Now standing in the doorway, she chirped with pleasure at the pure chaos spewing from every corner. The Boy was a slob, the worst she'd ever seen, but who cared? In her opinion, the bed was the only thing that mattered, and her eyes turned with reverence to the scarred and peeling four poster. Salvaged from The Boy's childhood, it was jammed against the wall, rumpled sheets carelessly tossed over the edge, and a drooping comforter concealing the mound of junk bulging from beneath. Everything from text books to fast food sacks, lay shrouded in dust... all kicked beneath the bed to be dealt with later. Later meant never, and protected by The Boy's resistance to order, Blitz's treasure trove had flourished.

Squirming beneath the bedding, she crept over a frayed towel from yesterday morning's shower, and snuggled into her nest. Before her, a bright red Christmas bow peeked from a house shoe along with six cough drops, a hair brush, headphones draped with Mardi Gras beads, and finally, Blitz's latest and most cherished acquisition...the cell phone. She touched its shiny black surface with awe, and for one brief moment considered letting The Boy's future unfold without her. But those were the naughty thoughts of a hoarder, she thought, not a hero. Fame beckoned and with it, came sacrifice. Gently, Blitz took the phone in her teeth, backed slowly out from under the bed, and bumped into something soft. Dropping the cell, she whirled in surprise.

Aluna crouched on the floor behind her, and the River Cat wasn't alone.

* * *

Mr. Krell was definitely up, because Axel could hear him banging around in the kitchen and detected the rich smell of coffee wafting down the hall. A white haze of fear engulfed the dog, and he pressed against The Boy's hip, his mind desperately seeking a plan. There was none. Even if he wanted to defend his friend,

they were chained so close together he could barely move, let alone attack. Axel thought of Mr. Krell's ever present baseball bat and cringed. The bathroom was tiny, there was nowhere to run...
...or hide.

A beefy hand reached in and pulled back the curtains. "Morning fellas," Stuart said pleasantly, stepping over The Boy and turning on the tub's shower.

Axel watched wide eyed from the floor, as the water became hot and steamy. Mr. Krell didn't have a weapon. Maybe he'd changed his mind and didn't want to kill them anymore. The dog whined hopefully.

"So, how did everyone do last night?" Stuart wiped a foggy swath across the bathroom mirror with the back of his arm, and studied his face in the sweating glass. "I'll bet you guys bonded all over the place." Grinning, he bent down, his face close to the young man's ear. "Today-is-the-day-they-give-turtles-away," he said in a sing-song voice; then laughed and stood up. "But first, how about a little privacy?" With a loud grunt, Stuart shoved The Boy away from the tub and into the hallway with his foot. Axel stumbled behind, the leash twisting hard and tight against his throat. The curtain was yanked shut, and The Boy groaned on the floor and tried to sit up.

Familiar sounds of Stuart's morning rituals filled the trailer. Spraying water battered a plastic shower curtain, the squeaky medicine cabinet opened and closed, and the yellowed toilet flushed through groaning pipes.

Axel sat in misery, wondering how such mundane things could signal the end of their lives.

Finally, Stuart pushed through the curtains, his rotund body swathed in a grimy robe, his pudgy feet leaving wet stains on the tile. "You drink coffee, College Man?" he asked.

The Boy, who had managed to prop himself against the hall wall, nodded slightly.

"Okay. I'll just take this good ol' dog out to do his business, and be right back with some java." Stuart plucked the leash from the floor, undid the clasp from around Axle's neck and slapped his massive terry clothed thigh. "Come on dummy." He said, lurching down the hall toward the front door.

The dog felt a thrill of joy. He was free! He wasn't going to die! With a puppyish wiggle, he trotted briskly behind Stuart, and then stopped. What was he doing? He couldn't leave The Boy. What if Mr. Krell hurt him?

"Axel! Come!" Stuart shouted from the living room.

The Boy looked up as though reading the dog's mind. "Go on, now. Go on." He whispered, lifting one hand as if in farewell.

Axel cocked his head and panted with confusion.

"Go." The Boy said once more.

Turning slowly, the pit bull walked to his friend, and tentatively licked the pale, outstretched fingers. He'd go outside, but he'd come right back. With his big head high, Axel padded for the front door. Canine Law plainly said that dogs were never to leave their masters. Unfortunately for Mr. Krell, Axle's definition of 'master' had taken a clear and surprising turn.

CHAPTER 27

The cockroach skittered through the carnival grounds, his shiny mahogany back glistening in the narrow shafts of sunlight that filtered through the clouds.

From above, Theda watched him from her perch on Bennett's head, her mind a black screen of fury. The roach was cruel and smug and had treated her with disrespect. Why? What had she ever done to deserve such a vendetta? But Theda knew the answer before it was asked. He knew what she really was.

A murderer.

Choking back a sob, she hoped Bennett's flapping wings covered the sound. Soon they'd all know who she was, and they'd hate her, too. A tear of despair dropped onto one of the bird's silvery feathers and quivered there, before rolling away in the wind.

Far beneath them, La De Da and Orie scurried among the shadows. Their attention riveted on the roach, now veering away from the park and onto a tree lined boulevard.

"Be careful!" Theda shouted in the parrot's ear. "We're going into a neighborhood and someone might think you've escaped from the zoo or something."

The bird soared upwards, his tightly tucked legs barely skimming the tops of trees, and his beating wings fighting a chilly head wind. "We're pretty high now!" he called. "Can you still see them?"

Theda squinted her multiple eyes, trying to focus on the blurry ground whizzing beneath them. Yes. There they were, the lizards

swerving on the sidewalk and the awful roach running just paces in front. But they were going in the opposite direction of the trailer, and she knew instinctively that Orie wouldn't stay long before returning to the warehouse…and she would be forced to go inside.
No
Unwanted images swirled in her mind. *Dead things on the ground. Amber eyes in the shadows…hungry, hungry.* Theda took a shaky breath. But the roach was smart. Everyone could see that. Maybe he'd figure things out and she wouldn't have to be scared anymore.

Of course her crime could never be changed. Redback spider; how she despised everything it implied. For the hundredth time, Theda swore an oath of pacifism. She would never harm anything again. Not even the despicable roach.

"Hold on!" Bennett shouted. With a sudden tilt of his wings, he banked sharply to the left. The earth tilted sideways, and the clouds puffed like gray cotton where the ground should have been.

The spider gasped, her grip loosening on Bennett's feathers, then suddenly they dropped, soaring past house tops and alleyways and finally skimming to a jarring stop on a concrete parking lot. Leaping from his back, she wobbled in a dizzy dance of nausea until the spinning stopped.

The lizards dashed from between two parked cars, and the roach stood at a distance, watching.

"Everyone okay?" Orie asked, his sides heaving with exertion.

Theda saw the worried look on La De Da's face as she watched him struggle to breath.

"Fine and dandy." Bennett said, staring skyward. "Is this the place?"

A small, one story building jutted from the pavement as though added to the street as an afterthought. Faux columns book-ended a crumbling entrance of dirty beige bricks and above it, a dented aluminum door the words: Fairmount Library – Established 1949 was carved into a cement block. The surrounding neighborhood wasn't much better. Rows of dilapidated wooden houses and crumbling duplexes lined the streets. Last year's Christmas lights still looped from sagging rooflines, and grassless yards featured rusted cars, and brown perennials.

The roach waved his front legs proudly toward the library. "Here we are," he said, "my home and supreme place of knowledge." Smiling with imperial satisfaction, he gazed at the silent cluster of animals gathered around him and fluffed his wings. "Ready?"

"Whatever." La De Da muttered.

Orie flashed her look of disapproval, and then stamped with impatience. "Come on, come on!"

The creature scurried up the brick and leapt on to a leafless trumpet vine. "There's a vent on the other side of that gutter," he called, pointing to a small black square with his antennae. "A corner is pulled lose, so just go through it until you see light. A couple more steps and you're in." Without waiting for a reply, the insect darted into the opening and disappeared.

"I don't like him." La De Da said, her stance defiant.

"Neither do I," Orie said, climbing up the brick, "but he's all we have at the moment, and I need Theda to go in that warehouse." He looked down at the female and frowned. "You coming or not?"

La De Da balked, her mouth set in a stubborn line. "I've never been inside a building before."

"You'll like it." Bennett said, his voice bright with encouragement. "They're very nice places."

"It has roaches," La De Da huffed, "how nice can it be?" But she scurried behind Orie as he started up the wall.

A spatter of raindrops blew through the parking lot, and Bennett fluttered to the ledge. "Come on, Theda and I'll meet you guys inside.

The spider gave one last wave of encouragement, and then hunkered into a protective ball amidst the bird's tail feathers. She held her breath as he squeezed through the narrow opening, and noticed a change of temperature.

The passageway was warm, dirty and narrow, with only a pinpoint of hazy light to guide them. Dust particles swirled in the air and somewhere behind them, she heard Orie sneeze.

"I'm in! Bennett's voice echoed. "Everyone needs to take a hard right at the end and step down!"

One by one, the animals trailed from the opening, their eyes squinting in the harsh glare of the library's flickering fluorescent lights.

Someone had left the heaters on, and the room was hot and musty. Cracked plaster walls were painted a muted green, and tall metal racks lined the perimeter, their bowed shelves so crammed with books that they threatened to snap. A Formica counter stood in the middle of the room, its pristine surface divided into two meticulous segments. One sector contained neat stacks of magazines and flyers, and on the other sat an old computer, its screen an inky black.

"Amazing, isn't it?" The roach asked, gazing around the room with teary eyed emotion. "I'm the luckiest bug in the world." Dropping to the floor, he scuttled through the desks, and crawled up the side of the counter. "Inside this box," his antennas waved toward the computer, "are all the answers of the universe." He stared imperiously at the animals clustered below. "Any questions so far?"

"Just one." La De Da said. . "Can those who think you're a windbag with wings be excused?"

The roach stiffened with anger. "And what exactly does that mean?"

"It means!" Orie shouted. "That we're not here for a darn MENSA meeting! We're here to find out about the thing in the warehouse." His voice lowered with barely contained wrath. "Is that clear enough?"

"Of course." The insect sniffed. "You're incapable of complex thinking, I understand perfectly."

Orie puffed his throat in warning, "Listen, bug. In the interest of time I'm going to let that pass, but don't push me." With a nod to La De Da, he scurried up the kiosk, jumped onto the counter and jostled for space atop the periodicals. Bennett followed, landing lightly on the rim of a coffee mug which held pens, pencils and paper clips.

"I've never seen one of these before." Theda said, emerging from the bird's feathers, and lowering herself by a silken thread on to the computer's keyboard. The growing hostility between Orie and the roach had frightened her, and they needed to get back on track. "I've always been fascinated by technology." Settling awkwardly on the Shift button, she averted her eyes from the approaching cockroach, fearful that he'd see the lie beneath the charm. "I'm impressed."

"At least there's one bright light among you."

Her ruse had worked. "So what now?" she continued.

"Now, my spotted back lovely," he answered with a courtly bow, "I access information." With a whir of wings, the roach jumped up and down on the Enter key until a blinking message appeared on the screen. *Welcome to the Fairmount Library-No Password Required.* With a smug smile directed at Orie, he popped hard against the same key, and a narrow box appeared with the word: *Search.* "Who would like to be my assistant?" The insect's gaze slipped past the lizards and landed on Bennett. "You seem easily amused. Care to loan your beak to the project?"

The parrot blinked. "Sure, what do I do?"

"See these letters?" the roach asked, indicating the board.

Bennett hoped forward, stopping inches from the computer's edge and nodded. "Now what?"

"Now," he indicated a key with one hairy leg. "Hit 'A'."

CHAPTER 28

The ferret hoped she was hallucinating. She wasn't. Two cats were sitting in The Boy's bedroom. One was Aluna casually sprawled amidst a tangle of sweat pants only inches behind her, and the other was a wiry gray tom. He lounged in the doorway, his heavy lidded eyes flat and unreadable.

Blitz smelled a whiff of decay, and noticed an abscess along his jaw.

"What a coincidence." Aluna said, cocking her head. "I was just telling my friend, here, about our adventure this morning." She glanced back at the tom. "Wasn't I?"

"You were." Gently, he scratched at his wound, and winced.

"And then we saw you enter this house, and decided to come on in and say hi." Aluna's eyes widened with earnest concern. "We're not disturbing you, are we?"

Blitz shook her head, instantly wishing she'd lied.

"Good." The cat continued. "Because I'd like my friend to meet you." She turned to her tabby companion. "This is the ferret who's best friends with the Legendary Lizard."

The cat nodded, and Blitz nodded back. This was no coincidence, and a queasy fear rolled through her mind. They'd obviously followed her here for a reason...but, why? "Look, Aluna," the ferret said, deciding to be honest, "I realize that you're mad at me, but..."

"...Not at all," Aluna interrupted. "In fact, I'm glad we've run in to one another, because I wanted to apologize for my outburst in the park." She gave a wide, fang filled smile. "I was completely out of line; too little sleep, not enough food. You understand." She paused, her green eyes sad with regret. "Friends?"

"Friends," Blitz repeated, amazed by the heartfelt apology. Maybe she'd misjudged her.

"So, did you ever find Orie?" Aluna asked.

The ferret considered the question carefully. Aluna seemed pleasant enough, but her prior interest in Orie had been anything but casual. "No," she said, opting for caution, "I guess he forgot our plans, because they'd all left by the time I found the trailer. Anyway," she said, eager to change the subject, "I'm surprised to see you inside a house. I thought you didn't like humans."

Aluna's eyes widened with mock amazement. "Humans?" She craned her neck in an exaggerated search of the room. "I don't see any humans." She turned to the stripped grey tom who was rubbing his jaw on a chair leg. Do you see any humans?"

Shaking his head, he grinned. "Not even a little one."

The cats watched Blitz in smug silence, their thinly disguised code blatantly clear. They knew she was alone and wanted her to feel vulnerable.

So much for friendship, Blitz thought. Backing against the bed, she straightened her posture. "Actually, people are in and out of here all the time." Her eyes scanned the room, hoping for an escape route. There was none. "So, if you don't want to be trapped or something, you should probably move on."

"Thanks for the warning." Aluna indicated the cell phone now gleaming between the ferret's front paws. "What's that?"

Blitz took a quick step forward and sat on the phone. "Nothing. Just something I promised I'd get for Orie." The gadget was hard and cold against her rear, and she readjusted her tail. "No big deal."

"I know what it is." The tom said. "It's a cell phone. Humans carry them everywhere… sort of a primitive form of mind talk, only louder and more annoying." He craned his neck for a better look beneath the bed. "What else have you got in here?"

The ferret's heart thumped with an alarming new thought. Was this the reason for their visit? Did the cats want her stash? She thought of the carefully collected treasure lovingly arranged in the dust, and her tail bushed with anger. No one was getting her stuff, and they'd be sorry if they tried.

Aluna stretched and sniffed The Boy's rug. "Nice place. It's been awhile since I was an Indoor." Her bright green stare was piercing. "How about showing us around?"

"Yeah," her companion echoed, rising to his feet, "how about it?"

Nice try, Blitz thought, but she wasn't going anywhere. "Sure, why not?" Her voice sounded amazingly normal. "You came in through the kitchen. This is the bedroom, and a bathroom is down the hall." She gave a goofy shrug. "Tour's over! Stop by the gift shop on your way out."

The two cats sat in humorless silence.

"So, what does Orie want with that?" Aluna finally asked.

Blitz dropped onto all fours, the phone now completely hidden by her stomach. "With what?"

"The phone." Aluna's eyes narrowed to glittering slits. "The thing you're lying on."

"Oh, *that*." Blitz swallowed, but held her position. "Well, it belongs to The Boy I told you about. You know, the stupid human who's is in trouble? He's in that trailer, and Orie needs the phone for some type of escape plan. It's nothing you'd be interested in, hating people and all..." She trailed off, suddenly aware that Aluna and the tom had exchanged subtle glances.

"Hey!" The male crouched low on the floor, his eyes dilated to black. "What's *that*?"

Confused, Blitz followed his line of focus to a wadded bit of paper on the floor. "I don't know, it could be trash, or..."

"...or a toy!" The cat shouted. With a yowl, he leapt to his feet, hooked the paper with one paw, and in an amazing display of dexterity, batted it like a hockey puck across the room.

Blitz watched transfixed, her nerves buzzing like flies at a picnic.

He crept along the perimeter of the room, then rushed toward the paper ball and smacked it again. This time, it ricocheted against the wall, landing in a pile of underwear by the bed. The tom swaggered in a circle, feigned to the right, and then neatly hooked the 'toy' back to the sagging comforter. It rolled to a stop inches from the ferret's nose.

Flash bulbs of pleasure popped and glowed in the darkness of Blitz's mind.

He wanted to play!

With a ferret dook of joy, she sprang to her feet and war danced through the rubble. Springing left and right, she flopped on the floor, and with a screeching whoop, rocketed to the bedding, grabbed the paper in her mouth, and bolted for the door. The cat pounded behind her, finally leaping onto her flanks and pulling her down in the hallway.

Squirming free, Blitz sprang into the kitchen where she hid behind the stove and ambushed his tail as he entered.

Both animals rolled on the tiles, biting and screaming with mock fury, and then they burst through the pet door, and into the back yard. Misty raindrops coated their fur and dripped from their whiskers, but still they wrestled and spun, until finally spent, they both lay panting on the wet grass.

"What a rush!" Blitz chortled. "Wasn't that great?"

"Yeah." Licking mud from one grey paw, the tom squinted against the rain. "I'm going to the porch."

"Okay." Blitz flipped on to her back, reliving their first glorious moment of physical contact. "Boom," she whispered. "Pow!"

Pewter clouds thickened the sky, and rain splashed in chilly droplets against her belly. Blitz rolled on to her side and yawned. "Why don't we go back inside until the rain stops and then have a little rematch? I don't have any food, but..." Shaking the drizzle from her head, she yawned again, her eyes suddenly heavy. An empty flower pot sat beneath a lawn chair, and in one motion, she snaked inside, snug in the comforting darkness. "Maybe we could...could..." The ferret's eyes closed and she gave a long shuddering sigh of release.

"Is she awake?" Someone asked in the distance. But the pot was so cozy and the voice so far away beneath the rumble of thunder that Blitz decided not to answer. Paws covering her masked face, she curled her body into a tight little ball, and counted the raindrops gently tapping the chair. "Can't wait for that rematch," she murmured.

But first she had to sleep.

CHAPTER 29

Soot hunkered against the rain, his thin black coat parted by rivulets of water. The morning's promise of sunshine, had dissolved into a dreary noon, and the temperature had steadily fallen. Wincing, Soot shifted weight off of his bad back leg. The change in weather had added a deep ache in the bone that made walking difficult and running almost impossible, and he longed to abort the day's errands and return to the little space beneath the pawn shop. Sometimes the owner's wife left scraps for him after lunch, and he didn't want a possible meal ruined by the downpour. But there was still much to do before evening.

He wasn't far from the river, and his mind turned to Aluna. With any luck, he'd find the River Cat quickly, share his concerns, and still have time to get back to the alley and check on his mate's new litter before dark. He smiled at the thought. There were four in all: three tortoiseshell females, and a yellow tom the spitting image of Soot's father, Buddy. All were sleek, bright, and healthy and Soot was determined to keep them that way, which meant no River Cats. With one last flex of his crippled limb, he hobbled up Cantey Street and headed for the park.

* * *

The trailer was cold and Stuart pulled a ketchup stained corduroy jacket over his sweater and considered turning on the electric heater. Instead, he gazed out his bedroom window, amazed at the torrent of rain now pounding against the splattered panes. Lowering the blinds, he grinned. Today's weather worked to his advantage, because no one went to carnivals in the rain. He'd take a quick look at the warehouse, pay off the few employees who'd actually shown up for work, and close the whole thing down for the season.

Turning off the lights, he headed for the bathroom. If things went well with the kid, he'd never see the lousy trailer or experience another summer in this hell-hole of a state again. Let Jerry move the rides and deal with vendors, Stuart thought with pleasure. He'd be long gone with one of the most valuable and endangered animals in the world sitting right by his side.

College Boy slumped against the wall just as he'd been earlier. His eyes were shut, and both hands were wrapped around a mug of coffee which sat untouched on his lap. Stuart watched silently, his mouth twisted in thought. The kid didn't look good, and the dog was sticking to him like gum on a school desk. Good. By the time Stuart returned from the warehouse, the choice between College Boy giving up the turtle and allowing something to happen to the dog would be an easy one. "Well!" He said with enthusiasm, slapping his palms together in a hollow clap. "I've got a few things to deal with at the carnival. When I get back, we're going to have that very important talk I mentioned." Stuart stared at the young man on the floor, the jovial brightness gone. "And I'm not kidding, friend. You're gonna tell me where the turtle is or things are gonna get ugly."

The Boy opened one red rimmed eye, and then slowly closed it again.

"Oh, and breakfast is over." Stuart jerked the mug from the young man's hands, stepping back as tepid coffee slopped onto the floor. Dragging him back into the bathroom, he chained Axel to the kid's ankle. "Put your hands behind you." The Boy did as he was told, and Stuart bound them with tape, using the last strip on the roll to cover his mouth. "I'll see you later." Grabbing the baseball bat, Stuart strode toward the door. "And when I do... it's gonna be turtle time!"

* * *

136

"Okay," the turtle said, shutting his eyes in concentration, "you're friend's name is Soot, right?"

Zekki and Pris nodded in unison.

"And what exactly do you want me to say?"

The white cat licked his chops with worry. "This is tricky, because we don't have any proof..."

"...we don't need any," Pris said. "We know what we know." She turned to Cuff, her tone authoritative. "Tell Soot that The Boy hasn't shown up and we're worried. Ask him if he knows anything."

The turtle bobbed his head as she spoke, memorizing the message. "Is that it?"

"Yes," Zekki said, "and I just want to thank you again for..."

"...excuse me," Cuff interrupted. "I don't want to seem rude, but you need to be quiet, now... both of you."

Pris started to speak, but the white cat shook his head. "Do your stuff." he said.

The turtle stared at the wall, his tail still, eyes unblinking.

An ambulance wailed in the distance, and the clock ticked from the living room.

Cuff's tail drooped, his legs wobbled, and without warning, he sank to the floor.

"Oh my gosh, we've killed him!" Pris wailed.

Zekki crept towards the domed shell. "Hey," he nudged the creature's leg, "are you okay?"

Raising his head, Cuff flashed a weary smile. "Mission accomplished," he said, "we've made contact."

CHAPTER 30

The ferret's eyes opened to dusty darkness. Her legs felt cramped, and at first she panicked, believing that she was still in the pet store. But memories of the wrestling match came rolling back and she replayed them, reveling in the pure physicality of their game. Wondering what time it was and how long she'd been asleep, Blitz stood, stretched, and then draped her paws over the pot's rounded edge for a better look. The rain had stopped, but murky puddles dotted the back yard, and water splashed in sluggish droplets from the chair above her. Yawning, she slithered from the pot, and onto the grass. Perhaps now was a better time to dig for grub worms since the ground was drenched and malleable.

With a happy chirp, Blitz scurried to a weed-filled flower bed and vigorously plowed into the sodden earth. The plan was fruitful, and moments later, her mouth crammed full, muzzle coated with dirt, the ferret chewed thoughtfully. The cat's wild-eyed face floated behind her eyes, and Blitz giggled. Their rematch would be spectacular, and she wondered if he was rested and ready to go. Rising onto her hind legs, Blitz swallowed the last of the grubs, and peered at the porch. Its wooden steps were slick with a fine glaze of mist, and only clumps of soggy leaves dotted the now empty deck. "Aluna!" She called. "Where are you?"

Two beetles marched across her tail, and a Grackle strutted in the flower bed, brazenly exploiting Blitz's labor. Other than that, the yard was hushed and still. A pinch of worry furrowed her brow. Where were the cats? Only a vague feline odor remained in the yard, and she sat, wondering why their absence should cause such uneasiness. Her sleep addled brain conjured a bleary order of events. Aluna had appeared in the house and introduced Blitz to a fellow River Cat who'd turned out to be a great sport. But was that all? Hadn't the cats talked about something?

Talked about what?

The ferret shrugged at the question, because they'd discussed all kinds of things...humans, the house, Orie...

Orie!

Blitz squealed and jumped backwards. How could she have forgotten? Scrambling onto the porch, she burst through the pet door and rushed down the hall to The Boy's room. Panting with fear, Blitz crept to the bed and stared at the crumpled comforter.

The cunning little cell phone had vanished!

What to do? Blitz war danced through the room in a fit of despair, and then stopped, her whiskers quivering. She had to retrieve it, but how? Obviously, Aluna had taken it, but the River Cats ruled the park in ever increasing numbers. It was unlikely that one lone ferret could intimidate an entire colony into returning stolen property. A long ago memory unfurled through her mind, and her ears twitched in thought. Was she alone? Maybe not.

* * *

Bennett blinked at the word he'd so carefully pecked out on the computer's keys. "I can't read," he said, looking from animal to animal. "What does this mean?"

The roach pressed close to the screen, careful not to touch anything. His mouth moved, silently sounding out the string of letters. "I don't know," he said, "but that's what the computer is for." Shaking his glossy brown body, he stretched his front legs. "Here we go." With a plop, he leapt onto the key marked ENTER, and waited as the computer screen jumped from blue to a long list of printed references. "There," he said, after a quick scan, "let's try that one." He tapped an arrow key until the second reference highlighted, and jumped on ENTER again.

Orie stood to the side. He'd noticed a change in his body since their trek to the library. He felt woozy and weak, and his chest felt strangely tight and heavy. A horrible thought burbled to the surface. Had old age finally caught up with him...chasing him down like some pest busting chemical just as a whole new life was unfolding? He peeked at La De Da, whose adorable face glowed against the light of the computer. Fate had brought them together, he thought with a wistful sigh, and instead of sharing slugs in a moonlit garden, they were stuck in a mildewing library watching a cockroach. Even so, there she was, food on her face, snout protruding, so dainty, so lovely....

La De Da slapped him with her tail. "Stop looking at me, you're creeping me out."

...And what a witch. Orie pulled his mouth into a tight little frown. Females were such a galling gender, who needed them? Annoyed, he turned to the roach. "What does it say?" he asked, purposefully ignoring La De Da's gaze.

"This can't be right." The insect said in a halting voice. "I must have spelled it wrong."

A sudden chill coursed through Orie's body, stark and cold amidst the stifling heat of the room. The roach was lying. Something was wrong. "Of course you spelled it right," he pushed. "You're wasting time. What does it say?"

The roach clenched his mandibles and looked at the animals who grouped anxiously around him. "It's a jackal."

"That's all?" Bennett asked.

The insect backed away from the computer. "Not...exactly."

"Okay, it's a jackal." Theda lowered herself from the parrot's back. "Why is that so scary?"

The roach stared at the dark monitor, eyes unblinking. "Because, it's not just *any* jackal."

"If you don't tell us what you're talking about!" Orie screamed. "I'm going to eat you right here!" Bullying forward, he blocked any hope for the bug's escape. "Once and for all, what's its name?"

"Anibus," the roach whispered, "the Egyptian God of Death."

CHAPTER 31

Stuart Krell cheerfully swung his car into the carnival parking lot and switched off the engine. The rain had slowed to misty droplets, and heaving open the door, he crunched across the gravel without his umbrella.

A teenage boy, his cheeks ablaze with acne, and a spiky-haired young woman lounged against the Tilt O' Whirl. Their heads bent against the biting wind, and their eyes squinted against the cigarette smoke spiraling against their faces.

"Hey, Mr. Krell," the girl said, flicking a scatter of ash from her sweater. "What're you doing here so early?"

"We're shutting down for the season." Stuart said, briskly. "Close the entrance gate and secure the booths."

The boy looked surprised. "But our contract says we're here 'til November."

"Sue me." Stuart tossed an envelope marked 'payroll' to the young man, and sauntered on. "Distribute those to the rest of the crew, and get out of here," he called over his shoulder. "Jerry will dismantle the rides tomorrow." Striding to the ring toss, he stopped and looked back, making sure his instructions were being followed.

With angry murmurs and obscene gestures, the two employees slouched through the grounds, calling to cohorts and enjoying their roles as Pimpled Paymaster and Mistress of Bad Tidings. Within twenty minutes, the last of their cars had screeched out of the parking lot, and Stuart was alone. Pulling his jacket closer around his neck, he marched toward the warehouse.

Gray clouds roiled like waves against the murky sky, and the temperature had gone from crisp to bitter, Stuart inhaled the biting air, and winced as a molar ached in protest. Once again, he hadn't dressed warmly enough, and shivering, he dug into his pocket, produced a ring of keys, and unlocked the warehouse door.

The stench was overwhelming. It was obvious that Jerry hadn't cleaned the cages or fed and watered anything since the kid's abduction. Just another reason to get rid of the guy, Stuart thought, holding his breath and peering into the gloom. The tarp had slipped off of the black mamba's cage, and Stuart briefly wondered if he should take the snake with him. The reptile watched with a glittery eyed intensity, its smooth silver scales camouflaged amidst the dirty woodchips. Stuart backed away, strangely rattled.

Other creatures hadn't fared quite as well. Two more birds were dead, and others were listless and ill. An inexplicable fear raised goose bumps up and down the big man's arms. He'd take one last look at the hyena thing, and then get out of here forever.

"Its name's not A anymore."

Stuart put on his glasses, marched to the cage, and released a sigh of relief. Jerry was right about one thing, the smelly creature's name wasn't "A" or apparently anything else, because the identification tag was gone… probably stuffed inside Jerry's pocket along with beer receipts. "Dumb drunk," he muttered, tucking the spectacles back in his pocket, and smoothing his hair.

Next, he checked the thing's cage. It was asleep, its narrow head tucked beneath its tail. Vindicated, Stuart nodded. "Just as I thought," he muttered. "That door is locked and everything's in order." Or was it? Something in the pen caught Stuart's eye, and he blinked. He leaned down and moved closer, his vision adjusting to the room's darkness. The animal lay as he had first seen it, but it wasn't sleeping on wire like the others. Instead, it curled on a lumpy square of fabric; blue, with zippers, and straps…and a big safety pin. College boy's backpack!

Stuart stood so fast he overturned a stool, and almost lost his balance. This wasn't possible! Had Jerry put the backpack in the cage to frighten him? To show him who was boss after Stuart's instructions to burn it? Worse yet, was Jerry trying to blackmail him? The fat man braced himself against a table, his startled mind fumbling for answers. There was only one scenario that made sense: Jerry had concocted the story about the creature's name and the unlocked door to ensure Stuart's visit to the warehouse today. Could this be a set up? A feeling of paranoia burned its way up Stuart's chest and into his throat. What if the cops were outside right now, waiting for him?

"Get hold of yourself, Stu." He said in a loud, firm voice. "Jerry would never think you'd be here so early in the morning, which might be a good thing. You'll get the turtle and skip town with a huge head start on everyone." But what if the police did come and found the backpack? The carnival was in his name, not Jerry's. They'd come looking for him when the kid never showed up. A dull pain throbbed at Stuart's temples and he rubbed his head and stared at the cage. All he had to do was open the wire door, push the creature away with some sort of a stick, and take the backpack. Heart hammering, he looked for something to use, and found nothing. The room was eerily neat, filled only with cages, a stool, and a table. Stuart snapped his fingers. The baseball bat! He'd left it in the car.

With a whimper of relief, he lunged out the door and shambled to the parking lot, his legs throbbing from exertion. With the weapon finally in hand, his terror morphed into steely resolve, and Stuart walked with quick, determined steps back to the warehouse.

The door listed open, swinging on its hinges, and he stopped, trying to remember if he'd shut it. But his exit had been so quick, so shrouded in fear that he couldn't remember. It didn't matter. All he needed to do was grab the bag and get out. With a firm grip on the bat, Stuart crossed the thresh hold, turned to the cage, and gaped.

The wire door was locked, but the creature and the back pack were gone.

CHAPTER 32

Eyes wide with shock, Soot crouched beneath a picnic table, trying to digest the blast of mind talk he'd just received. The Boy was in trouble! The Cat Master's beloved friend and rescuer, and the human Soot had promised to watch over after Buddy's coronation, had vanished.

The caller identified itself only as a 'friend' of Zekki's and Pris's, but it was plain from the dialect that it hadn't been feline. That wasn't important. It had spoken on behalf of two cats, and if they needed him, Soot was honor bound to help. There was only one problem, he didn't know how.

Awkwardly, he limped across the wet grass, taking refuge inside a stone pavilion. Usually, the park was teaming with people, but today, the weather was incompatible with outdoor recreation, and Soot had the place to himself. Licking the wetness from his coat, he took a deep breath and tried to regroup.

Only The Cat Master was allowed to use mind talk for mass communication. Other felines were limited to one on one contact, and Soot had no idea whom to call first. Aluna crossed his mind, but he decided against it. Though his only cousin, she was notoriously inhospitable to all but her own colony, and had ignored his past attempts to reach her telepathically.

His thoughts turned to The Boy, whom he hadn't seen in years. In fact, Soot's only visit to Buddy's old Sixth Avenue address had been to guide Zekki and Pris there after The Cat Master's coronation.

Soot shook, partly from the cold and partly from anxiety. He'd answered the nameless caller's message immediately, assuring Zekki and Pris that he'd do whatever he could to help. And now he had to create a plan, and fast.

Thunder grumbled from the east, and the darkening sky promised more rain. Hobbling down the flag stone steps, he followed the Trinity River's quiet gurgle through the park. His eyes scanned the leafless landscape until they found what he'd been searching for; a thick stand of bamboo that separated the zoo from the picnic area. Rumor was that Aluna's colony hid there during the day, and creeping closer, his nostrils probed the pungent wetness of water and vegetation. Could they know something about The Boy? Most felines knew the young man's name from the Cat Master Legend, and if his cousin had information, she was more likely to tell him in person.

Squirrels fussed and shouted above him, and a zebra brayed from its enclosure, but Soot pushed on, his eyes fixed on the canes, his senses alert for Aluna.

* * *

The ferret scampered down the glistening pavement, dodging through brown yards strewn with leaves and wind snapped branches. Carved pumpkins sat on doorsteps, their maniacal grins and triangular eyes frightening even in daylight, and fluttering paper bats and dangling scarecrows hung from porches for heightened Halloween terror.

Blitz found the displays both startling and intriguing, and it took real restraint not to abandon her mission and examine each ghoulish presentation down to the last detail. Fortunately, the panic and shame she felt at having lost the cell phone kept her on track, and after crossing two more yards and being chased by a squealing group of children who thankfully lost interest, she raced up the driveway of her former home.

Slinking to the porch, she climbed onto a window sill and peered through the rain streaked glass. The living room was empty, but the soft leather couches and bright open kitchen brought back a rush of memories Blitz wanted to forget.

Connie Jo, the woman who'd adopted her, was a cheerful high school teacher with tousled blonde hair and warm brown eyes.

The charming little house had everything a ferret could possibly want, with one glaring exception, and that was a dachshund named, Frank. From the moment Connie lifted Blitz from the carrier, the little dog had hated his new roommate, and no amount of good will on the ferret's part could change it. It was only a matter of weeks before Frank's pushy pointed nose had discovered Blitz's secret. Having been there such a short time, her stash only included three measly items: an antique ring, the car keys, and an unopened jury summons. From a ferret's perspective, it was nothing to get excited about. How wrong she'd been.

After a visit from the constable followed by three crazed days looking for her car keys, Connie Jo collapsed in frustration, and Frank led her straight to Blitz's nest. His triumphant bark was the last thing the ferret heard before her return to the pet shop.

It had been a devastating blow, even from a felon's point of view, and Blitz vowed never to steal anything again…a vow that had failed miserably, and was precisely why she now stared through Connie Jo's window into the snarling face of Frank.

* * *

"The Egyptian God of Death?" Orie asked, not quite understanding what the cockroach had said. "What in the heck does *that* mean?"

"It means," the insect said, clambering down the counter and onto the floor, "that I'm never going to the warehouse again, and I'd suggest that you do the same."

Bennett and Theda stood in frightened silence, and La De Da pressed hard against Orie's flank, shivering.

The lizard puffed his throat, desperate for clarity. "So you're saying that the thing in the warehouse, the animal that you've all seen, and that we've all been talking about… isn't real?"

"I'd say it's very real." The roach said with a nervous flutter of wings. "Death comes in many forms, and has many names, why not a jackal?"

Bennett shook his head. "I don't get it."

"Me either." Theda jumped on to the computer's keys and stared at the screen, as though all of their answers were written there. "If the jackal is really the God of Death…shouldn't we be dead?"

A visceral feeling of terror oozed through Orie's core, and a rush of memories flickered behind his eyes like a silent movie.

"Dude! This is Graeme! I forgot to tell you some guy's been trying to reach you..."

"...Krell wants the turtle...Mr. Krell doesn't like it when he doesn't get what he wants."

"...all the answers...all the answers...all the answers are at the carnival."

And suddenly Orie knew, beyond all reason and understanding, why the creature in the warehouse hadn't harmed them. The jackal god had no interest in crazy parrots or legendary lizards.

Anibus had come for The Boy.

CHAPTER 33

Stuart Krell roared through the park and turned with a spray of mud into his parking place by the trailer. The plans had changed, and he had to move fast. Grabbing his bat, he lurched from the car and pushed the front door open. "Hey kid!" he shouted, rummaging through the closet and finally finding his shotgun. "Time is up!"

Stuart yanked back the curtains so fast that they tore off of the rod, sagging to the floor in a crumpled heap. The kid sat against the tub, firmly tied, with Axel curled by his hip. With a grunt, Stuart ripped the tape from the young man's lips. "Here's the deal," he said, spittle flying from his mouth. "I'm in a hurry, and now's the time to give up the turtle or die here with the dog." Standing tall, Stuart aimed the gun at Axle's head. "What's it gonna' be?"

"Stop!" The Boy licked his lips. "I—I need to know what you're going to do with the turtle."

"What do you think I'm going to do?" Stuart snorted with irritation. "I'm going to sell him to the highest bidder, and he'll end up in some collector's herpetarium or in a private zoo or something. Forget the turtle. What really matters is what I'm going to do now." He pushed the gun against the pit bull's throat. "I'm waiting."

Axel growled softly, his eyes rolling toward Stuart, and the hackles along his back slowly rising.

The big man stared at the pit bull with surprise. "Shut up!" He shouted, cocking the trigger.

"Wait!" The Boy's voice shook and his shoulders sagged with defeat. "Don't hurt the dog, I'll tell you everything."

* * *

"Get off my porch, weasel!" The dachshund's lips trembled in a snarl.

Blitz stood her ground, heart racing. "Please, Frank." She said. "I just want to talk to you."

The dog stepped back, his brow furrowed with suspicion. "Why?"

"Because I've gotten myself in to a little trouble, and I need your help."

Frank gave a derisive snort. "What did you steal this time, a car?" He pawed at a dirty yellow tennis ball and nosed it toward the kitchen. "Beat it!" he shouted over his shoulder.

"It's about The Boy!" Blitz's voice reverberated in the porch.

Frank paused and turned around. "*The* boy? The human who rescued The Cat Master? *That* boy?"

Blitz allowed herself a tiny squeak of victory. The dachshund was interested. Maybe all wasn't lost after all. She nodded. "Can't we talk? It'll only take a minute."

"I hate you," he said.

The ferret shrugged. "I know."

"And don't even think about coming back here."

"I won't," she said, trying to look sincere.

Frank shot her a nasty look. "Wait there."

Blitz sat on the porch, her tail bushed with fear. The dog had already betrayed her once. What if he used this as an opportunity to finish her off? She started at the sound of a screen door banging in the back. In a few moments, she heard wheezing grunts as he squirmed beneath the fence, and then the click of his nails on the driveway.

The dog stood by the steps, his tail held straight and high with aggression.

"Hi Frank," Blitz said, trying to ignore the mud clumped on his belly and paws, "You're looking great."

"I know that," he said, eyes bright and wary. "I'm busy and you reek, so if you're asking for a favor the answer is no, and whatever else you want to say, make it snappy."

And she did; the words spilling out in a torrent of emotions that surprised her. By the time she'd told him about Orie's search for The Boy and Aluna stealing the cell phone, Frank's hostility had faded to worry.

"So where do you think the cats are now?" he asked, "back at the river?"

Blitz nodded.

The dog sniffed the air and casually lifted his leg against the porch railing. "I don't get it, why would cats take a cell phone?" He stared at the ferret, his bright brown eyes boring into her hers. "It's not exactly a twelve pack of tuna."

The question was something Blitz had never considered, and it caught her off guard. Why *had* the cats taken it? Desperately, she tried to remember her first meeting with Aluna, and what she'd said. The answer took form, incomplete but undeniable; the River Cat had lied. Aluna didn't revere Orie, she hated him. It was her martyred uncle, Jett whom she idolized. "Aluna blames Orie for The Cat Master's rise to power," the ferret's voice shook with discovery, "and also for Jett's death. He's a big hero to The River Cats."

Frank nodded, "and?"

"And...she tried to trick me into leading her to Orie, but I was too smart for that." The ferret paused, waiting for praise which didn't come.

"I think there's more," the dog said quietly.

"Well." Blitz chewed the inside of her cheek, fighting for clarity amidst the torrent of thoughts now jostling for attention. "It's common knowledge that Orie would die for The Boy, and Aluna knows he needs that phone to escape."

"Exactly who told her that?"

"A very good question...," Blitz stalled for time. She couldn't tell Frank that she was the snitch, or he'd leave. "...guess I never thought to ask her, but the cell phone is definitely bait. Aluna's using it to lure Orie to the river, and he'll go because he needs it to save The Boy."

"What happens when he gets to the river?" The dachshund asked.

The ferret's unblinking eyes met his. "Aluna will kill him as revenge for Jett's death."

"And since when do you care about reptiles?"

Frank was smart, she thought, carefully choosing her next words. "Well, I never did before, but Orie and I are roommates, now, and things have changed. We both love The Boy and I'd do anything for either of them."

"You're lying as usual." Frank said, licking at a puddle. "Normally, I don't do favors for weasels"— He stared pointedly at Blitz — "Or lizards, but Orie was close to Tenba, one of the greatest canines who ever lived," the dog paused, his voice suddenly tender, "and I think she'd want me to help him." Taking one last look at the sky, he shook himself and sighed. "It's going to rain and I hate to be wet, so let's get moving."

"But how are we going to do this?" The ferret asked, slinking down the steps to follow him. "Aluna isn't going to give the phone back just because we ask her to."

Frank rolled his eyes and trotted to the curb. "Who said anything about asking?"

CHAPTER 34

"Theda has to get back in the warehouse." Orie said, scrambling off of the counter so fast, that he slipped on a paperclip and almost fell to the floor.

"But the roach just told us what's in there!" The spider's eyes rolled with fear. "How can you still ask me to do that?"

"Because," Orie said, "the Anibus isn't after us, it's after The Boy. That's why the turtle ended up at our house, and why The Boy was eventually led to Stuart Krell's carnival, but Krell is a pawn as well. I've been going over and over each clue, and the answering machine messages tell the story. Everything that's happened was designed to bring The Boy to Krell's warehouse," The lizard paused, "and then... to his death."

Bennett hopped protectively toward Theda. "But Orie, you can't be sure of that."

"He has a point." La De Da said from the shadows. "What if you're wrong and we all die?"

"But I'm not wrong!" Orie shouted. "It's the only thing that makes sense." The lizard took a deep breath. "With you or without you, I'm going back to the carnival." He turned to the cockroach who watched from a chair. "Thanks for your help. Coming here was necessary, but it's cost us valuable time. We have to go."

"Go?" The roach's eyes widened with disappointment. "What's your hurry? I mean, the computer is old, maybe it was wrong and the jackal is just some perfectly normal animal who's as much a victim as Theda. You're probably all worked up about nothing. We haven't even eaten yet." He circled in a frantic little dance of appeal. "Come on! It's nice and warm in here, I rarely have company."

"Sorry." Orie said. "You're on your own." He waved a claw toward the others. "Everybody back into the vent. We'll meet out front."

"Wait!" The roach's voice cracked with desperation. "I have a better idea! Why don't I come *with* you? I know all kinds of things. You need me!" He hoped to the floor, and scurried after La De Da's fading form

"No." Orie said, standing solidly in his path. "I don't even like the friends I have, and I'm not looking for new ones." Ignoring the bug's stricken face, Orie leapt onto the wall, and disappeared into the vent.

You're wasting your time, lizard!" The roach shrieked, his angry voice echoing through the ducts. "No one cheats death! Not even you!"

* * *

Soot crouched by the bamboo, ears scanning, and whiskers thrust forward and alert. Someone was watching him. He'd sensed it the second he'd left the pavilion. At first he thought it might be an animal from the zoo. Two antelope exhibits backed against a bluff overlooking the river, and the wildebeests were particularly nosy. But, generally, its inhabitants stayed indoors during cold and rainy days.

Leaves rustled to his left, and Soot darted up a mesquite tree, his claws gripping the wet bark. "Who is it?" He called from his perch.

A raccoon ambled along the river, and a startled sparrow fluttered skyward, but otherwise, there was silence. "I know someone's down there." Soot tried again. "Come out."

Beneath him, the bamboo parted, and two green feline eyes looked up from between the glistening leaves. "What are you doing here, cousin? You're in River Cat territory." The foliage parted, and Aluna emerged, her mud splattered body thin and trembling from the cold. She gave a mocking smile. "Isn't the Prince of the Alleys a little far from home?

Jumping to the ground, Soot stared in distress. The last time he'd seen Aluna had been years before her capture by children, and subsequent abandonment. He remembered her once vibrant beauty and luminous green eyes so much like their uncle, Jett's and a sodden sadness tugged at his heart. The Outs had not been kind to her, and he stood at a distance, worried that she was diseased. "I have two things to discuss," he said quietly. "One deals with territorial issues and the second," he paused, "has to do with a human."

Aluna's eye narrowed. "Why come to me about humans? You know where I stand on that subject."

"This isn't just *any* human." The black cat's crippled leg throbbed in a dull, rhythmic ache, and his mind shifted to the warmth of the pawn shop. "It concerns The Cat Master's trusted friend, The Boy. I have reason to believe he's in trouble."

A fleeting look of wariness crossed the female's face, and her eyes drifted to the bamboo.

"Have you heard anything about it?" Soot pressed.

"No," Aluna gave an exaggerated shrug, "nothing."

Soot sat silently. Something wasn't right. Something he couldn't name, but felt instinctively to be true. "Aluna," he tried again. "As The Cat Master's heir, I speak for him in his absence. If you know anything about this human, anything at all… you're compelled to tell me. It's The Law."

"The Law!" Aluna sprang forward, ears flat to her head. "The River Cats have never acknowledged Buddy's ascension to power! I answer to no one but my martyred uncle, Jett, and thanks to you and the lizard, he's dead!"

Startled, Soot took a quick step back. He'd heard of The River Cats hatred for Buddy, but he'd never realized to what extent, or that it also included himself and Orie. "You're wrong, cousin," he said, tone firm, "Jett caused his own death through greed, and a lust for power. Buddy and I are as much your blood as Jett was. You have no reason to feel the way you do."

"My reasons are my own." Aluna spat. "The River Cats' allegiance is with the ferals, just as yours are with the Indoors."

Soot tried to protest, but she held up one paw.

"And don't deny it. Everyone knows about your 'problem'." She emphasized the word, pleased by his stunned reaction. "First you defected to the old woman's house, and now you're being fed at the pawn shop. The moment they open their door, you'll be gone…again." She leaned in, face pinched with malice. "But you know what they say, Soot, like father like son."

Her words floated in the frigid air, and Soot listened in stony silence.

"As for the territorial issue you wanted to discuss," she continued, "It concerns the River Cats infiltrating your neighborhoods. Right?"

"It does." the black cat said, his mind still numb from the insult, "I've had a lot of complaints and I can't allow it."

Indolently, she assessed his crippled leg. "As though *you* could stop us." Turning away, she flashed him one last look of contempt. "Find another human, Soot…it's where you belong." In an instant she was gone, the canes swaying in the wind behind her.

CHAPTER 35

Blindly, Orie ran through the library parking lot, his mind black with anger. How dare Anibus target The Boy! God of Death or not, he'd have to get past the Legendary Lizard first!

"Where are you going?" Bennett cawed from the roof. "Wait a minute!"

"Back to the warehouse!" Orie shouted, finally so out of breath he had to stop. "I'm not afraid of the jackal!"

La De Da rushed to him, her claw gripping his leg. "Handsome one," she said gently, "I know what saving The Boy means to you, to all of us…but the phone isn't in the warehouse. If it was, Axel would have seen it."

It was true, the lizard thought, forcing himself to accept the facts.

The answer is at the carnival.

Not the answer, he thought bitterly, just Anibus lurking in the shadows, altering lives, creating havoc, all for one human soul. Orie grimaced with determination. No! They wouldn't give up!

A sudden vision of Tenba came to mind. Not only had she been wise and brave, and loyal…but *big*! He thought of the pit bull in Stuart's trailer. "We need Axel," he said, with renewed focus. "Forget the carnival, we'll go back to the trailer and beg the dog for help. What we need is a better nose. Something that can track scents and run fast and…" Desperately, he looked from one animal to the other. "I mean, isn't that what dog's do… fetch and bite and drag things around with their teeth?" He stared helplessly from one animal to the other, aware that he sounded pathetically out of control.

"I guess we could try." Theda offered. "But it's pretty far from here."

"It's not far if you fly." The parrot said. "Why don't I carry everyone? We're running out of time, and no offense," he glanced shyly at Orie, "you're a little slow, lately."

Normally, such an observation would have offended the lizard, but today, it sounded like the perfect solution. "That's a good idea," he said. Gazing heavenward, he wondered how it would feel to plummet from Bennett's back and land in a squishy little blob on the pavement. He swallowed. "I mean, unless La De Da and I are too heavy."

"Naw," the parrot said, "you're light, jump on."

Without hesitation they scurried onto Bennett's back, positioning themselves above each wing as ballast.

"Wait!" Bennett cocked his head, suddenly alert. "There's something crouched in the bushes over there. I think it's a…."

"Cat!" Orie screamed.

A wiry, grey tom burst from the shadows, almost reaching the parrot before he took off with a whoosh. Feathers flying, he rose into the air, wings beating for balance, as the lizards scrambled for footing.

Caught off guard, Orie struggled to hold on, but disoriented and dizzy, his grip slipped, and he tumbled to the ground. In an instant, the cat was upon him, one fat paw firmly pushing him against the wet pavement. The lizard squirmed and flipped beneath its grasp, finally dodging a second claw filled swipe, and sprinting toward the safety of the library wall. With adrenalin masking his pain, Orie zigzagged over the sidewalk, and with the cat closing in, launched on to the bricks, and safety.

Above them, the bird cawed in anger. "Get away from him!" he shouted. Shaking La De Da and Theda onto the library's roof, Bennett flapped through the air in angry circles.

"Wait!" The tabby crouched on the pavement, ducking his head against a possible attack. "I'm not here to hurt anyone, I've come in peace!"

Orie's chin had been cut in the struggle, and a smear of blood stained the brick. "You don't seem very peaceful to me!"

"I'm sorry if I came off that way, but I have some very important information, and I was afraid you'd all fly away before we could talk. I had to catch you."

Orie's heart lurched in to overdrive and he forced himself to breath. "Information?"

"Yes." The feline sat on the sidewalk, eyes warily watching Bennett who'd settled on the roof. "Why don't you come down here?" Painfully, he scratched an abscess on his jaw and tried to smile. "It's a little hard to communicate this way."

The parrot fluttered to Orie. "Don't trust him."

"Exactly who are you?" the lizard asked, defiantly.

"I'm a River Cat, and I bring you a message from our leader, Aluna. You *are* the Legendary Lizard, right?"

Orie puffed his throat. "Of course I am."

"Good." The tom beamed; his fangs a dull yellow against the pallor of anemic gums. "First, she wanted me to impart just how much our colony admires you."

"Who doesn't?" Orie rolled his eyes. "What else?"

"In honor of your celebrated service to our *beloved* Cat Master, the River Cats would like to help a certain human whom we know to be your friend. He's in terrible danger."

Was it possible? The lizard held his breath, had The Boy's luck changed? Had *his*? "Exactly what human are you talking about?" he asked, trying to appear calm.

"The one in the trailer, in the park."

"Go on."

"We have something you've been searching for."

"Oh yeah?" Orie clutched the bricks, his heart banging. "And what's that?"

"The Boy's phone," the cat said, "do you want it?"

* * *

Stuart yanked his underwear drawer open and dumped the contents into an already bulging suitcase. Breathing hard, he scanned the room for one last look. Everything was done; the bed stripped, closets emptied and the shotgun carefully loaded and propped by the front door along with his trusty baseball bat.

Despite the chill, sweat rolled from his forehead, dangling on the ends of his lashes. Impatiently, he blinked it away, his mind trying to make sense of what he'd seen at the warehouse. Who had opened the creature's cage door and where was the backpack? Someone was playing games, and Stuart didn't like games, especially ones with rules he hadn't written.

But there was good news. College Boy had relented just as Stuart had hoped, so all that remained was to get the turtle, and blow town like a rocket. He looked at his watch. It was a little past noon, and heavy storms were predicted until evening.

Closing the suitcase, Stuart grabbed it along with the duffel bags and an umbrella and headed for the hallway. Everything would be fine, he told himself. Soon he'd be far away from backpacks, and warehouses, with plenty of money in his pocket and nothing holding him down. Breathlessly, he shuffled to the front door. "Here we go." he whispered, twisting the lock and turning the knob.

White daylight spilled into the darkened room, and outlined in the doorway, his ruddy face blank with surprise...stood Jerry.

CHAPTER 36

Soot trudged through the park, Aluna's hateful comments ringing through his mind.

"...you know what they say, Soot; like father like son."

Normally, he would be proud at the comparison, but, in this case, he knew what the statement implied; Buddy had been born a feral and ended up as an Indoor. Feral extremists had never forgiven The Cat Master's perceived betrayal, and apparently, were now watching Soot. Anxiously, he licked his chops. But there was nothing to know, or was there? So what if he missed the old woman and his former life as an Indoor? He'd accepted his role as Prince of the Alley, hadn't he? Wasn't he here, doing his job as best as he could? But Aluna knew about the pawn shop, and Soot's pulse quickened with guilt. Had she seen him staring through the barred windows, looking for the owner's wife, and hoping that one day she'd invite him in? He cringed at the undeniable truth; he was addicted to humans and always had been.

Cracks of lightening split the sky, illuminating the dingy soccer field and rotting bleachers. Scurrying beneath their leaky protection, Soot licked his flank, miserable and shaken. He wasn't alone in his illness. There were many cats skulking through gardens, and staring from porches, desperate for an open door and gentle hand, but none of that mattered.

Rain pummeled the boards like buck shot, and he slunk further beneath the risers, his soul sick with disgrace. Stomach growling, he wondered if the pawn shop's owners had thrown him their leftovers, and then groaned at his inability to forget their seductive pull.

"Find another human, Soot. That's always where you've belonged." The River Cat's words rang in his ears and Soot felt a flash of anger mixed with pride. Maybe he did crave human contact, and perhaps the feral life wasn't something he'd wanted, but he was also Prince of the Alleys, and the Cat Master's trusted son. Buddy had overcome the 'sickness' and so would he. With a deep breath, he lifted his chin in defiance.

The Boy was missing, and Aluna had the answers. Soot turned, and limped back toward the zoo.

* * *

The parrot, spider, and La De Da clustered around Orie, eyes watching the gray tom below.

"Don't believe him," Theda whispered, "something sounds wrong. I mean, where did this supposed 'River Cat' come from, how does he know about The Boy, and how did he know we'd be here?"

"I'll tell you how," La De Da, said, pushing protectively against Orie, "he's been following us. I don't know why or how, but he must have been."

The lizard listened calmly to their protests. Bennett asserted that all cats were dangerous, and the others agreed, their voices so loud that two doves abandoned their nest beneath the eaves, and fluttered away. "None of these matters," Orie said. "The River Cats say they have the phone, The Boy needs it, and I'm going to get it." He waved to the cat. "Okay, we're coming."

"Not them." The cat licked his chops. "Just you."

The animals were mute with shock, and only the steady drip of rain on the library's roof broke the silence.

Orie frowned. "Well, if…"

"…no freaking way!" La De Da interrupted. With a huff she scrambled down the bricks, stopping only inches from the cat's head. "I don't care if you have twenty phones! You're not taking the Legendary Lizard anywhere without us!" Her body pumped up and down with fury. "He's celebrity, we're security. Live with it."

Ears flattened with anger, the cat assessed each creature with a long, slow stare. Finally, he forced a tight little smile. "If that's how you feel, come on. The River Cats have nothing to hide." With a flick of his tail, he turned and trotted purposefully across a neighboring yard. "I'm headed for the park!" he called. "Meet me at the back of the zoo, by the bamboo grove."

The animals clambered onto Bennett's back, and he whistled with relief. "That was scary." He turned to the lizard with an apologetic smile. "You're not going to believe this, but for a minute I actually thought you were leaving without us."

"I was," Orie said, "let's go."

* * *

The ferret's whiskers dripped with water and a chill shook her body. Though she and the dachshund had been out for some time now, very little progress had been made. This was partly due to the rain, which Frank claimed blurred his vision, and partly due to human traffic, but mainly it was because of Frank's inability to pass a female dog without stopping to leer.

Blitz was appalled. So far they'd been sidetracked by three spaniels, a poodle mix, and now a gigantic, black Newfoundland with paws the size of soup bowls. The dog lolled against a chain link fence, her eyes fixed on Frank, and twin streams of drool dangling from her jaws.

"So anyway," the dachshund's tone was soft and intimate, "I've always admired a gal who could pull things."

"Come on," Blitz pleaded. "We've got to go."

Frank shot her a dark look of warning, but pushed on. Once past Willing Avenue, they crouched beneath a parked car, watching as traffic chugged by, drivers squinting through fogged windshields and rhythmically whooshing wipers. Finally the street cleared, and they dashed to the corner, turning onto Eighth Avenue and staying close to the curb.

"How will you find the phone, Frank?" Blitz asked, panting beside him. "I don't even know where Aluna lives."

"Stop worrying." Head down, the dog's pointed nose slid through the glistening leaves. "I've seen the River Cats before. They have a definite scent that's easy to trace."

Blitz watched anxiously as he tracked through lawns, and up and down driveways. What if Orie had already fallen into Aluna's trap? No lizard meant no story, and even worse, no fame which was completely unacceptable.

Suddenly, the little dog stopped, one stubby paw tucked up under his chest.

"You found something?" Blitz asked hopefully.

The dachshund nodded, his eyes focused on a distant house.

"Cat?" She whispered.

"Chihuahua," he said. With a piercing yip, Frank galloped up the street. "Senorita!" he howled. "Viva Mexico!"

CHAPTER 37

"Where do you think you're going?" Jerry asked. A chew of tobacco ballooned one cheek, and a slow scowl crimped his forehead. "What's with the suitcase?"

Stuart stood in the doorway, his posture as stiff as petrified wood. "Well, I—I was just headed over to your place," he lied, dropping the bag, and rubbing his wrist with a shaking hand, "because, we need to talk."

"Why?" Jerry's small blue eyes narrowed with suspicion and he peered past Stuart's fleshy bulk into the trailer. "Where's the kid?"

"In the bathroom," The big man said, solidly blocking entrance. "Here's the deal. The weather is bad and I've decided we should shut down the carnival and get out of here."

A freight train rattled in the distance and the two men stood in strained silence.

"Anyway," Stuart continued, trying to sound matter of fact," why don't I get going, take care of things at the carnival, and when I get back, we'll talk about moving the equipment?"

"I just came from there," Jerry said, a slow stain of color flushing his cheeks. "The place is shut tight with a closed for the season sign out front."

"Right." Stuart licked his lips, his mind groping for a believable answer. "Yes, I almost forgot. After you left last night, I was worried about the thing in the warehouse. I—I couldn't sleep so I decided to go on out there. And you were absolutely correct,

Jer," Stuart searched the man's face for a flicker of culpability, "something's definitely wrong in the warehouse." He forced a laugh which sounded broken and shrill. "I guess I panicked and put the sign out, because, really, Jer," he cleared his throat, "we need to get out of here."

"So," Jerry spat a hard stream of tobacco juice against the trailer, "let me get this straight. You bop on out to the warehouse and decide without even asking me that we're closing down." His tongue made an ugly sucking sound from behind his front teeth, and his eyes trailed to the duffel bags. "And now, here you are, all packed, and ready to split." Jerry stepped forward; his breath coming fast, his chest bumping Stuart's. "Well, you're sure right about one thing, *partner*," he said, hand coming up in a meaty fist. "We do need to talk."

* * *

Aluna paced by the bamboo, ignoring the unrelenting cold that pierced her body. Why hadn't the grey tom returned with Orie? As the River Cat's best tracker, he'd been searching for the lizard since leaving Blitz's house. "I have the cell phone," Aluna muttered. "All I need now is the lizard."

Remembering the Crippled Prince's visit, she scowled with disgust. How could such a weak, ineffectual creature be related to her? The River Cats would conquer the alleys with no trouble at all. Soot wouldn't have the mental or physical fortitude to stop her.

Twigs crackled in the distance and she darted behind the dripping canes, her eyes alert for movement.

With a groan, the grey tom pushed through broken branches and viney tangles. "I found them," his boney sides heaved with exertion, "they're on their way!"

"What do you mean '*they're*' on their way?" Aluna hissed. "The plan was for you to capture Orie, *alone*."

"Be happy he's coming at all. He's traveling with a parrot, a spider, and another lizard." Frustration twisted his face. "He got away, and after that none of them trusted me. The whole group insisted on coming with him. There was nothing I could do."

"Are you telling me," Aluna asked, her ears flattened with disapproval, "that even with a full set of claws, you couldn't catch an arthritic old lizard?"

"Don't underestimate him." The cat's tail flicked defensively. "He's tricky and tough, but so are we. I'll take care of his 'friends' later. You can count on it.

"Make sure that you do." Aluna shivered and gave a conciliatory nod. "I never thought this opportunity would come, and everything has to go perfectly." She pushed next to his ragged coat for warmth. "At least I got rid of Soot. He came by to 'warn' me about trespassing in the alleys, if you can believe that." Chuckling, she allowed her fur to be groomed. "I imagine he's back at the pawn shop by now, begging some human for love."

The tom cocked his head. "No he's not."

"What?" Aluna asked. "How do you know?"

"Because I just saw him, he's here in the park."

* * *

The white cat perched on the back of the living room couch, his pink nose pressed against the cold window. It had been hours since the turtle's telepathic conversation with Soot, and the day dragged on with grinding predictability. Rain streamed down the window panes and lightening scattered bursts of luminosity against the smoky clouds.

Zekki and Pris had endured the passing hours with stoic agony, wondering why no word had come of The Boy, and whether or not their call for help had arrived too late. At one point, the pet sitter dashed through the house in a flurry of shopping bags and laundry. Thankfully, she ignored the bathroom, only staying long enough to replenish cat food, and water before racing out the door.

Through it all, Cuff had snoozed beneath the dining room table, blissfully unaware.

Pris curled in a ball, watching the big wooden clock tick away the minutes. "Why hasn't Soot contacted us? Cuff said he'd reached him."

"I don't know," Zekki licked one paw. "Maybe he doesn't have any information yet."

"This is ridiculous." The calico stood, and trotted toward the dining room. "I'm going to ask."

"Let the turtle sleep!" He called, as she disappeared through the hallway. "Haven't we given the old guy enough trouble today?"

166

Joints stiff from the cold, the white cat stretched long and hard before jumping to the floor, and listlessly heading to the kitchen. The room was clean and cheerful, and despite his fear, Zekki's spirits lifted. Cat food and water brimmed from colorful ceramic bowls, and a hand full of treats lay on a rug by the pantry. He sniffed everything, but worry had dulled his hunger and he settled for water instead.

Pris appeared in the doorway, nostrils pulsing. Her soft, round belly almost touched the ground, and it was plain that her appetite was disaster proof. "You're not going to believe what Cuff's done," she said between bites. "He's tipped over the water bowl in Mrs. O'Connell's bathroom, dragged some dead flowers out of the trash, and," she grimaced, "he's obviously never used a litter box. There are puddles everywhere and I stepped in a pile of 'you-know-what'." She flicked one pristine paw at the memory. "Turtles are revolting. I can't wait 'til he's out of here."

"I'll make him stay in the kitchen," Zekki said, taking one more lick of water. "Where is he?"

The calico chewed thoughtfully. "I don't know. He wasn't in the dining room."

"He wasn't?"

"No," she said. "Come to think of it…I didn't see him anywhere."

A blip of worry tugged Zekki's mind. "Maybe he's stuck beneath something. I'll go check." Trotting to the hall, he stopped. There was a faint scraping sound coming from The Boy's old bedroom. Normally, the door was closed, but today it stood slightly ajar. "Hey, Pris!" he called, suddenly wanting company. But the calico didn't answer, too engrossed with food to hear.

Cautiously, Zekki moved toward the noise, and pushed through the door's narrow opening. He stood quietly, surveying the room. Mrs. O'Connell had long since replaced The Boy's furniture with an overstuffed chair, computer desk, and treadmill. Shutters were drawn against the cold, and the room smelled vaguely of pine from a forgotten Christmas candle still in its holiday holder.

The rhythmic scratching grew louder and seemed to emanate from an open closet.

Zekki slunk forward. "Who's there?" he whispered.

The noise stopped, and then started up again.

Taking a deep breath, the cat entered, pressing through folds of summer skirts, sandals, and dresses drooping from hangers…and then stopped, eyes adjusting to the lumpy form moving in the darkness.

Cuff stood on his hind legs in the furthest corner of the closet, his front feet dully scrabbling at the cedar wall.

"You're not supposed to be in here," Zekki said.

Startled, the turtle swung around. "I—I thought this led outside," he stammered. "I got a message, and I'm trying to find a way out of here. Where's the door?"

"A message?" The cat stumbled forward, his heart tight with hope. "Was it Soot about The Boy?"

"No." Cuff lowered his voice. "It's from a species I don't know, and don't *want* to know." Turning toward the wall, his scratching intensified. "No more favors. I'm not contacting anyone; I'm through."

"Wait a minute, at least tell me the message."

"Something bad is coming," Cuff said, his face obscured by the shadows. "It's on its way… and looking for me."

CHAPTER 38

Bennett flew across the park with Orie clinging to one wing, his wind-burned eyes squinting in protest. Though they'd tried to keep up, the River Cat kept low to the ground, finally disappearing beneath the shadowy underbrush a short distance from the library. Briefly, Orie wondered why it hadn't waited to lead them, but soon the zoo sprawled beneath them, and his mind let it pass.

"Where are we?" Orie screamed from his perch. The parrot took a sharp dip, and the lizard's stomach roiled and lurched.

"We've just crossed the park and I've found the bamboo!" Bennett shouted, his voice trailing in the wet air. "There's a tall stand of it right by that dead hackberry tree!"

In moments, Bennett perched on its rotting branch, and the animals dropped from his back and onto the bark.

La De Da looked around. "I don't see the cat," she said impatiently, "is this some kind of a joke?"

"No," Orie said, indicating a shadowed form, "there he is."

The gray tom crouched motionless in the weeds, eyes fixed on Orie. "Welcome to River Cat territory!" he called.

"So, where's the phone?" La De Da blurted. "We're in a hurry."

Ignoring her, he held Orie's stare. "Aluna wants to introduce you to the colony. They're congregating over there, by the river." Following his gaze, the animals gasped.

Skulking along the sodden banks, their bodies camouflaged by brush, were the River Cats. Most were adults, their bodies rangy and malnourished, but fat litters of kittens also danced through the mud, their small tails up; faces open and inquisitive.

"Oh no," Bennett breathed, "there're so many! It's just like that movie, Gone With The Wind, where all those soldiers are storming Atlanta and…" He stopped, picked at a dwindling clump of feathers on his patchy, pink chest and shook his head. "We need to get out of here."

"I hate to push," the tom said evenly, "but it's cold and wet, and there're kittens to think of." Cocking his head, he smiled. "Come on down. The phone is right behind that clearing, and we have all kinds of festivities planned."

"We don't need a party," Theda whispered in Orie's ear. "Make them leave the phone at the base of this tree and we'll get it after they've gone."

Assessing the scene below, Orie swallowed hard. Never had he faced such danger with so little protection. His mind strayed to Temba, and he imagined her galloping to the rescue, cats scattering in panic, as she grabbed the lifesaving phone. But this was only fantasy, and the truth hunched before him, bloated with facts. The German shepherd was long dead, and The Boy's life rested on the aching shoulders of one Legendary Lizard with a bloody chin, and no backup.

He stared at the cat-covered river bank, and then at his three solemn friends. Despite her protests, Theda was obviously poisonous, but too small to threaten such large numbers. La De Da was fearless, but equally ill-equipped for feline combat, and Bennett's natural fear of cats made his true level of effectiveness unpredictable. The answer was painfully clear. Without the cats, they could never carry the phone. If Orie wanted it moved, he would have to negotiate and pray the cats offered transport. With a flick of his tongue, he puffed his throat in a thin attempt at assuredness. "So, here's the deal," he said. "I know on the surface that this all seems risky. But why would Aluna offer the phone if she really didn't intend to give it to me? I mean, come *on!*" Orie poked Bennett's leg in a playful attempt at humor. "I know I'm *special*, but all this effort to kill one stringy old lizard? I'd barely be a meal for one cat, let alone a whole colony."

His bravado fooled no one, and the group sat in taut silence; their faces drawn with worry, eyes large and sad.

"Please don't go." La De Da whispered. "We'll find another way to save The Boy."

Orie's determined smile faded. "There isn't one." With a nod to the tom, he started down the tree. "Strike up the band," he called, "I'm coming."

* * *

Despite the biting wind, and muddy puddles, Soot was making good time. He'd already passed the bleachers and was headed north toward the River Cats, when the wind shifted, sending a musky stench in to his nostrils. Darting beneath a picnic table, he lifted his head trying to determine the scent's location, and level of danger. Another gust brought a second odor that Soot new well…the smell was dog, and it was close. Sprinting for cover beneath a tangle of fern, he turned just in time to see two creatures trot across the soccer field. One he recognized as a dachshund, an irritable, tenacious breed the black cat had learned to avoid, and the other was a weasel like creature he couldn't identify. It hurried behind the dog in a humped back gait much like that of an inch worm, its eyes darting right and left. Repulsed by its smell, Soot shook his head and pawed at his nose.

The twosome crossed the miniature train tracks, and seemed to be heading toward the zoo.

Soot watched until their figures faded in the distance. For some reason, he found the encounter unsettling. Why would such dissimilar creatures be together, and for what purpose? Hoping to avoid further contact, he bolted toward a jogging trail. Though more densely populated by humans, this route was quicker, and worth the risk. What he needed was to speak with Aluna. What he didn't need, was a dog.

* * *

Aluna paced by the river bank, trying to calm her racing heart. It had happened! The lizard was here, and there was no room for errors. Crouching behind a stump, she focused on Orie and his three companions. At first, she'd feared the reptile suspected something, because it seemed he'd never come down from the tree.

But now, she could see his small form inching slowly down the bark.

Nervously, she licked her chops and rehearsed her speech for the umpteenth time. How often she'd thought of this moment; pictured her colony perched by the river, and imagined the sweet juice of revenge. Jett would have been so proud, Aluna thought, with a moment of chin quivering emotion. Then rising to her feet, she strode through the brush to meet her uncle's murderer.

"Welcome," she said, surprised by a numb calm flooding her body.

The lizard's posture was wary and he stood, poised to run. "Right." He said. "Where's the phone?"

Aluna stared at the figure before her. Was it possible that this small, arthritic reptile, with a swollen toe and discolored skin was the Legendary Lizard? She wanted to laugh, and then remembered the grey tom's warning. This creature might be small and ugly, but he was also devious, hateful and responsible for Buddy's ascension to Cat Master. He must be handled carefully. "The cell phone is here," she said pleasantly, "but first I'd like to introduce you to my colony."

Orie fidgeted with unconcealed irritation. "I don't want to seem rude, but The Boy is in danger, and the phone his only hope for escape, so," he paused, tapping his right front claw with nervous energy, "could we skip the hoe-down, and get right to business?"

"I understand completely," Aluna said, careful to keep her voice steady and smooth. "Luckily, the phone is very near the colony, so we can take care of 'business' and still introduce the Legendary Lizard to the *equally* legendary River Cats." She cocked her head. "You've heard of us, right?"

The lizard shrugged. "I guess so. I don't keep up with cats much."

"Well," she smiled, "I'll try to make this a memorable occasion for all of us." With a nod for him to follow, she trotted briskly to the widest part of the river, and gazed at the crowd of hungry felines gathered there. "Attention please. I would like to introduce someone very special to you, a creature who's been as much a part of our species' illustrious history as The Cat Master."

The crowd reacted with barely concealed hisses, and Aluna noted the lizard's startled reaction. "Don't be alarmed," she said quickly, "they're thrilled to see you." Orie said nothing, but his eyes darted upward, and Aluna saw the parrot perched in a mesquite tree close by. Birds could be dangerous, and she leaned toward the lizard. "Would you mind moving a little closer?" she asked, indicating her front paws. "I want to make sure they can all see you."

From above, the parrot cawed in frantic protest, but Orie took three tentative steps forward, and stopped. "Hurry up," he muttered.

Aluna nodded. "And now, my friends, without further delay, it's my privilege to introduce Orie: Legendary Lizard," her voice hardened, "and assassin of Jett, the greatest feral who ever lived!" In one lightning motion, she clamped her teeth around the lizard's back, and raised his thrashing body into the air.

A gust of wind swirled tiny eddies of leaves along the banks and the cats yowled with excitement. "Hail Aluna!" they chanted. "Death to the lizard!"

A cacophony of beeps and sirens came from the tree as Bennett screeched and fluttered in horror, the spider wide eyed beside him, and La De Da clutching his wing.

"Kill him, kill him!" the throng intoned, and Aluna raised her head, preparing to crush the squirming lizard as they sang. Suddenly, the wind shifted and she paused; nostrils quivering.

A mélange of odors wafted from the park, and the River Cats quieted, their noses also probing the air. A skinny tortoiseshell whirled on her haunches, fangs bared with fear. "Run!" She shouted, darting toward the underbrush, "dog!"

CHAPTER 39

Beneath the rumble of thunder, and the 'whoop' of a distant car alarm, Soot heard a cat's scream. It was strangely muffled, and it didn't last long, but the sound stopped him; his ears pricked and alert. Where had it come from? Lifting his head, he tested the air for answers. The day was cold, and many scents blended, then faded in the steady drizzle around him. But one thing was certain: The cry had come from the river. With renewed energy, Soot broke into a run. His back leg wobbled through mud and slippery grass, but his pace was strong, passing the zoo's bamboo lined boarders in no time.

Feline distress calls filled his ears. Not the opened mouthed yowl of a fight, but a garbled moan from deep in the throat, and this time it was close. Icy wind blew rain into Soot's face, and once he slipped, almost going down in a tangle of slippery nettles. Wet and panting, he finally crested a sloping hill to the river and stopped, astonished by the scene before him.

Sliding down a dripping tree, ears back, and clawless paws wildly grasping the truck for footing, was Aluna. And beneath her, its jaws snapping inches from her tail, was the dachshund whom Soot had seen earlier.

But there was something else, something so surreal that Soot shook his head twice for clarity. Dangling from his cousin's mouth, front legs thrashing the air in a mad dance for freedom was a lizard; and not just any lizard, but Orie, the legendary reptile he'd met years before. Soot's heart pounded, mind alive with memories.

174

The chow dead by the tool shed; a battered German shepherd lying beside him.

It would be Soot's first and only meeting with the lizard, who'd come looking for his friend Tenba that night, and found cats instead.

The black cat thought hard. What had Buddy said that night as he, Zekki and Pris hungrily eyed the reptile?

"Leave the lizard alone. He's a friend"

"Stop!" Soot shouted, rushing forward.

The dog turned in confusion, and Aluna slipped lower, her de-clawed paws only slowing the descent, not stopping it.

"Get out of here, this isn't your business." the dog's tone was threatening.

"I'm afraid it is," The black cat said. "My name is Soot. I'm not part of this colony, but it's my job to protect them, which I'm going to do. Please get away from the tree."

Aluna watched from above, her eyes wide with surprise, but her mouth firmly clamped on Orie.

The dog glanced at the shadowy form of a ferret crouched beneath some leaves. "Who's this guy?" he asked.

Blitz assessed the black cat, and shrugged. "Never seen him."

"Well, Soot," the dachshund continued, "my name is Frank." Pointedly, he lifted one hind leg against the tree. "The lizard up there is an old pal of mine, and your cat friend needs to drop him. Also, she's stolen a cell phone that belongs to a very important human who needs it. I'd love to visit, but it's getting late and there's a very saucy Latin type who's expecting me. Tell her to let go of the lizard, and then give me the phone. Once that happens, I'll go away and everything will be fine. But if she doesn't," the dog gave a warning snarl, "then I'll wait until she falls, which she's definitely going to do, and maybe kill her. I haven't decided yet."

Every nerve in Soot's body tingled. "What human are you talking about?"

"We call him The Boy," Frank said. "He belongs to The Cat Master or I wouldn't even be here." He glanced at Blitz with disgust. "It's sure not because I like hanging out with ferrets."

The black cat felt dizzy. Frank knew where The Boy was! "Aluna!" he called, his voice rising in the chilly air.

Her mouth full of lizard, Aluna growled...angry but listening.

"What you're doing is wrong! " Soot shouted. "Release Orie, and give this dog the cell phone!"

Eyes slitted with anger, the cat shook her head violently, and Orie's body snapped back and forth like a doll.

Ignoring the dog, Soot stalked forward, and stared up at his cousin. "If you refuse to do the right thing, I'll stay here and defend you, even if Frank kills me." He blinked. "But, your colony is watching."

Though the river bank appeared empty, hundreds of eyes peeked from various hiding places in the weeds, and Aluna glared down; paws curled around a small branch that bent with her weight.

Soot indicated the hackberry tree, where La De Da, Bennett and Theda looked on, their faces blank with fear. "More importantly, *other* species are watching, and I'm asking that you show the world that felines are a fair and honorable order, and that we don't persecute others through association." He paused, staring pointedly at Aluna's declawed paws. "Because we, of all creatures know the sting of injustice."

From above, Aluna's eyes met his, their expression deep and troubled. Rain slowly drizzled from shining branches, and Soot felt time shifting. The dachshund and ferret stood close together, and a cat would have little chance against both. His thoughts drifted to the pawn shop, so safe, so warm, so far from here. I could leave right now, he thought. Just turn my back on all of this and live my life as an Indoor. But, he knew that he wouldn't. With renewed resolve, he turned to Frank. "The Cat Master commands me to protect my species, and it's a job I take seriously. For the last time, I'm asking you to leave."

"Not without the phone and Orie," the dachshund said. His lips pulled back in a snarl and Soot hissed in response.

A sudden rustling from above sent a shower of dead twigs on-to their heads, and startled, both animals looked up.

Aluna struggled awkwardly down the trunk, her paws grasping for balance, the lizard still locked in her jaws. Finally reaching the ground, she turned, and with a toss of her head, flung Orie at their feet. "The phone is behind that bush," she spat at Frank. "Take it."

* * *

176

Orie lay on his back in the mud, staring at the gauzy grey sky, and feeling strangely relaxed. It was an odd reaction that he wanted to share, but his head felt so light and balloon-like, he wasn't sure if he could talk. Flexing all four legs, the lizard carefully twitched his tail, and flicked his tongue. Everything seemed in working order. Apparently he really was alive, and aside from dripping with cat saliva, which was almost worse than death, it was a happy realization.

"Are you okay? Are you hurt?"

The lizard narrowed his eyes for sharper focus, and recognized the worried face of the parrot peering down. Theda dangled from his beak, and La De Da hovered beside them, clasping and unclasping her front claws.

"Everything seems fine." Orie said.

"I thought she'd killed you!" La De Da burst in to tears and then turned away, embarrassed by such emotion.

"Slimed but not dead," The lizard wanted to say, but a musky scent, thick and familiar clogged his nose, and he choked, and sneezed.

"Bless you!" a chirpy voice said.

Orie's eyes widened, and he flipped on to his feet. "Blitz!" He croaked. "What in the heck are you doing here?"

The ferret hopped in a circle, her bright eyes shining, pointed nose quivering with excitement. "I saved you! I saved your life!" She spoke so loudly that Orie's friends stepped back. "I knew the River Cats had the phone and wanted to hurt you, so I brought Frank to help."

The lizard scowled, not sure he'd fully understood. "Really? This was all *your* doing?"

Frank busily sniffed the ground, and Blitz stopped her dance of joy and lowered her voice. "I guess the dog helped a tiny bit, but the plan was all my idea, and now The Boy can be rescued, and—she ducked her head and looked humbly at the ground—I'm just grateful I could be part of it in some small way."

"Way to go ferret!" Bennett cawed, hoping forward. "Hey, everybody! This is our house mate, Blitz! She found the phone!"

La De Da and Theda joined in the congratulations, and the ferret basked in the attention. "Well, what are friends for?" she demurred, making sure Orie was listening.

The lizard said nothing. His euphoria had vanished, and he felt sure that this was somehow connected to Blitz. His thoughts were interrupted by Frank, who bounded toward them, tongue lolling with good will. "Orie!" The dog howled. "How many times do I have to save you, anyway?"

The lizard bristled. It was true that Frank had rescued him many years ago, carrying Orie home after The Cat Master's coronation, but to mention it seemed rude. "Hopefully never." The lizard said, begrudgingly grateful.

"Good," the dachshund winked, "because you're killin' my love life."

Orie remembered Frank's weakness for females and scowled with disapproval. "Where's Aluna?" He asked, suddenly realizing that both she and her colony were gone.

The dog snorted. "The rest of the cats left, but she's over there in the bamboo. Don't worry about the phone," he said quickly, "Soot is guarding it. I'm glad I didn't have to hurt him. He's Buddy's son, right?"

"Right, Orie said, inwardly thrilled by the sturdy dachshund's presence, and what it meant. Transporting the cell phone was solved, with no cats attached. "The Boy is being held in a trailer right beyond the park. It's not far from here, but the phone is too heavy for us. Would you mind carrying it?"

"Sure." Frank wagged his tail. "I had a date, but what the heck. This is for Tenba, right?"

"Yes, and she would have been…."

"…so, what's happening next?" Blitz interrupted. "Where are we going now?"

The lizard felt a flare of anger at her intrusion, but why? Shouldn't he be grateful? Thanks to her, they now had the phone and a courier, and if not for Frank, Orie would have ended the day as lizard pot pie. He looked at the ferret's wide, expectant eyes, and tried to feel appreciation, but couldn't. Something didn't feel right, and he'd almost grasped what, when three loud pops broke the silence.

The animals scattered, and Bennett flew to a tree.

"What was that?" La De Da whispered from beneath a rotted log.

Frank raised his head, ears forward and alert. "It was gunfire," he said, "and its close."

CHAPTER 40

Axel pounded through the trailer, the chain still attached to his neck, and whipping against walls and furniture as he ran. First, he checked the bedroom, his nose greedily sniffing every scent, broad head thrust into open drawers, and closets. Next he ran through the kitchen. The room was small, and empty with crumpled paper sacks, and plastic utensils strewn on the counter, cabinets ajar. Even the refrigerator door swung loose on its hinges, cold air drifting from its glowing interior. The dog stood on his hind legs. Only a carton of milk, and a long forgotten Chinese take-out box remained on a wire shelf.

A fresh burst of rain clattered against the trailer's metal roof, and Axel's heart banged like a blacksmith's anvil. Where was The Boy? Things had happened so quickly that his mind felt tangled and thick. Sitting with a thump in the hallway, he tried to calm his quivering muscles, and forced himself to concentrate.

They had been in the bathroom; The Boy lying by the tub with Axle's chain wound tightly around his ankle, and then attached to the dog's collar. Since Mr. Krell now knew the turtle's whereabouts, Axel hoped that he would leave the trailer and never come back. But that didn't happen, because they'd heard him hurrying through rooms, slamming doors, and throwing things on the floor. Then someone knocked on the door. At first the dog was relieved, hoping a stranger had come, someone who'd save them if Axel howled and whined loudly enough. But the visitor was Jerry, Axel recognized his voice immediately. He didn't like

Jerry, and neither did Mr. Krell, but the dog had never heard them screaming at one another the way they had today.

Alarmed, The Boy had struggled to sit, desperately trying to free his hands from the duct tape. Footsteps grew closer and suddenly, instead of Mr. Krell, Jerry stood before them, his face red and angry. Quickly, he undid the chain from The Boy's ankle, and, then retied the pit bull to the base of the sink.

Helplessly, Axel watched, as Jerry shoved the stumbling young man toward the living room, amidst the sounds of Krell's cursing. And then, the dog swallowed hard, eyes squeezed shut, that's when he heard gun shots. There were three of them, in quick succession, followed by a door opening, and then the sound of a car screeching in to the distance. After that, there was only the tapping of the rain…and silence.

Fortunately, Jerry had been careless when rewinding the chain and it only took minutes for Axel to pull free. That's when he'd smelled the blood, rushed into the living room…and seen the body.

* * *

"Did you say 'gunfire'?" The spider asked, her mandibles clicking with tension. "How do you know that's what it was?"

Frank shook a glob of mud from one wet ear. "Because the human I live with had a boyfriend who hunted, and we went with him once. That was definitely a gunshot."

"If the sound came from the trailer," Orie said trying to ignore a throbbing ache at the base of his skull, "we need to move fast." Still focused, he took a quivering breath, in spite of the gnawing fear now threatening to swallow him, "Frank, you've got the phone, right?"

The dachshund nodded, indicating The Boy's black cell between his splayed paws.

"Everyone back on the bird! I'll catch a ride with Frank, if it's okay with him." Orie gave the dog a questioning look.

"Like old times," Frank said amiably.

"What about me? I'm coming, too, right?"

The animals turned to see Blitz sitting on a tree stump, her black masked face alert and determined.

180

Orie paused. There was no denying her contribution. What harm could it do? "Sure," he said, trying to hide his reluctance, "why not?" With one quick hop, he vaulted to the dog's flank and scrambled on to his head. "Thanks for everything!" he called to Soot who stood with Aluna by the bamboo.

"Wait!" Soot called, running to Frank's side. "Who took The Boy, and why? Zekki and Pris are worried sick."

"The man's name is Stuart Krell," Orie said. "He's an illegal animal trader. Apparently, The Boy rescued a rare turtle Krell wants, and he's willing to kill for it." The lizard shrugged, deciding to leave the jackal out of it. "I'd like to talk more, but we're running out of time and need to get going."

Soot dipped his head in acknowledgment. "I'll pass it on."

* * *

"Pris!" Zekki called, "come quick!"

The plump calico galloped into The Boy's old bedroom, and slammed to a stop in the middle of the room. "Where are you?" she called.

"Over here." The white cat stood in the doorway of the closet. "Cuff is in there," he rolled his eyes in a 'here we go again' pantomime, "and he thinks he's in danger."

Pris huffed with annoyance. "Cuff!" she screamed "You haven't *done* anything in there have you? That's where Mrs. O'Connell keeps all her summer clothes and…."

"No." Cuff's muffled voice answered. Garments swayed on their hangers and the turtle's wizened face finally emerged from beneath a gauzy green skirt. "I'm just trying to get out of here. Something reached me with mind talk, and told me to run." He blinked at both cats. "And that's exactly what I'm going to do."

Darting into the closet, Pris firmly nudged him back into the room. "What do you mean, 'something'? wasn't it Soot?"

The turtle scrunched his face into a wrinkled ball and thought. "No, and I've never mind talked with anything like it. The voice felt sort of canine and yet not exactly, but it called me by name."

"Look," Zekki said, "we're all on edge. You're waiting for The Boy, we're waiting for Soot, Mrs. O'Connell is gone," the cat sighed with fatigue, "and everything's turned upside down. It's

181

made us all paranoid." He gave Cuff an encouraging smile. "Right?"

The turtle scratched his nose with one gnarled claw, and glanced back at the closet. "Yeah, I guess so."

"Well, isn't it possible that escaping from the tub was so exhausting that you fell asleep and dreamed all of this?" Zekki asked. "Nightmares can seem very real."

"Makes perfect sense." Pris nodded with confidence. "I'll bet that's exactly what happened."

A steady downpour drummed against the window panes, and the frigid room reflected a continuing drop in the day's temperature.

Zekki shivered. "It's cold in here. Let's go to the kitchen where it's warmer."

The turtle stood quietly, his head down. "You know what?" A sudden smile crossed his wrinkled face. "I am pretty tired, and it probably was a dream. Thanks, guys, I feel a lot better."

"So, can we please get out of this room?" Pris whimpered. "My paws are turning to ice."

Cuff nodded, and with agonizing slowness, plodded through the door and into the hall.

The cats trotted to the kitchen, and Cuff veered toward the dining room.

"I thought you were going to make him stay in here." Pris frowned. "You know what he's been doing all over the house."

"Let him go where he wants," Zekki said, picking at a cat treat. "He doesn't need any more stress, and I want him to be alert and focused when Soot finally gets back to us."

The calico gave a troubled stare. "You mean, *if* Soot gets back to us. It's been a long time since Cuff contacted him and so far…nothing. And if there really was something telling him to escape, who or what was it?"

"I don't know," the white cat said. "but…"

"Hey!" The turtle called, his voice reverberating through the house. "Does Mrs. O'Connell have a friend who plays baseball?"

Bewildered, Pris and Zekki walked to the dining room.

The turtle stood with both front legs propped against the French doors watching the street.

"I don't know." Zekki flicked his tail. "Why would you ask that?"

"Because," Cuff said cheerfully, "there's a guy in the driveway, and he's holding a bat."

CHAPTER 41

Soot and Aluna watched as the parrot flapped skyward, while beneath him, the dachshund galloped toward the trailer, Orie clinging to his back.

The rain had stopped and though it was late afternoon, the clouds had scattered and the sky was clearer than it had been all day. The black cat's leg hurt, but aside from the bone biting cold, he felt invigorated. A murder had been thwarted and all that remained was to contact Zekki and Pris about The Boy's situation. This was something he'd repeatedly tried through mind talk for the last hour with no success, and a nagging worry had replaced irritation. "I guess I'd better get back," he said to Aluna, who hadn't moved from his side since the cell phone's return.

The female glanced at him and looked away. "I—I want to say something first."

"It's okay," Soot said, "you don't ..."

"...but I do." Aluna interrupted. She turned and faced him, her wet fur outlining each protruding rib and hip bone. "You would have died defending me, and I..." she licked her chops nervously, "...I've been horribly disrespectful toward you."

The black cat listened silently.

"Please try and understand. Buddy is considered a traitor by many ferals, and being his niece has compromised my status with the River Cats. I thought avenging Jett would make up for that, cement the colony's respect for me as their leader, but I didn't understand what that really meant until today. Respect isn't won through violence, and revenge isn't really justice. I was wrong to target Orie," her shining green eyes locked with his, "and I'm proud to call you cousin.

"Same here," Soot said with a smile.

"The River Cats won't invade your territory; you have my word. If humans take our home, we'll find another one," Aluna jutted her chin, "we always do." Kneeling before him, she bowed her head. "Hail Soot. Heir to the Master, Prince of the Alleys."

Soot saw that the River Cats had reappeared by the river banks, their heads lowered as well.

"Like father like son," she whispered, and with a flick of her tail, she was gone.

* * *

The trailer loomed above them, its rusty white roof glowing in a shaft of sunlight now peeking through a gap in the clouds.

"Stop here," Orie said. Frank obeyed, dropping the phone on the ground and the lizard scrambled from his back.

Bennett fluttered down beside them, and La De Da and Theda nestled amidst his feathers, their eyes wide, waiting.

"Hold on," the dachshund's nose sniffed the air, "there's another dog around here... Nuts," he snorted with regret, "it's male."

"We know." Orie said. "He lives with Krell, but he's a friend to The Boy, and knew we were looking for the phone."

"Whatever." Frank raised one leg against a dirty tire. "But this is now officially my trailer." He stopped, and thought for a moment. "And maybe the park, too, I haven't decided."

"Hey." The parrot said, flying on to a low hanging sycamore branch. "The front door is open."

Orie crept forward, his eyes on the sagging front porch, and flickering glimpse of shadow inside the trailer. "Axel?" he called softly, "are you there?"

A dark figure lurched into the doorway, its huge head held low, deep growls rumbling from its throat.

"Axel?" Orie spoke carefully. "It's me, the lizard."

"I'll take care of this," Frank said, strutting forward, but Orie held up one claw, motioning for him to stop.

185

"Remember us?" Orie continued, his eyes focused on the pit bull. "Good news; we found the cell phone, and we're here to help The Boy."

There was a second of silence, and then Axel stumbled down the steps. Muzzle thrown back, he uttered a heartbroken howl. "I tried to save him!" he wailed. "I was ready to kill Mr. Krell if I had to, but they tied me up."

"Tried... to... save... him?" Orie asked, his throat suddenly raspy and dry. "*Tried?*"

"There was a fight." The dog's words tumbled on top of one another. "Mr. Krell's partner dragged The Boy out of the bathroom, and I heard gun shots, and..." Axle's voice trailed off.

"And what?" La De Da asked, scurrying down the tree and protectively standing with Orie. "Spit it out! What!"

"And then I pulled the chain loose." Axel said, shaking his head until the dangling links jangled against his neck. "I ran in to the living room..." The dog looked up, his eyes vacant and tired as though awakening from a dream. "And that's when I saw... the body."

A brisk wind whipped through the park, blowing fat gray clouds away from the sun and warming their backs for the first time that day.

But no one noticed.

The animals stood as if frozen, and even Frank stopped snarling, and sat.

"It was Mr. Krell's partner, Jerry." The pit bull said. "Mr. Krell knows where the turtle is, and he's killed Jerry, and taken The Boy somewhere. I've tried to pick up their scent, but the rains washed so much away." He gave a shaky sigh. "They could be anywhere."

Anywhere. The word reverberated in Orie's head, and he pictured The Boy lost and alone with nothing between him and the jackal but a hand full of animals with good intentions and zero power. He sagged to the ground in weary despair. Krell probably had the turtle by now, and then what?

The boy's answering machine...one message in particular.

The recorded phrase echoed inside his head, *"the thing in the bathroom"*. He couldn't quite place the voice, or interpret the meaning, but it triggered a profound truth. "Wait a minute!" Orie shouted, jumping up so quickly that the world spun. "The Boy would never leave a treasured animal with strangers." The lizard squeezed his eyes shut with concentration. "He'd pick a place familiar...."

"...that he knew was safe." La De Da interrupted.

Bennett fluttered with excitement. "Like the college?"

"Maybe with a friend?" Theda offered.

"Or!" The lizard's voice rose with discovery, "at his mother's house! I remember her phone message, now. She said she was leaving town." His brow furrowed, and he worked his mouth slowly to get the words just right. "And that a pet sitter would feed the cats as well as '*the thing in the bathroom*'." Orie slapped the ground with his tail, amazed he hadn't questioned the cryptic reference sooner. "That's it! The thing she referred to was the turtle. The turtle is at Mrs. O'Connell's!" For the first time in many years Orie leapt in to the air, his sore toe forgotten, then suddenly stopped, his exuberance smashed by an awful realization. "Krell and The Boy are headed to Sixth Avenue to get it."

"So?" La De Da asked. "Let's get going!"

"It's too late for that." Orie paced up and down, his tail leaving tiny rivulets in the mud. "They've had too much of a head start. By the time we get there they'll have left, and then The Boy will really be lost to us."

"But we have to at least try." Bennett said, head feathers raised with confusion. He looked around. "I mean, don't we?"

The lizard felt ill. What should he do? They were so close to saving The Boy, and now, this. His mind flashed on a horrifying visual; the Jackal God, Anibus, slinking through the rain, hunting The Boy. Was it on him now, talons red with blood, amber eyes wild? Orie shook the thought away. Just when he'd solved the cell phone problem, another one had arisen. Desperate for solitude, he noticed the trailer's open door. So what if it held a corpse? He'd always had a certain fondness for the dead...they were motionless, quiet, and never had opinions. "We need a new plan and I have to think," he called to his friends. "Give me a few minutes." With a determined sigh, he trudged up the rickety steps, crossed the threshold, and stopped... mute with surprise.

Crouched on the floor, paws furiously digging through the pockets of the sprawled and bleeding body, was Blitz. Shiny car keys and a small bag of tobacco lay by her tail, and lodged in her jaws, its sleek case wet with saliva... was the victim's cell phone.

CHAPTER 42

Zekki and Pris pressed their faces against the rain streaked glass for a better look. The turtle was right, a man stood in the driveway with a baseball bat. Hugely obese, he approached the house, his left hand fidgeting with keys, eyes darting left and right. A vivid purple birthmark snaked across a thin upper lip and his corduroy jacket was spattered with large red stains which had also streaked his trousers.

"What team does he play for?" Cuff asked. "He's not wearing a uniform."

"Get away from there!" Zekki shouted, pushing the turtle so hard, he almost tipped over.

Pris scampered away in horror. "What's going on?" she squeaked, from beneath the couch. "Who is that?"

"I don't know, but I've never seen him before, and something isn't right." A battered Ford was parked along the curb, and the white cat raced to the living room window for a better look. At first, the car seemed empty, but there was a sudden movement in the back seat, and a shadowy profile, its mouth covered with tape, briefly bobbed against the glass, and then fell out of sight. Zekki's temples throbbed, and he prayed for clarity. There was something painfully familiar about that trembling silhouette; the long, thin nose that turned up ever so slightly, the unruly shock of straight, brown hair falling across the high, pale brow. It was The Boy! The Boy was home! But why was he gagged and lying in the back seat of a strange car, and who was the man now approaching the porch?

"Pris!" his voice broke with emotion. "I saw him! The Boy's in that car!"

"Thank goodness." Cuff said from behind them. "He's come to take me home." With an unhurried gait, he trudged toward the living room. "It's been great meeting you," he called over his shoulder. "Gotta' go!"

Pris slunk into the open. "Why's The Boy in a strange car? What's happening?"

Zekki's brain pushed for the answer, thoughts darting through his mind like minnows. "Wait, Cuff," he said. "Tell me again what the scary voice told you, the one in your dream?"

The turtle swiveled his neck in the white cat's direction. "That something bad was coming, and it was after me."

"And you're sure it wasn't Soot's mind talk?"

Cuff thought for a moment. "Naw," he said, shaking his head. "Soot's been trying to reach me for the last hour. I'd know the feel of his telepathy."

Soot's trying to reach us?" Pris bounded forward. "Why didn't you say so?"

The turtle shrugged. "Because I didn't answer him. I told you I wasn't doing mind talk anymore."

A key rattled in the front door.

"Listen carefully, Cuff." The white cat's voice was strangely calm. "I want you to get back in Mrs. O'Connell's closet."

"No way," Cuff said pleasantly, lurching toward the front door. "It's too small, and besides, this is the way out."

The man cursed from the front porch, then rattled the knob, and tried the lock again.

Zekki blocked the turtle's path, his blue eyes wide and piercing. "What I said earlier was wrong. The voice you heard was no dream, it's real. Something really *is* after you, and I think it's the guy with the bat."

Footsteps retreated from the porch and crunched toward the back of the house.

The animals stood frozen in the hallway, listening.

"Oh—Oh ." Pris stammered. "The—the back door!"

Cuff stared at the cats in confusion. "Not a dream?"

"Not a dream," Zekki repeated, pushing the turtle down the hall. "We need to find out what's going on, and until we do, you need to hide."

189

There was a crash, followed by the sound of glass tinkling on the kitchen floor.

"Contact Soot!" He yowled, shoving Cuff through the narrow opening of The Boy's old room. "And do it now!"

* * *

"You're stealing stuff from a corpse?" Orie teetered on the threshold. "Even for you this is gross."

The ferret whirled around, her eyes wild with surprise. "I haven't done anything wrong! He's dead! It can't be stealing if he's dead!"

Orie assessed Blitz's stash, his eyes finally stopping on the man's cell phone. Cold drafts of air wafted through the trailer's open door, but he didn't care. Something was forming in his mind, something daring, and difficult, and probably impossible. "The guy on the floor is Stuart Krell's partner," he muttered, "which means they must have called each other on their phones a lot, right?"

"I guess so," The Blitz said. "Please don't tell on me, I'll put everything back, just let me keep the keys…"

"You can have his whole body for all I care," Orie said, pushing past her. "What I need is the phone. Hey, everybody," he yelled, "get in here!"

The animals ran up the steps, jostling one another for position, and finally surrounding Orie and the ferret, who sat with the cell phone between them.

"Who knows how to work one of these phone things?" the lizard asked, his eyes darting from one face to another.

No one answered.

Orie bit his lip in frustration, suddenly wishing he'd paid more attention to something other than himself. "Humans punch special numbers to call each other, right?"

Frank sat back and scratched his jaw. "Yep, that's how my Connie does it."

"Here's the deal," Orie said. "I'm convinced that going to Sixth Avenue is the wrong move. Even if we did get there in time, it's a busy neighborhood; we couldn't help The Boy without being seen, which would lead to all kinds of problems." The lizard took a deep breath. "What we need is for Stuart Krell to come to *us*."

"What?" The spider scurried forward. "How in the world do we do that?"

"We're going to call him," Orie said. "On that thing."

The animals exchanged worried glances.

"Are you feeling okay?" La De Da's eyes softened with concern. "I mean, this whole situation with The River Cats and…"

"Oh for heaven's sake!" The lizard snapped. "Stop looking at me like that. I'm fine!"

"Bennett!" He screamed, "Get over here!"

The parrot hopped forward, keeping a wary eye on Jerry's body which had now attracted two flies, and a scatter of ants.

The lizard stared at the phone's bright silver surface. "Krell's number has got to be stored in there. All we have to do is find it and…and…then push something to make it ring." He looked at the bird, hopefully. "You can do that, can't you?"

"Maybe," Bennett said, "if I knew what to hit." He pecked at his featherless chest, opaque eyes bewildered. "But once we call him, what do we say?"

"Not 'we'," Orie corrected, "you'. Parrots are masters at mimicry. Remember how you imitated the girl's voice from the answering machine earlier; the one where she talks about The Boy's backpack?"

The parrot nodded, his wings trembling.

"Well," Orie said, "there was more to that girl's message, and while we try and find Krell's number on Jerry's phone, I want you to practice doing her voice until you're perfect."

Bennett let out a shrieking train whistle that made Axel howl.

"Stop that!" Theda said, quickly. "You'll do fine."

The dachshund moved forward, his silky ears tipped with mud. "I'm not sure where you're going with this, Orie, but let's say we do reach Krell, and the parrot makes the call, then what?"

"Then," Orie said, staring into each animal's eyes, "Bennett imitates that girl's voice to lure Krell to the warehouse." There was a collective intake of breath from the group, and he rushed on before anyone could protest. "I remember one last message left for The Boy, by a friend of his from college. If I'm right, there's something in that warehouse as dangerous as the jackal, and if we can get Krell back in there, then maybe I've figured out a way to finish this thing."

Outside, the afternoon grew darker, flat grey clouds obliterating the momentary warmth, and a shiny black beetle plodded up the dead man's sleeve, and disappeared down his collar.

"That's all great," La De Da said, finally breaking the silence. "But first we have to find Krell's number on Jerry's phone." Frowning, she circled the cell and looked up. "Let's get real here, does anyone know how to do that?"

"Automatic re-dial," a voice said from behind them.

Startled, the animals turned toward the door.

Framed against the waning light, antennae lightly waving, stood the cockroach. "Of course you've made it painfully clear that you're not interested in either my brains or my company, so I guess I'll be on my way." With a sweeping gesture of his front leg, he turned. "Good bye, then. Nice to see everyone still looking so...." He gave a smug little snort. "...dumb."

"Don't go," Orie said, not quite believing what he was about to say. "I was wrong, you're a genius, please help us."

The cockroach squinted with suspicion. "Do you mean that?"

"Yes, you pompous pile of protein," the lizard screeched, "I mean it!" He felt his patience dwindling along with The Boy's chances for survival.

"Thank you, Orie." The roach said in a dignified voice. "That had the true ring of sincerity." Skittering to the phone's pad, he moved quickly over buttons and arrows, his antennae testing and stroking the glossy surface. With a satisfied smile, he looked up. "This is doable."

"Good." Orie gathered the animals around him. "Theda and Axel, tell me everything you know about the warehouse."

Axel licked his chops with uncertainty. "Everything?"

"Yes," Orie said. "I need to know the layout; where are the cages, lights, windows, how things lock and unlock, and most importantly," he paused. "I want a detailed description of every animal there."

CHAPTER 43

Stuart Krell stood by the shattered patio door, listening for any sounds. A television blared from a neighbor's house, but no one seemed aware of his presence, and dogs barked from across the street, only to be brought inside by their irate owner. Satisfied he hadn't been seen, Stuart reached through the broken pane, flipped the lock, turned the knob, and walked in. Stepping lightly across the jagged shards, he lifted his bat ready to swing. "Anybody home?" he called in a pleasant voice. "Hello?"

A damp wind rattled through the jagged hole, fluttering dish towels on their hooks, and scattering crumbs of cat treats across the rug. Stuart looked down and smiled. The Boy had said there were cats here, so far so good. Creeping through the hallway, he stopped and peered into the living room. A linen sofa stood by the plate glass window, with two Queen Anne chairs positioned across from an oblong coffee table for easy conversation. Pot plants flanked a baby grand, and a library ladder leaned against a wall of book stuffed shelves.

But no turtle.

The dining room yielded little more. A solid mahogany table gleamed in the soft, pewter light from floor to ceiling windows, surrounded by simple wooden chairs upholstered in a bold ethnic print.

Not a reptile in sight.

Stuart rhythmically slapped the bat across his palm, and thought. Where would he put such a valuable creature?

Plowshares were land turtles, so he knew not to look for a tank, and turtles were also notoriously messy, so restraining them in something that was easily cleaned was a must. The faint sound of water dripping from a faucet echoed from the hallway. "Bingo." Stuart said, then threw back his head and laughed. It was the first time he'd allowed himself to feel anything but white, gnawing fear since leaving the trailer...and of course, Jerry. He was surprised at the rush of excitement now zapping through his body. He felt good; powerful, as though he were no longer Stuart Krell; loser, fat kid, and petty criminal, but a portly master mind; shrewd, rich, and up to his neck in worshipful women...and pretty ones, too, not the sloppy bar types he usually attracted.

The bathroom was easy to find, and he padded toward the dripping sound. A night light by the sink emitted a soft, yellow glow against its pale green walls, and Stuart looked down, and frowned. A plush beige rug was bunched in unsightly folds near the shower, and a wash cloth lay on the floor by the toilet. This seemed odd considering how pristine the rest of the house appeared. Mentally crossing his fingers, Stuart looked in to the tub. A water pan, and withered clumps of chopped vegetables were positioned neatly beneath the faucet, and trails of excrement had dried on the porcelain.

But no turtle.

He clenched his jaws with frustration. Was this a trick? Did College Boy actually think he could lie to Stuart about the turtle's whereabouts, and still save himself and the dog? The stupid kid was tied up in the back seat of his car for God's sake! Angrily, he cracked his bat against the wall, then turned and stalked through the house.

One after another he charged through rooms, rummaging in cupboards, and slamming doors. Mentally he checked off a linen cabinet, utility closet, hot water heater, the basement, a bedroom and bath, and finally, one last closed door located off the hallway

Huffing with exertion, Stuart pushed against its sturdy frame. The door creaked on its hinges and slowly swung open.

The room was large and cold, obviously fashioned for hobbies, exercise, and privacy. Stumbling against a treadmill, he banged his knee against a small table and cursed. A candle fell to the carpet with a thump, and his hip grazed a recliner that gently rocked in the chilly dimness. Fuzzy light filtered through slitted plantation shutters, revealing nothing but home furnishings and space. This was the last place it could be, and a horrible fear tightened Stuart's chest. What if someone had already taken the turtle? Was that possible? His mind darted back to the warehouse, and focused on what he thought he'd seen in the cage. Stuart shook his head. No, he *had* seen it! The hyena thing was asleep on college boy's backpack, until suddenly, the pack wasn't there anymore, which meant someone had to have taken it. And he wasn't stupid. Jerry had made the mistake of thinking so—Stuart smiled bitterly—and now Jerry didn't think at all.

"Come on, where are you?" he called, shoving the treadmill aside and fighting an irrational urge to get on his hands and knees and look under the chair. His eyes scanned the room, finally stopping on an open closet door. Bright summer fabrics filled the space; clothes jammed so tightly on the rod that it bowed. Shoe boxes were stacked in the entranceway, some tipped over, their lids askew.

Despite the cold, Stuart's shirt was wet with sweat. Opening his coat, he unwound the muffler and sighed. What was he doing here? No one kept turtles in a closet. Either the kid was messing with him, or someone had intervened without either of their knowledge. He set his jaw. Whatever the answer, he and his bat were going to find out.

Kicking a sneaker across the room, he started to leave, and then stopped.

There was a faint tapping sound coming from the closet. At first Stuart thought he'd imagined it, but tip toeing closer, he realized that he hadn't. Something was moving in the darkness, and holding his bat a little higher, Stuart shoved back a skirt, and looked in.

* * *

Soot limped across the rail road tracks, his paw pads cold against the iron rails and gravel. He was troubled. Soon it would be dark, and after multiple tries, he still hadn't been able to contact Zekki through the mystery caller. At first, there was only silence to his telepathic probing, but the last two attempts had been blocked, as if someone were trying to contact him at the same time; a mind talk busy signal that went on and on.

Leaping a puddle, he wondered at the strangeness of the day. Aluna's tribute had touched him deeply. Her willingness for peace between the alley and the River Cats was a huge step toward a continuing collaboration, and Soot felt proud of both of their efforts. His mind turned to Orie, and he frowned at the memory of gun shots. Had the lizard and his entourage reached The Boy in time?

"Soooooot!"

The cat darted beneath a dripping privet hedge, and turned his thoughts inward. "What's going on?" He asked in mind talk. "I've been trying to reach you all day!"

"We're under attack at the O'Connell's." The voice answered. "The Boy is being held in a car outside, and a man is in the house. Do you know who he is?"

Two cars zoomed down the street, and Soot shrank deep into the foliage, remembering the lizard's words. "Listen closely, there's an illegal animal trader named Stuart Krell," he telepathed. "The Boy has a rare and valuable turtle that the man will kill to get. But Orie and some friends have an escape plan for The Boy, so be careful, and have faith."

There was such a long pause from the caller that Soot feared they'd been disconnected somehow.

"*I am* the turtle," the voice finally said. "If we never speak again… thanks."

Soot felt he might drown in the silence that followed, and with disheartened steps trudged across 8th Avenue toward home. The world was a cruel place, and creatures of all species were forever at its mercy. Memories of the Indoors beckoned, and looking up, he was surprised to see that he was already at the pawn shop, its lights glowing in the twilight. A woman looked out from the window, her face softening with pleasure to see him. Carefully she opened the door and crouched on the stoop. "Here kitty," she whispered, shaking a bowl of tuna. "Here boy, are you hungry?"

Love was indeed an addiction, and Soot felt the tug of relapse. These were kind humans, and they obviously wanted him. Just a few, quick steps and he'd be back inside, shielded from evil, happy and warm. With a joyous meow, he started forward and then stopped, suddenly aware of the night and its subtle perfume.

Wood smoke curled from a chimney, melding with the earthy sweetness of rain and vegetation. The cloying odor of possum, and the acrid aroma of raccoon trailed from the bushes, and beneath it all, the clean, fresh scent of cats and their kittens warmed the chill; their very presence a gentle anthem of home.

Soot glanced once more at the kind human face…and walked on, past the open door and cozy bed, away from food, and comfort, and safety.

With a singing heart, he turned toward the alley; to his kind, their lives, and his promise.

CHAPTER 44

"I thought you knew how to work this thing," Orie snarled, his claws clenched with frustration.

The roach gave a contemptuous snort. "I do, but I'm not a magician. There are many numbers stored in this phone. We're half way through them, and I'm sure Stuart Krell's will come up eventually." He motioned to a button, and patiently, Bennett pushed it with his beak.

The animals strained forward, listening as the number clicked and finally connected.

"Pizza Barn," a young man's voice said, "take it out or eat it in, Pizza Barn's your tongue's best friend."

"Bennett," Theda whispered. "How about a rehearsal?"

The parrot nodded, cleared his throat and bent his head toward the receiver. "If you want the backpack," he mimicked in the voice of the girl on the message machine, "you'd better get out here, 'cause we know who you are and we're holding it for ransom."

"Huh?" The Pizza Barn boy said.

Bennett clicked off, and the phone disconnected. "How was that?" he asked.

Considering that his first six tries had ended in imitations of bombs exploding, a NASCAR crash, and the theme song for Bat Man, Orie felt Bennett had come a long way. "It was great," he said, "right on the money."

The roach continued his crazy dance on the phone pad, and Orie decided to discuss the final plan with the animals one more time. "Does everyone understand what to do when Krell gets to the warehouse?" The lizard looked around. "Axel?" The pit bull licked his chops with worry. "I—I think so." "Theda and La De Da?" "Check!" they answered in unison. "Bennett and the roach are already doing their part, and Frank is going back home." He looked at the dachshund, and fought a throat constricting wave of affection. "You've never let me down. Thanks for everything, and I hope we haven't spoiled your—the lizard grimaced with distaste—love life."

Frank gave a hearty shake, sending dried mud clots flying everywhere. "Not a chance." The dog winked. "Everyone wants the dachshund." He moved closer to Orie and lowered his voice. "But watch out for the ferret. She's a thief and a liar, and if I were you, I'd lose her. Good luck. If you still need The Boy's phone, it's on the steps." With a saucy yip, he turned and breezed past Axel. "Drop by if you're ever in the neighborhood," he called. "I know some girls who love the gangster type!"

Before Axel could respond, the roach squeaked with excitement. "I think we've got something!" he shouted. "There's a numerical repetition here that has potential!"

The animals rushed to the phone, watching breathlessly as Bennett punched in the last number.

It was only then that Orie sensed Blitz's absence. Maybe she'd headed home he thought, his eyes scanning the dark stand of trees around them.

But deep inside, he knew she hadn't.

* * *

The closet was dark, and it took a moment for Stuart's eyes to adjust. The tapping had stopped, but something was moving amidst the clutter. He bent for a closer look, than jumped back. Gliding along the floor, bright paisley scarf trailing behind, was a big, straw hat. The man blinked, what was going on? Squatting down, he tentatively reached out one hand, not noticing the four glowing eyes beside him.

With a guttural yowl, two figures burst upward, warm fur brushing his face.

One clung to his thigh, claws imbedded in his flesh, the other scrambled high and on to his shoulder. Falling backward, Stuart dropped the bat. Razor sharp pain slid from his groin to his knee, and then the thing let go, darting back in to the closet.

The creature clinging to his coat, and biting his scalp was a different story.

Rolling to his knees, Stuart reached behind his neck, grabbed a soft fold of skin, and flung the attacker on to the recliner. Clumps of white fur dangled from between his fingers, and as he shook them off, his eyes caught sight of a pale flash of movement rushing out the door.

"Cats!" Stuart shouted. "It's cats!" His back and thigh stung from the attack, and a wet patch of red was seeping through a rip in his new pants. His mind was a black hole of rage and frustration; reason a thing of the past. "I—I'm going to kill you!" Stuart bawled. Struggling to his feet, he grabbed his bat, and shambled to the hall.

Everything was falling apart, he thought, peering into the kitchen, and then the dining room It had taken months to find the kid and his turtle; he'd killed Jerry, risked everything, and all he'd found were cats! Well, he thought grimly, he wasn't leaving empty handed.

Something caught his attention. A feline had blundered into the hallway. Stuart blocked its path, and panicked, it darted to the bathroom. "Bad move," the big man whispered, slipping inside, and shutting the door behind him.

Frantically, the creature dashed from corner to corner, leaping on the sink, bouncing off the tub, and finally crouching in the shower, its blue eyes angry, and terrified.

"Gotcha'!" Stuart lifted his bat.

The sound of a telephone rang. Stuart stopped in mid swing, and looked around. Unbelievably, it was coming from his pocket, and perplexed, he reached in and pulled out his phone. It rang again, a bluesy little jazz rift he'd downloaded weeks before. Mechanically, he checked the Caller ID…and froze. It was from Jerry! Stuart took a lurching step back. This wasn't possible! And yet, there it glowed on the tiny blue window, a number he knew by heart and never expected to see again. With a yelp, he tossed the cell in to the sink, and put both fingers in his ears to block the sound. But on the fourth ring, he flipped open the cover, and with a shaky hand, brought it to his ear. "Hello?" He whispered.

"If you want the backpack," a girl's high pitched voice said, "you'd better get out here, 'cause we know who you are and we're holding it for ransom!"

Stuart felt his knees buckle, and he slumped onto the commode, eyes shut. "Wh—who are you?"

The caller repeated the message verbatim... and then there was silence.

Extortionists! He knew it! Someone had seen everything, and not just the kid's abduction, but the murder, too. Otherwise, how had they gotten Jerry's phone? "Where are you?" he asked, his heart thudding.

"You'd better get out here," the girl repeated, brightly.

"To the warehouse?" Stuart asked.

"If you want the backpack," she answered.

So there had been a back pack, and now someone had it. Stuart took a deep breath, suddenly angry. "How much do you want?" he asked. "I don't carry a lot of money, and its after banking hours."

Silence.

"Never mind," Stuart said in a rush. "We can work something out. I'm on my way. Just don't do anything crazy, okay?"

"Cause we know who you are." Came the teasing reply.

"I heard you!" Stuart shouted. "I'll be there in ten minutes. Don't leave!" He clicked the phone shut, and tried to catch his breath. There was something strange about the girl's voice. He didn't like the robotic cadence, and wondered how many others were involved, and if drugs were somehow at play.

With a determined groan, Stuart stood and smoothed his hair. He hadn't wanted to kill anyone else, but they'd left him no choice. Mind whirring, he took a quick inventory. He had his bat, and the gun was loaded and in the trunk. First, he'd take care of the blackmailers, and then he'd take care of The Boy. After that—he rubbed his eyes until they ached—he'd blow this town and never come back.

* * *

Blitz hid behind the trailer, listening to Orie's plan. The whole idea sounded ridiculous, but she really didn't care about that. What she cared about was the dead guy's shiny silver cell phone. It was one thing to have had The Boy's phone stolen by The River Cats, but to lose such a treasure twice, especially when she'd acquired this one so legitimately made her whiskers itch with fury. Who did they think they were? The ferret snorted with resentment and scratched her muzzle. She'd long since given up on being part of the group. It was plain by the way Orie had looked at her, even when she'd supplied him with The Boy's phone, that he hated her. Most likely he'd never intended including her in his story, and who knew what the stupid dachshund had told everyone?

There was only one thing to do: follow the animals to the carnival, wait until they entered the warehouse, and then take the dead guy's phone back... and run. Tough luck if they still needed it. The crazy parrot had been jabbering in it for an hour, and her head ached from the sound of the shrill, repetitive message.

Slinking behind a thick black tire, Blitz stretched out and watched the animals. They were still gathered around Orie, going over and over their part in his plan as though it was actually possible. The ferret yawned, suddenly tired of the whole thing. Once she'd taken back what was rightfully hers, she'd simply go home and make up a really good story to tell at the next meeting.

From the way things were going, no one here would live to dispute it.

CHAPTER 45

Zekki sat in the shower, his body trembling, and his mouth dry as dust. The bathroom reeked with the big man's odor, and the cat felt an urge to vomit. A door slammed in the kitchen, and footsteps thudded out the front door of the house, and down the driveway. Zekki scurried to the dining room just in time to see the car screech away from the curb, its taillights fuzzy in the misty darkness. The Boy was in that car, and the cat's heart ached with worry.

"Is he gone?"

Zekki turned to see Pris's dilated eyes peering from the hallway. Her brown and white coat was still bushed with terror, her tail twice its size. He trotted to her side and rubbed against her shoulder. "Yes. He's gone. He took a phone call, and couldn't leave fast enough."

"What about The Boy?" Pris asked, finally relaxing against the white cat's solid body.

Zekki sighed, and shook his head. "He's gone too. I don't know where they're headed." He thought of The Boy's face in the window and felt a searing anguish that threatened to choke him.

"What's wrong?" Pris asked, sensing his mood. "Are you keeping something from me?"

"No, no," he assured her, his voice light and positive. "The lizard's smart, I have faith that he'll save him.

"Help!" a voice called in the distance. "I need space! It's too tight in here!"

They both turned to see a big straw hat slowly moving up the hallway, its rim bumping the walls, and a short brown tail poking from behind.

Zekki waited until it got closer, then snaked out a paw, flipping it off.

Cuff blinked up at him.

"You almost blew everything by moving around," Pris scolded. "We told you to stay still."

"Sorry, but you know I'm claustrophobic. I stayed there as long as I could." He looked around. "Is Krell gone?"

Zekki nodded. "Because of that stranger's telepathic warning, you're safe."

"True." Cuff said, scrabbling toward the kitchen. "Which reminds me, I finally reached Soot. He says the lizard has a plan."

"He did?" Pris trilled. "What is it?"

"Don't know," Cuff said, heading toward the kitchen. "Any cat treats left?"

The cats watched him go, amazed at his cheerful resilience.

"The message from Soot is good news," Pris said. "Right?"

The white cat jumped to the top of the couch. "Yes, but it's not over yet. The Boy is still out there." He settled into a ball, making room for the calico, now snuggled beside him.

"But he isn't alone," she said hopefully. "There's a plan to save him."

Zekki stared sadly out the window, his eyes adjusting to the gloom. "I've always heard that Orie is special. Let's pray the rumors are true."

* * *

Afternoon had turned into evening, and the moon was only a pallid haze in the cloud covered sky.

The animals moved silently toward the carnival, their enthusiasm now dampened by fear.

Orie lead the way, with La De Da and Axel behind. Above them, Bennett circled among the trees, Theda clinging to his feathers, and the roach burrowed beneath a wing.

For the hundredth time, Orie processed Theda's and Axel's information. He now knew how the warehouse door opened, that there was only one window, the number of cages inside, how these were accessed, and what was inside them. But more important than this, he knew that an enemy more frightening than Stuart Krell was waiting in the musty darkness. One that terrified the others so badly, it had been hard to convince them to come, no matter how much they wanted to help.

"Not even you can cheat death." Isn't that what the cockroach had said? Orie squared his shoulders. They'd see about that. A muscle beneath his eye twitched with fatigue. Though he hadn't mentioned it, he'd started to feel the effects of Aluna's earlier attack. His side ached, and he feared a rib or two were cracked. But that could wait. Many things could still go wrong, and The Boy had so little time.

The gnarled landscape of the park gradually changed to mowed grass and concrete, and the carnival stood silhouetted against scatters of sullen gray clouds. A closed for the season sign drooped on a padlocked chain at the entrance, and a lone Ferris wheel, so thrilling in daylight, now towered sinister and huge beneath the darkening sky.

Below the flapping canvas, and shrouded in gloom, stood the warehouse.

Orie stopped. "Okay," he motioned at the group to form a circle, "we're here, and Krell should be driving up any second."

The animal's dread was palpable. They averted their eyes from the structure, and Axel whimpered quietly.

"You can do this," the lizard said firmly, and then waited in silence until each of them nodded their heads. "We have one shot at making this work so stick to the plan; any questions?"

Before anyone could answer, a car swung into the parking lot, its bright headlights suddenly dimmed.

"Speak of the devil," Orie said, "he's here."

* * *

The pit bull had stuffed both phones into his big, tooth filled mouth, and Blitz was livid. At first she'd pouted in the shadows before following Orie's entourage through the park, wondering whether she should settle for the dead man's tobacco pouch, and go home. That was until she realized they had entered the carnival, a place she'd heard of but never actually seen. A bitter wind rattled through the fairgrounds, swirling scents of rancid grease, corn

PEMBERTON

syrup, and peanuts through the air. Even in the darkness, she saw brightly colored flags flapping against ticket stands, the flimsy plastic popping and snapping with every gust. The place was a wonderland of twisted shadows, and mysterious structures, and she was enthralled.

Suddenly disinterested in cell phones, keys or tobacco pouches, Blitz watched Orie's group disappear behind a row of Port-O-Potties. Who cared about such serious matters? The grounds were alive with sounds and smells she'd never experienced before, and her heart did a skittering dance of pleasure. Clamoring up the side of a dingy kiosk, she danced along the plastic counter tops, her nose detecting stale popcorn, and fat. Aluminum soda pop tabs littered the gravel, and a vast display of stuffed dinosaurs and plastic hula girls, their heads bobbing in the wind, lined the shelves of an adjoining ring toss.

Mesmerized by the sumptuous selection, Blitz leaped to the structure, snatched a mask sparkling with glitter, and with wild dooks of joy, blasted across the grounds.

A car slowly wheeled past the entrance gate, its headlights illuminating her path, and she scampered beneath a Tilt-O-Whirl, where she lay in the dirt, ripping the mask to shreds, her paws shimmering with a fine glaze of sparkles.

Footsteps scrunched in the gravel, and a dusty pair of men's shoes moved past her hiding place. Looking up, she noticed a baseball bat trailing along behind the feet, and suddenly curious, she left her stash and followed.

* * *

Orie and Bennett hid on the flat roof of the warehouse, watching the big man approach. The sound of his breathing was raspy and fast, and he was hiding something behind his back.

"Hello?" Stuart turned in a slow, careful circle. "Anyone here?"

The lizard had expected something like this. He raised his head and whispered in Bennett's ear. The bird nodded and cleared his throat.

"Guess what I'm looking at?" Complete with giggling, the parrot repeated his perfect rendition of the answering machine's voice. "Your nasty backpack!

A bank of clouds parted, and Stuart's eyes shone like pale white orbs in a sliver of moonlight. "Stop playing games!" he said angrily, "where are you?"

Orie signaled to La De Da who began a furious scratching against the side window pane.

The big man jumped... his breathing now quick and rapid. "So you *do* have a key," he muttered, "I thought so." Shuffling to the warehouse door, he jiggled the handle. It was locked. "Very funny," he said loudly. "If you want to make a deal, open up and let's get this over with."

"Kristin and I are waiting," Bennett mimicked again. Only this time, he'd flown to the back of the building, the voice floating beneath the canvas sign's rhythmic flapping.

"And there're two of you. Stuart licked his lips. "Okay, let's all stay calm, I'm coming in." Tucking the bat beneath his arm, he pulled a ring of keys from his pocket, and opened the warehouse door. It swung on its hinges, scraping along the ground.

Directly above, Orie, Theda, and the cockroach skittered down from the roof, following Stuart Krell's heavy steps in to the gloomy interior.

Quickly, the man jerked at a string, and a light came on, its sickly glow casting patterned shadows against cages and walls.

It was exactly as Theda and Axel had described, and Orie's heart ached at the sight before him. The air was noxious and stale, and exotics of all description stared listlessly from their pens. But there were only two animals that mattered for the moment; one was Anibus, who's jackal form and yellow eyes were conspicuously absent, the other a black mamba; coiled and watching from a tall wire enclosure across from the door.

The lizard took a quick breath. It wouldn't take long before Stuart realized that something was wrong, and left. If things were to work, they had to move now.

La De Da had joined them on the floor, and at Orie's nod, the foursome split; the lizards crawling up the side of the mamba's cage, while the insects clung to the ceiling above Stuart's head.

The man stood squinting in the light, his eyes darting around the room. He frowned. "What's going on here?" he asked, suddenly realizing that he was alone. As if still not trusting what he saw, Stuart moved from cage to cage, looking into corners, and peering beneath the table. Finally he crept to the closed door, put his ear against the wood, and listened.

"He's getting ready to go," Orie hissed. Simultaneously, he and La De Da placed their backs beneath the latch on the mamba's cage, pushing upward, as Stuart put his hand around the door knob, preparing to leave.

"Now! Now!" the lizard shouted, still grunting against the metal latch that hadn't budged.

From the ceiling, Theda dropped onto Stuart's hand, and at the same time, the roach fluttered to the ground.

At first, the man simply flicked his wrist. But as soon as he saw Theda moving swiftly up his arm, her red stripe bright in the artificial light, he screamed. Twirling in the room, he desperately tried to shake her from his jacket. He'd almost jerked one arm out of its sleeve and was working on the other, when the roach rushed up his pants leg.

Grunting with effort, the lizards worked furiously to lift the latch.

It won't move!" La De Da shouted. "The darn thing is rusted or something."

From inside its cage, the black mamba uncurled its silvery body; flat ebony eyes watching their struggle. Tongue flicking, the snake swayed its head for a better look; mouth stretched in a permanent grin.

Orie stared helplessly as Stuart continued to wail, stamping his feet and whirling so fast that dust and feathers puffed around him. So far, the insects had managed to hang on, but it was only a matter of time before the big man dislodged them, and both Theda and the roach were in danger. The lizard's heart pounded. It was imperative for Axle's arrival to coincide with their accessing the latch, or the plan would fail. "Axel!" Orie bellowed in to the night. "Axel, where are you?"

There was movement in the doorway, and Orie felt a short lived sense of relief. It wasn't Axel who stood on the threshold, but Blitz, her black tail bushed, eyes wide with surprise.

CHAPTER 46

The ferret stepped back, stunned by the frenzied scene before her. The man was flapping his arms, and screaming in the middle of a tiny, cage filled room. And above her, clinging to a tall, wire enclosure, Orie and La De Da were pushing against a latch.

Amidst the excitement of the carnival, Blitz had forgotten the animals and their boring quest. She'd followed Stuart through the grounds, hoping to find more treasure, but there were so many distractions along the way that she'd lost him. Finally, she'd traced the man's scent to the ratty little building, and now, instead of romping through piles of glittering trinkets, she'd stumbled upon a weird and perplexing chaos.

"Axel!" Orie's voice echoed through the room. "Where are you?"

Of course! Blitz's mind jolted to clarity. She'd stumbled upon the lizard's 'plan' in action, and as predicted, things had gone terribly wrong. Crouching amidst the shadows, the ferret watched with smug satisfaction.

Theda zigzagged across Stuart's chest, when his massive hand slapped her away. With a shrill cry, she sailed across the room, slammed against the wall, and slid in a small black ball to the floor.

"Orie!" The cockroach shrieked, dropping from Stuart's pant cuff and running toward her. "Theda's been hurt!"

"No!" A familiar voice cawed from the open doorway. "No!"

Blitz looked up to see Bennett, his body framed in moonlight; opaque eyes wild and fixed on Stuart.

"I remember! The parrot screamed. "Now I remember!" He streaked into the room, his body a soft grey projectile aimed at Stuart. "It was you! You captured my family and brought us here, and now you've hurt Theda!" Talons extended, he soared through the opening, heading straight for the big man's face. "Get the net!" He shouted in a perfect imitation of Stuart Krell's voice. "Get the net!"

* * *

The lizards looked up from the latch, amazed at what they saw.

Bennett dove and swooped through the room, his razor sharp beak leaving a jagged, red slash across Stuart's cheek

"This wasn't the plan!" La De Da shouted. "What's Bennett doing?"

Orie didn't know. Suddenly, the world had tilted, any future hopes of success grinding to a slow and painful halt. Stuart was batting the bird with his hands, and moving quickly toward the door. Theda lay crumpled against the wall, the roach watching her in horror, and instead of Axel coming to the rescue, the stupid ferret had appeared instead.

From his out of body viewpoint, Orie felt a crazy urge to laugh. Of course the plan was failing, and why not? Humans were huge and powerful with easy access to the world and all it offered... Whereas, Orie and his friends were only animals; small, thumbless, and from the looks of things, amazingly inept.

Below them, Stuart's fear had quickly turned to aggression. Retrieving the bat, he swung at the bird, the thick wooden stick crashing against the table and knocking cages to the floor.

Soon, it would all be over, Orie thought with hollow detachment. The man would escape, and The Boy would die.

"Not true." A quiet voice said.

Orie jumped, and turned to La De Da, whose focus was back on the latch. "Did you say something?" he asked.

She shook her head, claws scrabbling at metal.

Movement caught the lizard's eye, and he smelled garbage, then rain...then the sea.

Sitting beside them, in what Orie could have sworn was an empty crate, was a dog like creature, its golden eyes piercing and direct.

"Anibus?" the lizard whispered.

"Look." the jackal said.

Axel had burst through the door, the chain still swinging from his neck. Growling with fury, saliva dripped from the pit bull's jaws, and its lips were pulled back from gleaming white canines.

Forgetting the parrot, Stuart stared with disbelief. "What's going on here?" he yelled, raising the bat with one hand and wiping the bleeding cut on his face with the other. "Axel, you idiot, it's me!"

The dog leapt up, his massive jaws clamping on the weapon, wrenching it from Stuart's grasp.

"No!" the man shouted, stumbling backwards. He tripped over carcasses and boxes, moving closer to the mamba's cage. "Down Axel! Down!"

"The latch won't move!" La De Da shrieked from somewhere far away. "We need help!"

A clear and sudden vision blazed through Orie's mind. He looked down at the ferret, and their eyes met and held. "This is your chance, Blitz," he called, his voice rising high and strangely calm above the racket. "You don't need my story. A better one is right before you, truly yours, and happening now."

The ferret looked from the lizard to the latch, and then blinked with a sudden understanding. Quick as a gunshot, she war danced through the room, rocketed up the snake's cage, and in one swift movement, pushed the latch free with her nose.

Axel stalked forward, Stuart stumbled back, and the mamba's door swung open.

Pulling itself upward, flat silver head almost touching the roof of its cage, the creature watched Stuart's flailing approach.

As if sensing its presence, the man turned, saw the mamba, and tried to run, but the pit bull and parrot blocked his path. Hands flailing helplessly, Stuart gaped in shock as the snake's jaws opened wide, the inside of its mouth a glistening black.

The fangs found their mark.

Stuart's head snapped back...and he screamed.

CHAPTER 47

The warehouse was silent, a bare bulb swinging slowly from the ceiling, its waving light casting eerie shadows on the walls.

Stuart had staggered to the doorway before collapsing, and now lay across the threshold; his head and torso face down in the mud, legs and feet inside.

Quietly, the animals emerged from their places; Bennett gently carrying a bruised but conscious Theda in his beak, Axel and Blitz striding from the shadows, and La De Da and the roach boldly approaching the man's body.

"Is he dead?" La De Da asked.

"Very." The cockroach announced after checking the big man's pulse.

A torrent of rain burst from the heavens. The hard drumming against the roof and carnival grounds sounding like applause from a thousand bystanders.

"We did it," Axel said, in amazement, "Orie's plan worked...." The dog stopped; his broad face bewildered. "Where *is* Orie?" he asked.

The animals turned in surprise, their eyes searching for the lizard.

"But he was right there by the latch." Blitz said.

"I'm here," a soft voice whispered. Orie lay on the floor beneath the mamba's cage. In spite of a crushing pain now spreading through his chest and down one leg, he felt surprisingly happy.

Rushing to his side, his friends circled around him. "What are you doing down there?" The parrot asked, nudging him gently. "Get up. Stuart's dead. The plan worked." Orie winced. "That's good," he said. "Great news."

Wind battered the window, and from every cage in the room the captive animals watched; eyes shining with hope for the first time in many months.

"Where's the mamba?" the lizard asked.

"Sleeping." An unfamiliar voice answered.

Startled, Orie twitched, and then suddenly remembered Anibus. The Jackal God of Death had finally appeared. It was lying beside him, its long, thin snout inches from Orie's face. "I was hoping you'd stick around," the lizard said, surprised at his lack of fear, "because I'd like to make you a deal."

"I can't understand you." La De Da said, her claws stroking Orie's brow. "What did you just say?"

The jackal understood him perfectly, and tilted its head, listening.

"I know you're here for The Boy." Orie inhaled the tangy scent of the sea, and he fought its heady pull. "But he's a special human with so much left to do, and I'm an irritable, tired old lizard with a lousy heart and bad behavior. Please let him live," he said, not caring that he was begging for the first time in his life. "Take me instead." And suddenly he was weeping. Fat, hot tears rolling down his snout, splashing the floor, and anointing the feet of Death.

The creature gazed at him for a long while, its expression inscrutable. "I'm not here for The Boy."

The lizard blinked. "You're not?"

"No." It said. "I'm here for you."

Time ground to a stop and the room grew dim. Though he hadn't known it until now, Orie suddenly understood that this was how it had always been between him and the jackal. The two of them side by side, day after day, year after year, separated by an invisible curtain called life… which would someday be drawn. And here it was.

And he was pissed.

Are you kidding!" Orie finally croaked. "You mean you put us all through this mess for nothing? Why didn't you just take me last week after lunch or something?"

"Because," Anibus said, "death has a specific time and place. This was yours."

Orie paused, digesting this new information. "So, you're saying The Boy is safe and always was?"

The jackal nodded.

"Hey, everybody!" the lizard cried. "Everything's okay, The Boy is safe!"

"He's conscious again!" Theda shouted. She turned her face to Orie. "I think you passed out a minute ago. Can you hear me?"

Of course he could hear them. Confused, the lizard nodded, wondering why none of them acknowledged the jackal's presence.

Axel wagged his stump of a tail. "You're right, The Boy *is* safe. I'm sorry I was late getting here, but when I saw him tied in Mr. Krell's car, I had to stop." The dog lifted his massive head. "He's my master, and his welfare comes first."

"Congratulations." Orie mumbled. "Does he finally have his phone?"

The pit bull nodded. "He'd managed to free one hand, and almost opened the car door when I found him. I pulled him out and dropped the cell at his feet. He picked it up."

"So it's really, finally over." The lizard sighed with relief. "Which leads me to one last thing. I won't be at the Meeting of the Spoken Word again, and there's something I have to say."

"Sure you'll be there." La De Da's voice broke. "Please don't say that."

"No, I won't," he said firmly. "I never had the chance to tell my story, and there's something that everyone should know; Tenba was the true hero of The Cat Master's ascension, and all the legendary stuff should go to her."

The roach stepped forward. "Everyone knows she took part. We've all heard about the shepherd, but just because she helped, doesn't mean you're any less of a hero. Sometimes two ordinary creatures come together and accomplish great things. That was you and Tenba."

"No kidding?" Orie said, deciding to ignore the word, 'ordinary'. "Well that was a lot of worry for nothing." He glanced at Death, now lying next to Theda. "By the way, I'm glad to see none of you are afraid of the jackal anymore, because he's actually a pretty good guy.

"Afraid of who?" Bennett asked.

"Anibus, the jackal." Weakly, Orie pointed to the spider. "He's right there, by Theda."

The animals looked uncomfortable; their eyes avoiding Orie's.

"They can't see me or remember my name anymore," the jackal explained. "Their part in this is over, and it's not good for the living to think of me too much."

"But that's nuts!" Orie hissed back. "Everyone knows who you are. We've been talking about you for days!"

Anibus shook his head. "They saw what I needed them to see. Now they can rest and forget."

A frigid gust of air rocked through the warehouse, and La De Da moved closer, shielding Orie's body with hers. "He's mumbling something about a jackal." She said. "Does anyone know what he's talking about?"

Orie longed to tell them that Death was right beside him smart as a whip and smelling great, but when he turned to speak, the saffron orbs had vanished. Instead, he stared into the soft, brown eyes of Tenba.

The German shepherd's tail thumped the floor with joy. "Time to go."

"I'd really like to," Orie said; surprised at how easily he could speak to dead things, "but for some reason the old heart's still ticking," he winced at the sudden pressure threatening to suffocate him, "and not in a good way." A distressing thought crossed his mind. "Is this just a visit, or are you staying?"

"Definitely staying, old friend." she said. "From now on, it's just you, me…and eternity."

The lizard grinned; a smile so wide and happy that it hurt his face. "Let's get moving!" he shouted, struggling to stand. But a searing pain jolted his chest and he fell back. It was infuriating; death or no death, patience wasn't his thing. "Theda!" he called.

The spider scuttered to his side.

"I need a favor."

Her multiple eyes shown with tears and she nodded. "Anything."

"First; I know you're poisonous, we all do."

She started to protest, but Orie held up one claw for silence. "The German shepherd is waiting for me, and even though I'm ready to go, my body's not cooperating. How about helping things along?"

"I don't understand," Theda said, but her horrified expression showed that she did.

Orie sighed with frustration. "Yes, you do."

There was a collective intake of air as the meaning of his request registered, and the group shifted with shock.

"What German shepherd?" Axel asked, gazing around the room.

You don't know what you're saying." La De Da patted the lizard's leg. "You're just confused. You'll be fine…"

"…oh for heaven's sake," Orie interrupted. "Of course I know what I'm saying, and I won't be fine. I'm old and tired. It's time to leave, Sho-Valla is waiting, and I'm ready."

The sound of police sirens blared in the distance, and he realized things were moving fast. The Boy had obviously called for help, and the authorities would be here to rescue the warehouse animals. His friends needed to leave, he wanted to die, and suddenly, he realized how many things were still left unsaid.

"Bennett," he paused, waiting for the bird to hop closer. "Look… everyone's life involves painful moments. The important thing is that you finally remembered them, which means you now have a past as well as a future. And by the way, stop the mechanical noises. They're irritating."

The parrot bobbed his head and whistled the first two bars of Taps.

"Knock it off," Orie said, and Bennett nodded, plucking the last remaining feather from his breast. Shutting his eyes, the lizard winced. "Where's the ferret?"

Slowly, Blitz slunk from the shadows, jaw set with defiance.

"It was you who took The Boy's phone in the first place. You're a manipulative, selfish liar without a shred of character," Orie shrugged, "which I actually admire. You're not particularly nice, but without your help, the plan would have failed. So tell your own darn story, and stop trying to steal things." He took a labored breath. "As for the roach…"

"Ready to assist." The insect interrupted, his antennae waving imperiously.

"You're an arrogant pedant and if I live until breakfast, I'm going to eat you. On the other hand," Orie gave a sigh, "you're smart and loyal, and I hope you'll keep an eye on Theda. Speaking of which," he turned to the spider, "how about it? Will you help me, or not?

"I—I can't." Her mandibles trembled. "I promised myself I'd never hurt anything ever again. I killed...well I killed a baby once. It was awful. Please don't ask me to do this."

The German shepherd leaned down, and whispered something in Orie's ear.

The lizard registered surprise, and then smiled. "The story you're so ashamed of is wrong, Theda, the baby lived. You're always assuming the worse, and because of that, you've suffered needlessly."

"That's not possible!" The spider drew back in shock. "How do you know?"

"What are you?" Orie screeched, "some kind of martyr? If you don't believe me, have the roach look up 'anti-venom'. And Theda," he said with a groan. "I'm a little bored with the garden spider thing. You're one of the most dangerous insects alive, which is pretty darned impressive. You don't have to hurt anyone but you don't have to lie either."

"You're right," she said, her face filled with wonderment. "I won't."

"One last thing;" Orie turned to La De Da, his eyes drinking in the sweetness of her face. "I don't think I ever told you this, or anyone, for that matter." He blinked, suddenly embarrassed by such blatant sentimentality. "But I—I mean, you..." He stammered to a stuttering halt, appalled by his inability to speak.

"I know, handsome one." La De Da placed her head next to his, a dribble of tears rolling from her eyes, and on to his nose. "I love you, too, and always will." Sobbing, she hugged him hard, and then turned away.

Sweet cold air had blown in from the opened door, and the little room smelled fresh....its inhabitants calm and expectant.

A sudden thought crossed Orie's mind, and he turned to the shepherd in wonder. "The answers really *were* at the carnival, weren't they?"

Tenba nodded. "Every last one."

The downpour had slowed to a lulling drizzle, and soft drops of rain plopped against the lone window, their gentle rhythm comforting.

But not comforting enough. The pain in Orie's chest had crept to his jaw, and he felt nauseous, and weak. Something tickled his face and he turned to see the spider, one fragile leg touching his brow.

"I—I just wanted to tell you, that we've all discussed your request," Theda said, "and under the circumstances... I'm willing." Her many eyes held his. "But, are you absolutely sure about this?"

Orie released a long, contented sigh. "Dead sure."

At his words, the group formed a circle around him; paw to claw, antenna to beak; forever bound by this moment of loss.

"Goodbye Legendary Lizard," Theda whispered, and with the gentleness of a kiss, let her venom flow.

EPILOGUE

No one witnessing Orie's death ever remembered his references to Tenba, or the jackal God. Anibus. Privately, they all experienced fleeting memories of saffron eyes and the salty smell of the sea, but these were dismissed as nightmares, their meanings best left unknown.

Stuart Krell's carnival was permanently closed; illegal exotics nursed back to health, and the warehouse destroyed. Cuff was returned to Madagascar and the care of his grateful countrymen, and Zekki, Pris, and Soot heard of the lizard's success, and subsequent passing through Aluna, whose River Cat colony now existed peacefully with the alley ferals.

Thankfully, The Boy recovered quickly. His fight for animal welfare, despite risk to himself, received international press, and photos showed a smiling young man, one hand resting on the head of a pit bull, who sat by his feet.

Cemented by grief and circumstance, other friendship's flourished. Theda and the cockroach formed a lifelong bond, and spent most of their time in the library, surfing the web, and watching children read.

La De Da went back to the park, and Bennett, Axel and the ferret returned home with The Boy. As far as anyone knew, Blitz never stole again, but years later a rusted silver cell phone was found behind the dryer; its owner never identified.

Days became weeks, weeks led to months… and the space beneath the kitchen sink remained empty.

* * *

A year passed, and once more fall brushed the park with strokes of dazzling color, and with it, came the Meeting of the Spoken Word.

Free of past confusions and excited to tell his story Bennett perched atop the gazebo, cawing loudly, and preening the new growth of down on his chest. Beneath him, Theda and the cockroach sat on the railing, and Axel joined a squirrel, coyote, and three armadillo on the leaf strewn steps. As usual, Sarge upheld rules, waving his striped tail in warning, and introducing the tellers. First on the list... was Blitz.

The ferret began with her life in the pet store, subsequent adoptions, returns, and escapes, and then ended with a moving account of her part in The Boy's rescue, a plan, she was quick to point out, that was Orie's, down to the last detail.

At the mention of his name the group sat in silence, the last rays of autumn sunlight filtering through the trees, their thoughts turned toward the reptile whose bold and crusty heroism had altered animal history.

"Hey," a lively voice rang from the steps, "this the Meeting of the Spoken Word, right?"

Startled, the animals looked up to see a female lizard standing in a golden slice of light. Traces of food stuck to her snout, and her chin dipped in a noticeable under bite.

"La De Da!" Bennett screeched, his wings flapping wildly. "It's you!"

Amidst shouts of greetings, the reptile acknowledged one old friend after another, and then, with a gesture of her palm for silence, moved quietly to the center of the gazebo. "A year ago today, Orie gave his life to save The Boy, and in doing so, gave meaning to ours."

Theda, Axel, Bennett and Blitz exchanged knowing glances, their expressions soft with understanding.

"And so," she continued, "in honor of his sacrifice, I offer you one last gift from the Legendary Lizard."

There was a murmuring from the group, and members strained to see, as a tiny figure scurried from the undergrowth.

Moving before them, his skin mottled green, was a young male lizard. Dashing up the steps he stood beside his mother; his defiant stance and puffing throat so achingly familiar that some of the animals turned away, unable to speak.
Placing one claw on the youngster's head, La De Da smiled at the group, eyes moist with pride. "I bring you Koo De Ta!" she cried. "Son of Orie, and heir to the Legend!" With a gentle prod, she pushed him forward until the last beams of sunlight touched his face. "His time is now. The future ours…and today his story begins."

THE END

ABOUT THE AUTHOR

Bonnie Pemberton spent thirty years as a singer, actress, writer and voice-over talent in Dallas and Los Angeles. An avid animal lover, she invented Sticky Paws® for Furniture, an anti-scratching product for cats, which is carried worldwide. She is a member of the Cat Writers Association and Trinity Writers Workshop. She lives in Texas with her husband Kipp Baker and their two cats.

Cover illustration: copyright Lisa Falkenstern © 2012

Made in the USA
Lexington, KY
13 February 2013